Last in Series

I stand on the riverbank and gaze at land that has now become foreign soil. Our country is rent in two, and hatred gathers like thunderheads. Yet, in the midst of fear and turmoil, love and hope still flourish... like a daisy pushing through parched, cracked earth. It is with hope, and because of love, that AJ and I will set out before the sunrise declares a new day. Father, guide our quest, protect the one we search for.

Prudence Willard
Marietta, Ohio
June 6, 1861

SECRETS OF WAYFARERS INN

Old, New, Borrowed, Blue

BECKY MELBY

Guideposts

Danbury, Connecticut

Old, New, Borrowed, Blue

CHAPTER ONE

Marietta, Ohio
June 3, 1861

Prudence Willard knelt between two rows of carrots and pulled one from the soft, sun-warmed dirt. Moses, just turned two, sat at the edge of the garden, using a spoon to shovel dirt into a brass apple butter bucket. Patience, their pet goose, stood watch over him.

"I will add a bit of maple syrup to the carrots tonight. Just the way thee likes—" Pounding horse hooves drew her attention to the dirt lane leading to the house. Patience squawked at the sound, hovering close to Moses.

Prudence rose to her feet and scooped up her son. By the time she reached the porch, the rider had dismounted. A tall blond man. In uniform. Her gaze swept across the field north of the barn, hoping for a glimpse of Jason, or even his dog. These were uneasy times. Though the man wore Union blue, she couldn't guess what his business might be. "Hello," she called. "How may I help—" Was it possible? That boyish grin… But he was so tall, so broad shouldered.

"Miz Prudence, do you recognize me?"

"Asher Bailey?" She stared from the stubble of beard to the gold bar on his coat. "*Lieutenant* Asher Bailey?"

In seconds she and Moses were engulfed in a hug from a man who had been a gangly boy of fifteen when last she'd seen him. Asher released her, then stepped back. "Your son?"

Prudence nodded, pride swelling in her chest.

"He has his father's hair but a look of mischief in his eyes like his mother."

"I cannot deny that. How is thee, Asher?" Seeing him in uniform brought an ache to her middle. She wanted to hear about his life before he'd donned the Union blue. "I have kept thee in my prayers all these years." *And will increase my fervency now.*

"Thank you, ma'am. The Almighty has seen fit to answer. Save but one problem, I live a blessed life." He looked beyond her, surveying the farm. "Uncle Henry and I got our own place up near Youngstown. 'Course, he's farmin' on his own now. I'll be training recruits at Camp Putnam, soon as it's ready."

"I hope thee can return to farming soon, Asher." She looked out toward the land beyond the Ohio, thinking of all the men, on both sides of the conflict, torn from homes, lands, and loving arms.

Asher nodded. "Is Mr. Willard well?"

"He is. His leg still pains him but a tad less each year. At least that is what he tells me."

"I hope to be half the man he is someday." Asher scuffed the dirt with the heel of his boot. "Are you still...involved, Miz Prudence?" His shadowed eyes searched hers.

"We are."

"I'm in need of some help. It's Salome's mama."

Prudence blinked hard, her eyes widening. "Thee is still in communication with Salome?" In the summer of 1854, Asher had accompanied his uncle, a trusted conductor, on a dangerous mission to free four slaves from a Virginia plantation. A young girl of fourteen was the only one who managed to escape. Prudence, married only three years at the time, had ferried Henry, Asher, and Salome across the river, and she and Jason had taken them in while Salome recovered from beatings, malnutrition, and an arduous journey. It was not hard for young love to recognize the same in someone else, but she could not imagine a safe future together for Asher and Salome. Fathered by the man who owned her, Salome had skin the color of coffee rich with cream, but Prudence knew firsthand that life as a mixed-race woman and escaped slave would still have its perils.

"We corresponded for years, and I have been to Canada a number of times in the past three years. I aim to ask her to be my wife." A slight smile crossed his face. "I love her dearly, but she is not going to make it easy for me to take care of her." He sighed. "She is adamant on coming back here to find her mother herself."

"Find her?"

Asher took his hat off, worrying it in his hands as he continued to kick the hard-packed dirt. "We made contact with some freed slaves who helped get Deborah off the plantation. We got word she'd made it to a safe place this side of the Ohio. She was injured, so they were going to keep her for a few days, but next morning, she was gone. They found this." He pulled out a folded paper.

Bring $800 to the Black Dog Tavern in Millwood, Virginny by 10 June or we will sell her or tak her bak to her owner for reword. Ask fer Joe. Do not bring uthoritees.

"Oh, Asher." Prudence felt her eyes smart with tears. "I am so sorry."

"I can get the money. I sent word to Salome when we found out her mama had disappeared. She wants to come look for her, but I didn't tell her about the letter. I have to do this, have to bring Deborah back before Salome does something she may not live to regret." He placed his hat back on his head. "I could use your help, ma'am. Will you come with me?"

June sunlight painted bright squares on Wayfarers Inn's age-distressed hardwood floor as it blazed through nine-pane windows. LuAnn Sherrill tapped her silver pen on one of the spiral-bound notepads in front of her as she gazed out at the Ohio River. Diamonds danced on the water but could not compete with the brilliance of the gem on the ring finger of her left hand.

Nine days. In nine days she would be Mrs. Bradley Grimes. She scrawled her new name on the page titled "Honeymoon Clothes." *LuAnn Grimes. LuAnn Sherrill Grimes. Mrs. Brad Grimes. Mr. and Mrs. Bradley Grimes.* It had been decades since she'd been giddy over a man. It still felt foreign, unnatural. But blissful.

Mrs. At sixty-five, she was finally going to be a Mrs.

Her phone vibrated. The name on the screen brought a sigh of strained patience. Irene Bickerton Martin. Brad's ninety-year-old second cousin once removed. The little woman was feisty and energetic and, especially recently, quite demanding.

"Good morning, Irene."

"The painter's here to redo the master bathroom." Panic tinged Irene's voice. "This time it's supposed to be more sea-foam and less robin's egg, but it just doesn't look right to me. I need you to come and look."

"I'm sure it will be fine. Potential buyers have their own color schemes in mind anyway. Brad says the only important thing is making sure the colors aren't too bold."

"I'd feel better if you came and had a look. My eyesight isn't what it once was, you know."

The thought of Irene's comically huge glasses with thick lenses that magnified her pale eyes brought a genuine smile. It was hard to stay annoyed at the little elf of a woman. "I'll be there as soon as I can."

"I'll give the painter snickerdoodles while we wait."

"Wonderful idea." LuAnn said goodbye then stacked her notebooks.

"Lu?" Tess Wallace, one of her two B&B and café co-owners and forever best friends, stepped up behind her. "Are you breaking the rules?"

LuAnn held up the top three notebooks. One labeled *MTDC*, one *Honeymoon*, and the other *House Decorating*. With a sheepish smile she said, "Just double-checking my packing lists."

With a "tsk-tsk," Tess picked up the bottom two notebooks, which were clearly for the purpose of wedding planning. "And what were you doing with these?"

Janice Eastman came down the stairs. As she set an envelope on the front desk, Tess tattled about LuAnn's infringement.

"Lu, what part of r-e-l-a-x don't you understand?" Janice shook her head and attempted to stifle her smile as she snatched the books off the table. "It's all under control."

"I just thought…maybe I forgot something."

Tess laughed. "You told us where to buy the exact shade of pink mints you want on the tables and how much ribbon, down to the inch, we need for decorating the pews. I don't think you forgot anything."

"Trust us, sister."

The gleam in Janice's smile was anything but trust-inducing, but LuAnn couldn't help but laugh. "I'm putting plans for the biggest day of my life into the hands of the people who short-sheeted the bed in my dorm room and put Vaseline on the door handle, and—"

With identical waves, her two best friends turned their backs on her and walked off, Tess to the kitchen and Janice back upstairs. LuAnn took a calming breath. Everything was under control.

She left the notebook labeled *MTDC* on the table. The newly formed Marietta Tourism Development Coalition, chaired by her future husband, would convene here at Wayfarers Inn Café at four o'clock, giving her just enough time to drive to the Bickerton mansion and solve the seafoam/robin's egg dilemma.

She stepped into the elevator, treasuring every creak and clang of the antique contraption. Though she'd still be working here five days a week after the honeymoon, life would be different when she no longer shared the fourth floor with her two best friends.

When LuAnn walked out of her sitting room, Janice was standing in their small, shared kitchenette dunking a tea bag in a chartreuse mug. LuAnn held up her keys. "Off to do the queen's bidding."

Janice laughed. "What doth Her Majesty requireth now?"

"A seafoam bathroom."

7

"I feel bad for her. Putting all this work into a house she'll never set foot in after she moves."

Hand on the door leading to the stairway, LuAnn paused. "I know. I do too. Even though she makes me a little crazy sometimes, I really do love her heart. It's like this is her way of saying goodbye, by giving the place a final dose of TLC."

"May we all have a bit of Irene in us when we turn ninety." Janice waved. "Have fun."

LuAnn recited the love chapter from 1 Corinthians as she drove. "'Love is patient, love is kind…'"

Irene stood on the back porch waiting for her. Her apple cheeks rose in a smile, causing her glasses to elevate. "Come, have a snickerdoodle and meet my painter."

I've met your painter. Many times. The man had been there for weeks, painting every single one of the twelve rooms. Was Irene's memory glitching like her older sister Thelma's?

LuAnn grabbed a cookie as she followed Irene through the kitchen. As they walked up the stairs to the second floor, LuAnn heard singing. A female voice.

The painter who stood on a ladder next to the clawfoot tub was not *the* painter. This painter had a blond ponytail and wore a flowered hat. The woman turned, smiled at them with large brown eyes, and pointed at the new color she'd used along the ceiling. "It's dry here. What do you think?" She spoke around a bulge in her cheek. A clear yellow cellophane wrapper on the bathroom counter explained the temporary speech impediment.

Where had Irene found this painter? After a plumber she'd found online had charged her double what he should have for installing a faucet, Brad had asked her to *please* touch base with him before hiring anyone new. Anxious to get back to the inn, LuAnn didn't ask questions. "I like the new color. It's lighter and fresher, don't you think, Irene?" She put her arm across the tiny woman's shoulders and felt them instantly relax.

"Yes. Fresher. Thank you. I just didn't trust myself to make the decision on my own." Irene stepped into the hallway. "Come say hi to Thelma. She's napping in the library, but I need to wake her, or she'll never sleep tonight."

LuAnn ran her hand along the railing that formed a rectangle around the staircase. Seven doors opened off the hallway that circled the second floor. As always when she stepped into this house, she wished she had a time machine. To be able to push a button and see the original wallpaper, eight layers beneath what the painter had scraped from these walls. To see women in bell-shaped dresses and children sliding down the banister. To hear the whispers in the walls…

The house had been commissioned in 1856 by the man who had intended to be the first Underground Railroad conductor at Wayfarers Inn, then called Riverfront House. Unfortunately, the man was murdered before he had the chance to set foot in his new home. Murdered by Thelma and Irene's great-grandfather. It was a piece of the history of the family she was marrying into that the "aunts" had covered up for decades.

Irene stopped at her son's room. Leo Martin, an almost fifty-year-old man who'd managed to skate through life without holding down a job, at least one that didn't involve gambling, was back home from another one of his continent-hopping escapades with his latest girlfriend, whom the family had yet to meet.

LuAnn stared at a framed picture on the wall above the dresser. Leo, standing next to a bright yellow Cessna. Though he'd had the discipline to get his pilot's license, he'd used it only for fun.

"Oh!" Irene turned pale blue eyes on LuAnn. "Did Leo show you what he found in the attic last week?"

"No. What did he find?"

"Come see. I made him leave it there. I didn't want him disturbing any clues. He took pictures, and I thought he was going to show it to you and Bradley. Maybe he talked to Bradley. Maybe he told me he did. I don't know. Sometimes I wonder if I'm getting as forgetful as Thelma. All this stuff to do. The lists you made really help, but…"

Irene continued her monologue as she opened the narrow door leading to the third floor and started up the narrow steps once used by servants, not giving LuAnn the space of a breath to protest. Though her history-loving spirit soared at the dusty, old-wood smell and the worn stair treads and faded pink wallpaper, she really couldn't let herself get caught up in the mysteries of the attic right now. She had to get back for the meeting. "Irene, I really—"

"There's a trunk. Leo found it behind an old wardrobe that's been here as long as I can remember. I never have liked coming up here. Leo thinks the trunk belonged to the original Howard Bickerton."

Shivers skittered along LuAnn's arms. She stifled a laugh. By "the original" Howard Bickerton, Irene was referring to the man her great-grandfather had shot in the back on a riverboat, pushed overboard, and impersonated for the rest of his life.

Irene pointed to a corner of the cavernous room, and LuAnn dropped to her knees. With reverence, she touched the curved top of the scuffed leather trunk framed in strips of metal and wood. She lifted the latch and slowly raised the lid. She expected to find clothes or linens. Old dresses and shoes, maybe. Instead, the box was filled with dishes packed in wood shavings that had all but disintegrated into sawdust. She lifted a saucer. An intricate pattern of flowers and leaves in blue and rust accented in gold. She turned it over. On the back, imprinted in blue were the words SPODE STONE CHINA. Beneath it, hand-painted in red, was the number 2059.

LuAnn felt her pulse skip a beat as she brushed off a teacup. "This whole trunk is full of china? A complete set?" She glanced up at Irene. "Do you know how old this is? It was probably made in the early eighteen hundreds. Do you think it could have been Marta's? Maybe they shipped it over before she died. I wonder if Charisse used it." After reading about Marta, the real Mrs. Bickerton, who passed away in England before the house was finished and who never set foot on American soil, and the imposter Charisse, LuAnn felt she knew them personally.

Irene shook her head. "Would you use another woman's chi—" She caught herself. "I'm sorry. That was different."

LuAnn nodded. "Yes, it was." Though she had to admit she had moments of struggling over moving into the house Brad had shared with Stephanie, his late wife. But Irene was right, her story was different. Diverting the conversation, she said, "This is an amazing find. It ought to be on display somewhere. Maybe you should have Margaret Ashworth come and look at it." The director of the historical society could give them a better idea if it was as old as LuAnn assumed it was.

Irene nodded. "Leo mentioned that. Though I think what he was after was an appraisal. I told him to leave everything exactly like he found it. I adore my son, but he'd sell...well, you know how he is."

No need to reply. LuAnn offered a sympathetic smile.

Irene's eyes glittered. "The china isn't the most interesting part." She pointed at something wrapped in faded burgundy velvet sticking up from a corner.

LuAnn pulled it out. "Feels like silverware."

"Open it."

A frayed ribbon wound around the middle. The thin velvet was bald in spots. LuAnn unrolled the cloth slowly. Burgundy fibers drifted onto her tan slacks. Two large serving forks lay on the cloth. And under the forks, a yellowed card. LuAnn grasped a corner, pulled it free, and looked at the single faded, handwritten line.

M's wedding pearls. Marietta house deed.

Goose bumps rose on LuAnn's arms. She glanced up at Irene, then looked at the back of the card.

Turn over
Twist R front R 2 turns
Turn over
Twist R back L
Turn onto L side. Tap
While R side up, turn L back left
Bottom will drop

"Did Leo show you this?" LuAnn asked.

Irene nodded.

"Any idea what it's for? If it's connected to what's written on the other side of the card…"

Irene squinted at the card. "Right… Left… Whatever it is, you think it might be telling us where to find the deed Brad's been hunting for?"

Turning the card over again, LuAnn whispered, "I hope so." There was no deed for the Bickerton estate on file at the courthouse, and Brad had searched through boxes of old papers trying to find it. He needed the deed before they could sell the property. If he couldn't find it, he would have to hire an attorney to help sort out ownership and chain of title before he could put it on the market. With the house renovations, wedding, and honeymoon, he didn't need that extra burden.

"'M's wedding pearls.'" LuAnn thought of the old sepia-tone photographs of the "original" Bickertons they'd found in an old brass box. She took out her phone and snapped a picture of the front and back of the card, then tucked the card back in its original position so she could show it to Brad exactly as she'd found it. "Could be Marta's pearls, don't you think?"

"I have no clue." One magnified pale eye winked at LuAnn. "But you know I love a good mystery."

CHAPTER TWO

Brad came through the swinging door leading from the café just as LuAnn stepped through the back door into the Wayfarers Inn kitchen. "How can I help get ready for the meeting, ladies?" he asked.

LuAnn walked toward him. Though he'd addressed all of them—Tess, Janice, and Winnie, their cook—his focus was on her.

She stepped into his embrace. "You can help me push a couple of tables together." LuAnn took his hand and pulled him into the café. "But first I need to show you something." She took out her phone. "Look what Irene and I found in the attic."

Brad leaned close to read the words. "'M's wedding pearls. Marietta'"—his eyes widened—"'house deed'?"

"Swipe to the next picture."

Brad's brow furrowed as he read silently. Confusion etched his face when he looked up. "Turn over, right side up, tap, and the bottom will drop? It sounds like directions for a magic trick."

"The big question in my mind is, do the directions have something to do with what's written on the other side? And if so, who wrote them? Irene and I think 'M' could be Marta. She's wearing pearls in their wedding picture."

Brad gave a slow nod, as if letting the implications sink in. "You think it's that old? So the real Howard could have written it, and this could be instructions on where to find the deed to the mansion?"

"It sure sounds like—" The front door opened, and Kimberly Daniels, the exuberant owner of the newly opened Happy Wanderer Travel Agency on Front Street bounded in.

"Hi! Thought I'd come early. Anything I can do to help? I brought chocolate." She held out a box with Putnam Chocolate's distinctive label. "And brochures. That's okay, right? I just don't want to miss an opportunity to network."

LuAnn and Brad exchanged a look that said "talk later," and LuAnn slipped her phone in her pocket and focused her full—well, most of—her attention on Kimberly.

They'd made room for sixteen people and set out plates of Winnie's "kitchen sink" cookies when the rest of the coalition members began arriving. As they took their seats, LuAnn marveled at the number of people she'd come to call friends in the past two years and how Marietta had once again become her home. She'd been born and raised in Marietta until she was six, but her few happy early childhood memories were overshadowed by flashbacks of the night her mother woke her and they packed in haste and fled. It was only two years ago she'd learned that her father—whom she never saw again—had witnessed a mob-related murder and spent the rest of his life under a different name to protect his family.

LuAnn brushed away the dark thoughts as Brad opened the meeting. She took notes and added a few suggestions of her own, including the idea of conducting a survey of visitors to Marietta. The group had formed as a subgroup of the Chamber of Commerce, creating a coalition of business owners who relied primarily on tourism. The colorful new MTDC brochures with tear-out coupons were the highlight of the meeting. Ninety minutes later, LuAnn had two pages filled with ideas for drawing people to the historical charms of the first permanent settlement in the Northwest Territory.

Brad closed the meeting, and LuAnn added, "Help yourself to more coffee and cookies. You're welcome to stay and chat as long as you want." Her phone buzzed on the last word. She pulled it out. Irene again. She stepped toward the foot of the stairs to answer.

"I just made the last apple cake I will ever bake in this oven. We need someone to share it with us. I tried calling Bradley, but he didn't answer."

LuAnn shook her head. Irene, the social butterfly. The upcoming move might be emotional, but it would be good for her. As Thelma, now ninety-six, was spending more time napping and was beginning to show signs of memory issues, the house had started feeling "too big and too quiet" for Irene.

"Brad's right here. I'll talk to him, and we'll be over in a bit." She said goodbye and slid her phone back in her pocket.

"Problems?" Harry Olson, owner of the Antique and Salvage Mall, asked.

"That was Irene. You know—" The door chime rang, and two of their inn guests entered. Davinia Richards and Lesley Doran, mother and daughter, owned a B&B near Wheeling and had heard about Wayfarers Inn from Leo. "Find any good bargains?" LuAnn asked.

"This the tourism group you were talking about?" Davinia asked, not answering LuAnn's question. "Mind if we mingle? Might need to start something like this by us."

"Mingle away." LuAnn introduced them to Harry, who had migrated to a group that included Emma Carpenter, manager of Antoinette's Closet, Maybelline Rector, director of the Marietta Underground Railroad Museum, and Nancy LaPiere, owner of Tie the Knot Wedding Designs.

"Irene okay?" Harry asked.

"Well…" She took a moment to explain to the newcomers that the woman her fiancé referred to as Aunt Irene was in the process of getting her massive Victorian house ready to be put on the market. "She and her sister are moving to Countryside Manor, an assisted living facility. I'm sure it's incredibly hard to leave the home you've lived in your entire life, but she's…well, let's just say I'll be very relieved when the work is done." No argument from LuAnn could convince Irene she didn't have to put so much work into making everything perfect before Brad put a For Sale sign out front.

"Could we look at it?" Davinia asked.

"You said my mother's favorite word," Lesley added. "She's all about anything Victorian."

"I'd like to see it myself," Harry said. "I've got a lot of memories of the mansion from back in the day."

"So would I," Maybelline added. "It's been years since I've seen more than the kitchen."

As more voices joined in, LuAnn laughed. "Let me talk to Brad."

LuAnn walked over to Brad and waited for a break in his conversation with the manager of the Ski and Skate Shack. "Irene baked a cake and wants us to come share it. Think she'd mind if we brought a few more guests?"

Brad turned to her with an amused smile that warmed her toes. "What's the planner planning now?"

"Just a little impromptu open house at the mansion." She nodded toward the group she'd just left. "One of our guests is a Victorian house fan, and the others are just curious. Might be kind of a fun distraction for the aunts, and it can't hurt to get some buzz going before you list it, right? I'll call Irene and make sure she's okay with it."

Brad stared at her, surprise—and a twinge of irritation—etched on his face. "It's not on the market, and for all we know it may be months—"

"I'm sorry. I know you don't have spec sheets ready or—"

"It's okay." The rigid angle of his jaw softened. "It's fine. I just don't have my spiel figured out, but I can wing it." He put his arm around her. "No problem."

But clearly it was.

LuAnn studied Brad's profile as they drove to the mansion. His usual easy smile had returned. She'd caught him off guard, unprepared. He could have said no to the tour, but that wasn't like Brad. Now she'd put him in a position of not being able to present himself as the consummate professional he was. *Note to self. Apologize thoroughly for not thinking before opening mouth.*

"Some curb appeal, huh?" he said as they pulled into the drive.

LuAnn felt transported back two years, to the first time he'd brought her here. She'd ridden past the house days before and admired the landscaping and the unique copper weather vane glinting in the sunlight. Walking up to the house with Brad, she'd felt almost dizzy from the kaleidoscope of color bordering the stone walkway. Petunias, impatiens, and sundrops seemed to be competing for attention with their blazing corals, purples, fuchsias, and yellows. The two-acre, perfectly landscaped lawn created a backdrop for several stone fountains, statues, and benches. While she wasn't generally a fan of yard art, these were tasteful, in harmony with the nature around them and the style of the house.

The house...she remembered thinking it towered over them like a mountain. Turrets, leaded glass windows, rich red brick, and cut stones with flecks of quartz that sparkled in the sunlight. She'd been surprised when Brad said he'd never liked the house, but now, having spent the past few weeks helping Irene clean out every nook and cranny, she could understand why the dark, heavily draped rooms and the somewhat creepy cherubim faces carved into the woodwork of the fireplaces could have been frightening to a young boy, leaving an impression that stayed with him.

"Let's go in the front door," LuAnn suggested, and Brad agreed. Their guests would miss some of the grandeur if they used the kitchen entrance.

They waited on the wraparound porch while everyone got out of their cars. Six people had taken them—*her*—up on the open house offer. Davinia, Lesley, Maybelline, Harry, Nancy, and Emma. Brad welcomed them. "The first thing you may have noticed as you drove up the hill is the massive weather vane. The eagle with its wings spread represents freedom. Our understanding is that this eagle carrying a lantern in its beak is one-of-a-kind, designed to be a sign of welcome and safety in the event the house would be needed as a place of refuge for runaway slaves fleeing"—Brad's words slowed as Leo's car pulled in the drive—"to safety across the Ohio."

LuAnn waved and smiled, but her stomach tightened as she did. Leo was unpredictable.

Brad cleared his throat and began the tour. "The house was commissioned by Howard Bickerton, a man whose wealthy father was one of the founding members of the British and Foreign Anti-Slavery Society. After antislavery laws were passed in England, Howard began supporting the cause in the States, eventually deciding to move his family to Marietta to join the fight. While still in London, he bought the Riverfront House, now known as Wayfarers Inn, sight unseen, and hired a contractor to build this house. Unfortunately, his wife died before they set sail, leaving him with an eleven-year-old son and a toddler. Due to circumstances we don't fully understand, the oldest son chose not to accompany Howard to the States. And in another sad twist, before he even had a chance to set foot in this house, Howard was killed, and his murderer assumed his identity." Brad paused as gasps of intrigue spread through the knot of people gathered on the porch.

LuAnn knew Brad had deliberately brought out that part of the story before they were in earshot of the sisters. For being unprepared, he was doing a fantastic job. As he held the door open, she gave his arm a squeeze of encouragement.

"The first things you'll notice are the custom-designed light fixtures and the grand staircase." Brad gestured toward the brass chandelier with etched globes hanging in the center of the foyer. "Howard Bickerton's original plans would have included gaslights. To your right is the back parlor. The box beam ceiling…"

LuAnn heard voices in the kitchen and slipped away. She paused in the front parlor, admiring the room now that the old brocade window treatments had been taken down and the walls painted a pale terra cotta, the color pulled from the glazed decorative tiles surrounding the fireplace. The aunts' oriental rugs had been removed and the oak floors buffed to a beautiful patina. Thelma's grand piano fit perfectly in the corner next to the stairway.

In the dining room, LuAnn ran her fingertips along the table that could extend to seat sixteen. The furniture could be sold with the house, if the buyer was interested. Since Brad and Irene had first talked about selling, she'd had fun imagining a new life for the mansion. Would it be bought by a large family that filled every room with fingerprints and laughter? Or a wealthy eccentric artist? As she'd mentioned to Tess and Janice with some trepidation, it would also make a very inviting B&B. Tess had laughed and quoted J. C. Penney. "A merchant who approaches business with the idea of serving the public well has nothing to fear from the competition."

She passed the library where Thelma dozed, once again, in her platform rocker, and walked toward the kitchen. White-painted cupboards met the ten-foot ceiling. Glass handles on the doors reflected light from the wrought-iron fixture over the table. A cake covered in lightly browned apple slices sat cooling on a wire rack on the counter.

Leo leaned against the new, high-end made-to-look-old white enamel stove, one arm crossed over his middle, his focus riveted on the phone in his hand. "I know the clock is ticking. I promise I'll find both documents."

LuAnn stepped behind the door, out of sight, peering at Leo through the crack above a massive brass hinge.

"Today?" The female voice held a hint of teasing.

"Today, yes." His smile and tone conveyed patient amusement. "They have to be hiding somewhere in my bedroom, or maybe in the attic. I'll call you when I find them."

"You're sure you're not getting cold feet?" The teasing had left her voice. "If you're worried about what this will do to your mom, I totally understand, babe."

"My mom won't be a problem. Nothing I can't handle. Talk to you soon." He blew a kiss at the screen and ended the video call.

LuAnn stood outside the doorway to the kitchen, questions swirling around her like a swarm of Ohio valley mosquitoes.

CHAPTER THREE

LuAnn waited a moment before walking into the kitchen, a moment to look like she hadn't been eavesdropping on Leo's conversation. She smiled, hopefully convincingly.

Leo raised one hand. His tan spoke of hours in a tropical sun. Leo was a surfer and parasailer. He waved. "Hey, almost cousin."

"Hi, Leo. Where's your mom? I heard voices."

Leo held up his phone. "Just talking to my sweetie. Mom's upstairs. She was worried the boxes I brought down from the attic looked"—he made air quotes—"unkempt." He laughed.

And you didn't offer to help her? "Okay. I'll go tell her we're here."

"Brad's doing his thing, huh?" He nodded toward the parlor where, from the oohs and aahs, people were probably admiring the fireplace.

"You mean selling the house?"

"Yeah." Leo ran a hand across a day-old beard. His gaze drifted to the backyard. "Used to have a swing hanging from that tree." His voice grew rough. "Gonna be hard to say goodbye."

LuAnn veiled her surprise at this rare moment of vulnerability. In the few times she'd seen Leo, he'd always come across as the kind of person who kept moving and talking to avoid the exact kind of transparency he was displaying now. "Has to be sad for you, leaving a lifetime of memories behind." *Unless...* Had he been talking to his girlfriend about finding the deed to the house? Did he plan to find it so he could destroy it before Brad could find it, then try to prove Brad had no right to sell it? The thought became words in her head before she could activate a mental lasso to take it captive.

Stop! Her overactive imagination had been a gift when she'd needed creative stories to hold the attention of a class-room full of distracted high school students, but there were times it caused her to jump to ridiculous conclusions and get her in trouble.

"Yeah. It'll be hard." Leo ran the back of his hand across his eyes and turned around. "Coffee?"

"Thanks, but I think I'd better let your mom know her visitors are here." She walked into the dining room just as Brad was leading the group into the library. He was in full tour-giving mode when she passed him, but he aimed a wink at her. A wink that shrunk all the concerns his earlier response had swelled.

"Irene?" LuAnn called as she hit the landing then made the turn leading to the second floor.

"In here." The slightly breathless voice came from Leo's bedroom.

LuAnn found Irene staring into a small hinged black box. "Things are missing. They're not here."

"What are you looking for?"

"My mother's wedding rings. Leo's girlfriend is coming for your wedding. Did you know that? I like this one. She calls me sometimes. None of the others called. She's so interested in everything about our family. I set some pictures aside for when she comes. I think this might be the one, finally." She dumped the box upside down. "I was going to put the rings in our safe, but you know Thelma's theory— 'Hide it in plain sight.' I wanted to be sure it was handy for him just in case..."

"Maybe Leo put them somewhere else."

"He was just up here a few minutes ago. He said he didn't take them."

"Maybe Thelma put them in one of your jewelry boxes."

"I checked hers and mine. She said they were here, in the box, the last time she saw them." Irene sighed. "Speaking of jewelry, I want you to look through mine."

"You and Thelma already gave me the necklace when we got engaged. That's going to be my something old."

"Maybe we'll find Marta's pearls, and you can wear two somethings old." Irene's entire countenance seemed to vibrate with anticipation. "Or maybe that would be considered something borrowed. You can never have too many somethings borrowed, right?"

"Absolutely right." LuAnn nodded toward the door. "I noticed Thelma sleeping again. Is she doing okay?"

Irene sighed. "She was all excited when I told her you and Brad were bringing company. And then a minute later she was asleep. Our doctor says that's normal at her age, but..."

LuAnn put her arm around Irene's thin shoulders. "Has to be hard for you."

"Maybe she'll stay awake more after we move. More intellectual stimulation than I can give her, you know."

"I think it will be good for both of you." She gently steered Irene toward the hallway. "Let's go down and greet the people who are here to see your beautiful house."

Irene patted her thinning white curls. "I suppose I should go be a gracious hostess, shouldn't I?"

"You're the hostess with the mostest, Irene."

She gave a tiny, girlish laugh. "Take a look at the finished bathroom before we go down. The painter said she'd come back to make sure it looks okay after it's dried. Not that my eyes are worth much, but I think it looks fine." She walked ahead of LuAnn into the bathroom that had two doors, one opening to the hallway and the other to the master bedroom, a room that hadn't been occupied since Irene's husband passed away. LuAnn had always wondered how the family dynamics had worked when Irene and her husband and son shared a house with her unmarried sister—who had "set her cap" for Fred Martin before he began courting Irene. Maybe someday she'd feel bold enough to ask.

The seafoam bathroom was stunning. "It's such a serene color."

"I like transformations and surprises, don't you?"

Did she? "I love transformations." Watching the inn go through renovations had felt like watching the earth wake up after a long winter.

"But not surprises?" Irene's sparse brows rose above her blue frames.

"I'm a planner. I like to stick to the program."

Irene's smile flattened. Was she thinking about Saturday's "surprise" bridal shower, the one LuAnn wasn't supposed to know about? "I do like some surprises. The fun ones. This color is a delightful surprise."

Irene nodded as if LuAnn had given the correct response. "You still have my credit card, don't you?" she asked.

"Yes." LuAnn kept her smile in place while imagining more to-dos on her "Mansion" list.

"Can you pick up a new shower curtain with some of this greenish color in it? Something 'serene,'" Irene added.

"I can do that. Anything else?"

"Whatever you think it needs. A couple of hand towels, maybe?"

"Will do." LuAnn moved toward the door before the shopping list got any longer. She let Irene go first down the stairs, gripping the rail and planting each foot firmly on the next step.

The group was still gathered in the library, speaking in hushed tones. Oblivious to the tour, Thelma was softly snoring. Irene greeted friends and strangers with, "Thank you all for coming," while gently nudging Thelma awake. LuAnn wondered when the subtle shift had started—the younger sister taking care of the older.

Brad and his brother, Grant, had packed up most of the books and heirloom pieces that had once filled the library, but a few pieces remained. A Civil War sword hung on the wall above a charcoal sketch of a World War I biplane. A vintage radio stood in the corner.

Harry pointed at the shelf beneath the sword. "Now there's a piece with a story." He picked up the brass box that had once been buried amid layers of salvage finds at his store. He held it out for Lesley and Davinia to get a closer look. "A couple of years ago, the Wayfarers Inn ladies found a loose brick in a secret room and I—"

"Secrets," Thelma muttered, looking dazed as she stared around the room. "They just get you in trouble."

With a laugh, Harry lifted the top of the brass box. A picture fluttered to the floor. He picked it up and stuck it back. "This box sure caused some trouble, didn't—"

"Harry." Brad lowered his voice. "Let's get on with the tour."

Harry's story would lead to details of the murder, which could easily send Thelma into a tailspin. Thelma was still traumatized by the childhood memory of hearing her great-grandfather's deathbed murder confession.

In an effort to distract Thelma, who was still muttering about secrets, LuAnn said, "Tell them about the radio, Thelma," and pointed to the polished wood piece that stood in the corner.

A smile flitted across Thelma's lined face. "Daddy ordered it from the Monkey Ward catalog. That's what we called Montgomery Ward when we were children. He ordered it in 1929, and it arrived on October 23." She looked up, waiting for someone to respond.

Harry nodded. "The day before the stock market crash."

"Yes!" Thelma's dim eyes sparkled. "What a dark, dark day. We were all huddled around the radio listening to…"

LuAnn marveled at the human brain that could recall small details of a day ninety years ago. She watched the faces of their visitors. Thelma had their attention.

The doorway darkened. Leo leaned against the frame, a half smile on his face. Unsure how to interpret the smile, LuAnn stepped toward him.

"Funny how she can remember that but loses her glasses a dozen times a day," he said.

"She's a good storyteller." LuAnn stepped out of the room, and Leo turned with her, away from the group clustered around Thelma. Exactly what she'd hoped for. She'd learned from Brad that when it came to Leo, it was wise to be proactive. She hated being cynical, but if the conversation she'd over-heard was about finding the deed to the house, she wouldn't put it past him to try convincing potential buyers that they really weren't interested.

"She used to make up these long yarns when I was a kid," he said. "Had me believing she and my mom had traveled the Oregon Trail in a covered wagon. It was her way of teaching me history. Too bad you didn't know her when you were teaching."

"I'm sure I could have learned a lot. You have a rich heritage."

"Rich." Leo made a sputtering sound. "That, I am not."

So many comments came to mind. She discarded them all. Leo was going to be family. Still, she wondered if anyone had ever tried directing him toward a career, a way of living that involved supporting himself. Maybe she could ease her way into the topic. "Every time I see you, you seem to be doing pretty well for yourself."

He huffed, looked her in the eye, and held her gaze. "I'm a sponge, Lu. And I'm pretty sure you know that."

The honest admission took her aback. "Well"—what should she say?—"it's not too late to change that." She held her breath, wondering if she'd offended him.

"No, it's not." Leo stepped out of the way as Brad led the group into the dining room. A spark of recognition registered on his face when he saw Davinia and Lesley. They greeted him with hugs and followed the group into the kitchen.

LuAnn was about to thank him for the referral when Leo's countenance darkened. He rubbed his hand across his face. "I was recently told I'm a lazy, freeloading, overgrown spoiled brat."

LuAnn blinked. "Who would say something like that?"

Leo gave an easy laugh. "The woman I want to marry."

"You still want to marry her after that?"

"Yep. For the first time in my life, somebody cared enough to tell it to me straight. Gotta keep a woman like that."

"She's good for you, then."

"Yep. I'm done sponging. I've got a whole new gig going." He pulled his keys from his pocket. "Gotta go. Nice chatting, almost cousin."

He turned and walked out the front door. Before she figured out a polite way to ask if the "new gig" was legal.

June 6, 1861

Prudence stepped out the kitchen door of the Riverfront House and walked around the corner, hoping for even the slightest breeze off the river. She and Elizabeth had been baking bread since before dawn. Now, though not yet noon, the heat from the stove multiplied the warmth of the day, sapping her energy.

The tiny blue cornflowers on her calico dress had faded. It was not the prettiest of the three she owned, but it was the coolest, the thin fabric allowing for some air to seep through. When would she be able to purchase material for a new one? Cotton was becoming scarce with the fear that products from the South would soon be impossible to acquire. How could she think of new dresses when cotton may soon be desperately needed for uniforms? And bandages. *Oh, Lord, please bring reconciliation.*

Less than six weeks had passed since President Lincoln had called for seventy-five thousand militiamen. Her heart broke as one by one Marietta's young men answered the call. And now there would be a camp within walking distance of their farm.

She pictured Asher in his meticulous uniform, full of excitement and drive. What would that uniform look like a few months from now? She shared the fears of women from both North and South. Fear for family, for their way of life.

In truth, it was the weight of the mission she would embark on tomorrow that wilted her spirits far more than the heat. Was Jason right when he suggested this was a fool-hardy journey Asher could well accomplish without her?

"No." She spoke the word aloud.

"Miss Prudence?" A rustle in the lilac bushes next to the building accompanied the small voice.

"Zephaniah? Is that thee?"

He peeked out, and Prudence motioned for him, but he seemed reticent to come to her. She walked to where he stood, and the eight-year-old boy, face drawn and pale, fell into her open arms, sobbing against her apron.

Zephaniah Bickerton had tugged at her heartstrings from the moment he'd walked through the front door of the Riverfront House three and a half years earlier with people claiming to be his parents and brother. As far as Prudence had been able to figure out, she and Zephaniah were the only ones who knew the truth. The man who introduced himself as Howard Bickerton was an imposter.

Prudence and Jason had written letters and passed them on through their contacts to people involved in the British and Foreign Anti-Slavery Society. They learned that Howard's father had been a well-respected member, and that Howard's wife had died, leaving him with two sons. No one seemed to know what happened to Zephaniah's older brother, nor did they know of other family members. When Prudence asked Zephaniah, then only four years old, if he wanted her to find him another family to live with, Zephaniah said no. "My father said Matthew will come. I have two beds in my room. The other one is for Matthew. I have to wait for him."

Though Prudence questioned whether Zephaniah's brother would ever come, she respected his wishes, and she and Jason had done what they could to watch over him and let the child know he was loved. It had been easy the first year when his "father" bumbled his way through running the Riverfront House, but since Mr. Siloam had taken over as manager, Zephaniah and his "brother" Romulus were rarely seen at the inn.

"What is wrong, Zeph? Why is thee crying?" It was a question she didn't really need to ask. She had seen the way the boy was treated. Hearing the way Romulus spoke down to him reminded Prudence of the Grimm brothers' tale of the ash girl and her cruel stepsisters. She knelt in front of Zephaniah, cradling the trembling child close to her.

"C-can I see my b-box?" He wiped his nose on his sleeve.

"Of course. May I ask why?"

"I'm going to r-run away."

CHAPTER FOUR

N ot under here." LuAnn smoothed the quilt back in place, but a lump remained on the bed right where she'd thrown the covers up to scan the floor for her wedding shoes. "Not in the mood, Tom." She sighed as she stood. She was tired, but she gave in, scratching a spot a foot away from the playful, darting paw beneath the covers. Tom, army-crawling between the sheets, attacked the spot. They repeated the game of chase before LuAnn lifted the quilt and called a halt to it. The inn's mascot cat leaped out and circled her feet.

"I wish I had even a tiny bit of your energy today." LuAnn stepped over the purring cat and opened her closet door. Again. "They have to be here." She'd bought the shoes on sale more than a month ago. Ivory satin with a low heel. They'd been just a tiny bit snug, so, after looking up a solution online, she'd stuffed a slightly damp hand towel inside each one. Now she wanted to see if that had done the trick, but couldn't find the shoes anywhere. "I'm sure I left them on the shelf in my closet." Right next to the matching purse. She stared at the purse and the empty spot next to it. Maybe, in spite of all her careful planning and surrendering of details to Tess and Janice to avoid becoming a stressed-out bride, the stress was getting to her anyway. Janice's words echoed in her head. *Lu, what part of r-e-l-a-x don't you understand?*

The shoes would show up. She walked back to the desk and looked at the next thing on her list. *Call florist.* She'd picked out bouquets, boutonnieres, and centerpieces weeks ago, but she'd seen an idea for vintage-inspired bridal flowers on Pinterest. Along with the dusty-pink and ivory roses she'd already chosen, the picture she'd seen added eucalyptus leaves. LuAnn was captivated by the way the muted green gave the arrangements a timeless feel, but she needed to be sure they wouldn't make the place smell like the essential oils Winnie used for her arthritis. Making the call might be "breaking the rules," but it was such a small detail, not worth bothering her friends. She picked up the phone and tapped the number for Blooms, the florist shop on Front Street.

LuAnn didn't recognize the voice of the woman who answered. "Hi. This is LuAnn Sherrill. I'd like to make a change to my order for next week."

"Can you spell your last name, please?"

LuAnn spelled it then waited until she wondered if the woman was still there. "It might be easier if I just talk to Katrina. She's the one my matrons of honor have been working with. Is she there?"

"Um. Yes. I'll...get her."

The wall clock ticked off the seconds. Six minutes passed. LuAnn was about to hang up when the woman returned. "Yes, well, Katrina said I should take a message, and she'll get back to you."

LuAnn held back a sigh. "Tell her I would like to add eucalyptus leaves to my bouquet and maybe to the other arrangements, but I'm wondering about the smell. I don't want the church smelling like cough drops." She laughed. The woman did not echo.

"Okay. I'll let her know. Thank you." Without asking if LuAnn had further questions, she hung up.

"Customer service is not what it used to be, Tom." She was about to call the bakery with a question about the size of the cake—should she order a half sheet to go along with the full just to be on the safe side?—when her phone rang. Brad. She smiled as she answered. "Hi there."

"Hello, Beautiful. Hey, I hate to do this, but Leo asked me to help him and a couple of other guys move Thelma's piano tonight. Found out they can keep it in the dayroom at Countryside. Anyway, I hate to cancel, but we'll have a lot of dinners together soon to make up for it."

Something about Brad's reason for canceling their dinner plans rang hollow, but she couldn't put her finger on it. "Yes, we will. Be careful you don't throw your back out. You have to carry me over the threshold in nine days." Not that she would let him attempt that, but it was a fun mental picture.

She loved his laugh, always close to the surface. "I'll be careful. See you tomorrow. Dinner at the mansion, remember."

"I remember. Makes me sad. I can't imagine how the rest of you feel." Although Brad had never been enamored with the mansion's charms, it surely held more good memories than bad ones. "I'm not big on lasts."

"Yeah." Brad sounded distracted. She heard a muffled voice and then a door close. "Well, I'm sure I'll talk to you sometime before tomorrow night."

For the second time in a matter of minutes, someone hung up on her without waiting for her to say goodbye. LuAnn looked at Tom. "Makes a girl feel kind of invisible." She tried to shove off the sense of disappointment, but wasn't successful. It wasn't just dinner. She'd planned on showing him the trunk. They hadn't had time to talk about the card with the cryptic instructions. She picked up her pen, but there was a knock at her door before she had a chance to tackle the next thing on the list. "Come on in."

Tess walked in, followed closely by Huck, the inn's mascot terrier-shih tzu mix. "I think he knows you're leaving." Tess bent and ruffled the wiry fur on the top of Huck's head.

The gesture warmed LuAnn's heart. When they'd taken in the stray pup, Tess and Huck's relationship had been anything but love at first sight. LuAnn stood. "Do you have plans tonight?"

Tess nodded. "Big plans. Nachos, ice cream, and *Saving Mr. Banks* with Janice. Where are you and Romeo off to?"

"Nowhere. He's helping move Thelma's piano to Countryside." She folded her hands in a pleading gesture. "Can I join you?"

"Um...sure. Yeah. Of course. You know you don't have to ask." Was it just LuAnn's imagination, or did Tess's enthusiasm seem forced? "I'll go tell Janice to use the whole pound of hamburger."

In seconds, Tess had turned and left the room. Without even mentioning why she'd come by in the first place. The door stood partway open after Tess walked out. LuAnn heard whispering coming from their gathering room at the end of the hall but couldn't make out their words. Most likely, she'd messed with her friends' plans to work on prep for Saturday's surprise bridal shower. She'd be happy when that was behind them so she could stop acting like she hadn't overheard Brad's nieces, Wendy and Saffron, talking about the shower planned for the Saturday before the wedding.

But what if it wasn't shower plans? What if her two best friends were simply moving on without her? Her chest tightened as she struggled to shove the thought aside. The three had stayed close after Tess and Janice had gotten married, made time for each other even after they'd had kids. Even though LuAnn hadn't married or become a mom, they'd never made her feel left out. Her marriage at this age wasn't going to change that.

Was it?

With a shrug, she closed the door, then looked down at Huck and Tom curled together on her bed. "Invisible," she whispered. "At least you two have each other."

"Before we start the movie, I have something to show you two." LuAnn, comfy in an oversized T-shirt and stretchy capri pants, settled on the couch between Tess and Janice. She told them about the trunk and the card she'd found wrapped up with silverware, then held her phone out so they could both see the screen. "This is one side."

"You think this is about the deed for the Bickerton house?" Janice asked. "Were there papers in the trunk?"

"I didn't take everything out, but it looked like it was just filled with china. Beautiful, old, and probably very valuable china." LuAnn swiped to the next picture. "This is the other side of the card."

"What in the world?" Tess leaned closer. "Is it some kind of code? Right front right. Left back left. Assuming *R* and *L* mean right and left. Maybe they're dance steps."

"Or an aerobics workout," Janice said.

LuAnn laughed, maybe for only the second time all day. "Get up and try it."

"Unh-unh. You're the athletic one." Tess nudged her. "Stand up."

Now this felt more like their usual relationship. For whatever reason, things between the three of them had been strained the last few days. Wanting to keep the easy feeling going, LuAnn stood and took a giant step over the coffee table. Janice scooted closer to Tess, held her fist to her chin as if she were holding a microphone, and made a beatbox sound with her lips. "Ready?"

Tess started tapping the coffee table to the same beat. Together, the two other members of the partnership they now called the Inn Crowd, who had once dreamed of singing around the world as the In Crowd, began rapping out what could have been an eighties exercise video soundtrack.

"Turn over. Twist right. Front right. Two turns."

LuAnn bent, twisted, hopped a hundred and eighty degrees, and turned again.

"Two turns. Turn over. Twist right. Turn onto left side."

LuAnn dropped to the floor and turned onto her left side. By the time they got to "tap," and she patted her belly, they all had laugh tears, and when LuAnn stood and did a deep squat on "Bottom will drop," they were all gasping for air.

As LuAnn plopped back onto the end of the couch, Tess prompted, "We will never be…"

Janice and LuAnn joined in, finishing the motto they'd promised to live by more than forty years earlier. "…boring or bored! And we will never act our age!"

When they'd all caught their breath, Janice reached out and grabbed their hands. "I love you guys. The past two years have been the best."

"They have been," Tess said. "It's going to be hard to be split up."

LuAnn blinked back sudden tears. "Oh, you guys will find somebody else to take my apartment, and you'll forget all about me."

"Did you get that For Rent ad posted, Janice?" Tess laughed, then picked up LuAnn's phone and read the words again. "It sounds like a sequence of steps to open the bottom of something."

"It has to be something small and lightweight enough to be able to pick up and turn over." LuAnn rubbed her temple. "But what could you pick up that has sides that can be turned? I can't picture anything."

"Maybe it's the key for a vintage Rubik's Cube." Janice read the words again. "Could it be some kind of safe?"

Tess bolted upright. "The brass box!"

LuAnn felt her forehead rippling into a myriad of unflattering lines. "I don't know why I didn't think of that right away."

"But…" Janice seemed reluctant to tarnish their excitement. "We opened it already. And I can't imagine the sides would turn. The sides are solid, aren't they?"

Tess sat back. "Yeah. You're right. This is probably referring to something that disappeared a century ago."

"Or went overboard with the real, dead, Mr. Bickerton," LuAnn added.

Janice grimaced. "That's morbid."

"I need a notebook." LuAnn stood.

Tess laughed. "What will we do without your notebooks?"

One foot in the hallway, LuAnn turned. "Don't think for a moment my notebooks aren't going to be here. You are not allowed to ever attempt solving a mystery without me and my silver pen. Got it?"

Her best friends smiled and nodded and said in unison, "Got it."

LuAnn returned with a new, never-written-in notebook and copied all of the right/left directions. When she finished, she turned to a new page, and Tess and Janice began firing comments and questions as fast as she could write.

"What is the code for?"

"Do the words on the front and back go together?"

"Could it be referring to a deed to a different house?"

"Who is M?"

"Was the card put in the trunk the same time the china was packed?"

"We need to take all the china out of the trunk and see if anything else is in there," LuAnn said. "Maybe there are more clues, something that will tell us for sure if the dishes, and therefore likely the directions, belonged to the first Bickertons."

Tess held up one finger. "You said Leo found the trunk. Did he see the clue card?" She tapped the phone.

LuAnn wrote "Clue Card" at the top of a page. "Yes. Irene told him to leave it just the way he found it. I guess I need to talk to him."

"Or not," Janice said. "Not to say anything bad about Leo, but from things I've heard you and Brad say, I'm wondering if maybe we should keep this to ourselves for a bit. He lives in the house. He might know exactly what this is referring to, assuming it's something still there. If he knows we're looking for whatever we're looking for, he might be motivated to get to it first. Maybe we don't need to encourage him to go hunting for pearls."

"Or the deed," LuAnn added. If he didn't already know where it was.

Tess tilted her head to one side. "I know Brad's been stressed about finding the deed, but I hadn't really thought through all the possible implications until now. If Brad and Grant can't find the deed to the mansion, is it possible Leo would step in and claim Right of Property for his mom?"

"Does that really matter?" Janice asked. "The Grimes brothers are honest. They've said they'll use the money from the sale to support the sisters for as long as they live. Even if Leo got the court to agree the house belongs to Irene and Thelma, the sisters will still ask Brad and Grant to sell it for them, right?"

"Well…" LuAnn was tired of badmouthing Leo in her head. She didn't want to do it out loud. But…

"Oh." Tess was clearly experiencing another light bulb moment. "Does Leo have power of attorney for his mom?"

"Only if she becomes unable to make her own decisions." LuAnn rubbed her temple.

Tess gave a slow nod. "If the court ruled in his favor, all Leo has to do is convince them his ninety-year-old mother is no longer in her right mind, and he could claim the right to sell the house as his mother's representative."

"And keep the money for himself." LuAnn's voice grew weak.

"Stop!" Janice held up a hand. "You just said the other day you thought Leo was turning over a new leaf. Don't let that incredible imagination of yours go to the dark side. Nobody's done anything wrong."

Yet. No, Janice was right. Once again, LuAnn was letting her emotions run alongside a made-up scenario. "You're right. Leo wouldn't do that to his own flesh and blood." *Would he?* "Okay, so what we have to do is see if there is anything left in the mansion that belonged to the real Bickertons that could be turned over, twisted, tapped, and has a bottom that will open."

"Yep." Tess nodded. "All while running an inn, getting ready for a wedding, and moving you into Brad's house."

"Easy peasy, girls." Janice took a handful of popcorn. "We are, after all, the still-mostly-in-our-right-minds Inn Crowd."

CHAPTER FIVE

Friday morning had dawned without a cloud in the sky. LuAnn would have loved a longer, more leisurely walk with Huck. As she walked up to the front door of the inn with a reluctant dog in tow, she said, "I warned you we only had time for a short walk." She tugged on his leash. "Maybe we can get out again after lunch if it's not too hot."

What would mornings be like two weeks from now? Would she and Brad linger over coffee every morning before heading to work? Would she still have the time or discipline for morning walks or her daily stretching routine?

She took Huck up to the fourth floor, filled his food and water dishes, took a moment to give Tom a bit of attention, then headed downstairs to help with breakfast.

Davinia and Lesley were sitting in the wingback chairs near the fireplace. Davinia was zeroed in on her laptop while Lesley paged through the photo album LuAnn had just finished a few weeks earlier. It contained old pictures of the inn, photos taken before and during remodeling, and scenes from the events they'd hosted. LuAnn greeted them.

Lesley looked up and smiled. "Good morning. Something smells really good."

"Our cook's famous cinnamon rolls. People come from miles around for Winnie's specialties." She smiled in Davinia's direction, but the woman didn't look up. "I hope you two slept well."

"I sure did. I love the room." Lesley's smile was the kind people labeled contagious. They'd put her in Moonlight and Snowflakes, a room decorated in shades of blue and silver and white. "I was so hot after we walked around town yesterday, and it felt absolutely luxurious to come back to those beautiful cool colors."

"I'm so glad you like it." LuAnn turned to Davinia, who still hadn't looked up yet.

"Mom?" A twinge of embarrassment cramped Lesley's voice.

Davinia waved her hand. "Slept great."

"How did you come up with your room names?" Lesley asked.

"Well, in truth, it was pure whimsy."

"I love that!" Lesley clasped her hands on the photo album. "Woodbine and Roses, Lilac and Sage, Sunshine and Daisies. The names are...lyrical. And I think you hit just the right notes with the decor of our rooms and, from what I've seen in these pictures, all the rest of them. Don't you agree, Mom?"

No answer.

Lesley's shrug seemed to be an apology. LuAnn gave her a warm smile. "Guess I'd better get into the kitchen."

Davinia looked up from whatever she was studying. "The Bickerton mansion has some very unique features. Did Howard Bickerton design the layout himself?"

"I don't know. I imagine he worked with an architect."

"Here, or in London?" Davinia looked at her as if her "I don't know" would suddenly morph into an answer.

LuAnn shrugged. "We have a lot of unanswered questions."

Davinia nodded. "Must be records somewhere. No… indication…of the builder anywhere in the house? Sometimes they leave their mark, you know."

LuAnn's shrug gave a curtain call. "The sisters might know."

"I'll have to talk to them." Davinia looked back at her laptop.

After another apologetic smile from Lesley, LuAnn walked into the kitchen where Winnie was clanging pots and pans louder than usual. "Morning, Winnie. What's on the menu?" She took a clean apron off the hook.

"Apparently not as many selections as they offer at the Paw Paw Patch B&B." Winnie smacked a two-pound bag of shredded cheddar on the counter.

"What?" LuAnn stepped over to Winnie as she tied her apron strings. She put a hand on Winnie's stiff shoulder. "What's going on?"

Winnie yanked a drawer open and grabbed the kitchen scissors. With a little more vigor than needed, she cut the top off the bag. "You know I'm a pretty easygoing person, right? I can take a whole lot. Except when it comes to my cooking. You know I don't always handle it well when you three make suggestions about changing the menu, but when a complete stranger walks into my kitchen and starts telling me what I need to change…" Her shoulders fell in a forceful exhale. "Forgive me, Lord, I just need to let it go."

"Maybe you do need to let it go, but if something's bothering you, Tess and Janice and I need to hear about it. No unauthorized people are supposed to be in the kitchen anyway. Who's trying to tell you what to change?"

"That B&B owner from up north."

"Mother or daughter? Or both?"

"The mom. She came strollin' in here like she owned the place. Half expected her to put on an apron, nudge me out of the way, and start making her 'best baking powder biscuits this side of the Mississippi.'" Air quotes accompanied a raised eyebrow.

"Davinia Richards. Their B&B is called the Paw Paw Patch? I would have imagined something more…sophisticated for a Victorian house."

"It's no Victorian. Sounds like a big ol' log cabin. The original house was built in 1824 by a surveyor for the Erie Canal. It's been added onto about five times, and now they've got six rooms and a loft for guests. And besides the biscuits, they serve up homemade pawpaw jam, eggs from their own chickens, and bacon from their own pigs." Winnie dumped the cheese into a mixing bowl. "She said it was good that 'at least' we use locally sourced meat and produce here."

"Wow. Davinia didn't strike me as the farm type."

"Me neither. I think her daughter and son-in-law do the work. I got the feeling she was…you know…trying to feel better about herself by bragging up their place. You know how people can be when they feel inferior. She annoyed me, for sure, but I kind of feel sorry for her. I think she wishes she had a place like this."

Or like the mansion? LuAnn bit her tongue, gave Winnie a quick hug, and started cracking eggs.

"Our last meal here together." Irene sat at the dining room table in a room filled with boxes. She looked from Brad to LuAnn to Leo, and finally Thelma, then opened the cover of one of the pizza boxes that had just been delivered. She dabbed at her eyes, though no tears were visible.

LuAnn knew that Irene, the eternal optimist, and not an overly sentimental person, was looking forward to their new home, and had a feeling her act was all for Thelma, who was having a harder time with the thought of the transition. Stuffing the tissue back in her pocket, Irene asked Brad to bless the pizza.

They held hands around the kitchen table. "Father, we are grateful for this food and this home. Thank You for all of the memories, and we pray that the next people to live here will fill this house with joy, love, laughter, and new memories. Amen."

"Amen," Thelma echoed. "Do you think the new people will let us come back and take a look once in a while?"

If they turn it into a B&B, they will. But you'll have to pay to stay here. LuAnn kept the thought to herself. She might be making an assumption that wouldn't prove true, but Davinia's questions about the mansion seemed to go beyond mere curiosity.

She looked out toward the parlor that appeared far more spacious without the grand piano. As the sun lowered toward the horizon, it cast diamonds of multicolored light from the stained-glass trim on the front window onto the newly polished floor. What would the next owner change? It shouldn't matter, but it did. LuAnn hoped the next person to live here would bring a lively and eclectic mix of old and new, breathing life into these rooms. She silently echoed Brad's prayer. *Joy, love, laughter, and new memories.*

"I guess we'll have to wait and see," Brad answered. He turned to Leo. "So we finally get to meet this woman of yours, huh?"

Teeth sunk into cheese and pepperoni, Leo simply nodded, but his eyes shone. There was definitely something different about him. What had changed since his last visit? True love? Or something else?

Leo swallowed then looked at his watch. "She was on a medical mission trip, so I haven't seen her for two weeks."

"M-mission trip?" LuAnn stuttered. Leo was dating a woman who went on mission trips?

"Yep." He grinned. "I know, shocking that I would be with a woman like that, right? Anyway, I'm leaving for Pittsburgh as soon as we're done eating so I can meet her when her shift is done. I'll spend the week with her family, and we'll be back for your rehearsal." He looked at LuAnn. "Mom asked if you had a room for her, right?"

"Yes. She'll be in Lily and Lace." Leo would be staying with a friend after moving out of the Bickerton mansion, and his girlfriend would be staying at the inn. Another thing that spoke volumes about either a change in Leo or the moral character of his girlfriend. Possibly both. "I want to hear more about her."

"You'll love her." Leo scrolled on his phone and proudly showed them a picture of a woman with a dazzling smile, short blond hair, and bright blue eyes. "She has absolutely the best sense of humor and biggest heart of anyone I know." His smile faded. "She's way too good for the likes of me."

"She's an RN?" Brad asked.

"Yep. Pediatric oncology. Gotta have a big heart to do that, right?"

"Have you met her family?" LuAnn asked.

"I have. Just spent a few days up north with them last month. We went to this incredible immersive theater thing at a museum in Wheeling and then spent a few nights at a bed-and-breakfast. That's where I met that mom and daughter staying at the inn. Giana's family's good, salt-of-the-earth people. They're originally from Texas, but Mr. Fontaine got transferred to Pittsburgh when Giana and her sister were in high school. She's still got a little bit of a twang."

"So, she has a sister. Any other siblings?" LuAnn felt like she should lower the light hanging over the table and pull a notebook out of her purse.

"Family interrogation night, huh?" Leo smiled and leaned back, crossing his arms over his chest. "Okay. I'll play. She has an older brother. The whole Fontaine family's been involved in this cool old restored theater. Very cultured, you know." He lifted his little finger as if sipping tea from a delicate cup. "Giana is thirty-nine, and yes, I know that's ten years younger than I am. She's five-foot-three and loves Chicago-style hot dogs and butterscotch sundaes and Monet and Norah Jones, and her favorite T-shirt says, 'Created with a Purpose' and some Bible verse. She sings in the church choir and helps direct a children's theater."

Pediatric nurse. Bible verse. Church. LuAnn felt a rush of repentance. *Lord, forgive me if I've let Leo's past cloud my perception of who he is becoming.*

Irene patted Leo's hand. "I think she sounds like exactly the person we've been waiting for."

"And waiting and waiting…" Thelma added.

Brad laughed, and LuAnn joined in. Thelma's dry wit was still firing on all cylinders.

When Leo took the last piece of pizza and said goodbye, LuAnn cleared away the boxes and paper plates, then tugged on Brad's hand and whispered, "Let's go exploring."

He followed her upstairs where she opened the attic door and then walked ahead of him up the stairs. "I didn't get to ask you. Do you think Lesley and Davinia are interested in buying the house?" She made it sound casual as she ran her fingertips along the wallpaper. Brad and Grant had decided not to touch the attic. They would leave this bit of original history for the future owners.

As she waited for Brad to answer, LuAnn released the reins on her imagination. She pictured herself a young house servant, living under the eaves when the house was brand-new. A hard life...rising before dawn and turning in at night only after the Bickerton family had gone to bed. What would LuAnn the Victorian Housemaid have figured out about the imposters she worked for? Would she have heard Howard and Charisse Bickerton—aka Stuart and Charisse Dawson—whispering at night about how they were going to pull off their monumental scam? Would she hear Zephaniah Bickerton crying for his father at night, or catch Romulus, the real son of Stuart and Charisse, ridiculing Zephaniah because he was adopted?

"They asked a lot of questions."

Brad's statement startled her. LuAnn stopped in the middle of the attic and stared at him. "Oh! Lesley and Davinia."

His easy, teasing smile warmed her. "Where were you?"

She loved being known this well. "I was right here." She pressed her teeth against her bottom lip in a sheepish grimace. "In 1857."

"It's going to be fascinating living with a woman who teleports to bygone eras. I wish you could take me with you."

She waited for him to reach her. "Close your eyes." When he did, she kissed his cheek.

His eyes popped open. "That was nice."

"But that's not why I wanted you to close your eyes. You need to exercise your imagining muscles."

"I have imagining muscles?"

"Yes. But they're flabby."

"I beg your pardon." He grinned, but obeyed.

"Now picture this room the way it looked right after the house was built. Smell the new wood and fresh paint?"

Grooves formed on Brad's forehead. "There used to be walls partitioning off rooms. More like cubicles without ceilings, Thelma said. Their father tore them down. So I'm imagining we're standing in a hallway between rooms. I'm a butler and you"—he wrapped his arm around her waist—"are the ladies' maid I snuck up here to see." Laughing, he opened his eyes and planted a kiss on her lips, then pulled away. "Now why did you drag me up here, my lady-in-waiting?"

She led him to the trunk, knelt, and opened it. He knelt beside her.

"There appears to be a full set of china, maybe service for twelve here. And look." She held up a handful of sawdust and touched a curl of thin wood that fell apart under her fingertip. "Irene agrees it could have belonged to the original Howard. Is it possible this was never unpacked?"

"Doesn't seem likely, but I guess it could be possible. Why do you think it was Howard's?" He gave her a quizzical look.

"This is not another one of my time travel fantasies. I can back this up with real evidence. First, it's a very old pattern. Irene didn't remember ever seeing the dishes. Second, people used wood shavings to cushion things for travel. Why would anyone who lived in this house order china to be shipped here and then never use it, or repack it in stuff that would make such a mess?" To illustrate, she picked up a plate and let powdered wood drift onto Brad's khaki-covered knee.

"But why wouldn't Charisse have used it? She didn't have a problem taking everything else that belonged to Marta. Including her son."

"It's a woman thing." She wouldn't touch on anything that would give Brad any hint that she was struggling with the thought of living in his late wife's shadow. She turned her focus to the contents of the trunk. She lifted the velvet cloth, carefully unwrapped it, and handed him the card. "Whoever put this in a box of china was either a scatterbrained packer or was trying to hide something."

Brad nodded as he read one side, then the other. "I know the secretary desk in the library was sent from England by Howard. I think the bed and dresser in Thelma's room were too. And maybe the buffet." He tapped his finger on his chin. "But all of those things are too large to..." His eyes gleamed. "What about the brass box?"

"That's what Tess suggested. But that opened with a key, and I'm pretty sure the sides won't turn."

"But what if"—Brad was halfway to the stairs before he finished the sentence—"we missed something. What if the leg thingies turn?"

Goose bumps cavorted up the middle of LuAnn's back. The box rested on small, round brass feet. She closed the trunk and hurried after him. They were practically running when they skidded to a stop in front of the library door.

The box was not on the shelf.

"Aunt Irene!" Brad strode toward the kitchen.

Irene met him halfway. "What's all the commotion?"

"Where's the brass box? Did you pack it?" He swept his arm toward the library.

"No. It's right on the shelf under the…" She pointed to the card still held tight between his fingertips. "Do you think…?" Pale eyes wide, she looked toward the library window with its view of the driveway leading to the road. "I have no idea where… Unless…"

LuAnn stared out at the haze of dust at the end of the drive. "Leo?"

Irene's shoulders drooped as she nodded. "Gone to Pittsburgh."

June 7, 1861

Asher's borrowed buckboard sat in front of the house, the horses nickering impatiently in the dark as if sensing the need to get on their way before light.

"Another cup?" Prudence stood by the fire, ready to take the boiling pot off its hook.

"No. Thank you." Asher lifted the leather sack she had filled with biscuits, a jar of strawberry jam, a tin of coffee, and cloth-wrapped jerky.

Jason stood by the window, hands on hips. "Blue was fidgety last night." He nodded toward the hound dog who stood on the porch, hackles raised. "I heard Charity whinnying around midnight."

Prudence stepped to his side. Though sure the normal night noises had only seemed amplified because of his concern for her, she put her hand on his back. "Does thee think that bobcat's back?"

"Possible." He looked over his shoulder at Asher. "Who knows thee is going?"

"No one. I asked leave for a family matter. Didn't tell 'em what for. I've got five days."

Prudence felt Jason's shoulders relax a bit. "Must be the bobcat," he said. "I will try tracking him after I take Moses to Tabitha. The ground is soft enough to see tracks."

Leaning against Jason, Prudence tried to memorize the feel of his muscled arm, the scent of sunshine on his shirt. She drew close enough to be heard in barely a whisper. "If a message arrives, thee will take it to Stockton." Her voice rose on the last word, as if it were a question, even though Jason would know it was not.

He nodded. "Of course." He wrapped his arm around her. "*Someone* must stay close to home to work the fields, tend the animals, wash the clothes, bake the bread, cook the meals, feed the boy, make the soap..."

She laughed and nudged him with her shoulder. "Thee has enough bread, eggs, vegetables, and canned venison to last a fortnight, and I am quite certain there will be no soapmaking or laundry washing while I am gone. At day's end, thee has naught to do but warm the meat and read to Moses."

Prudence stood on tiptoe and kissed Jason, then walked into the corner bedchamber to brush her lips across her son's forehead one last time.

With a last glance at the warmth and safety of her home—the lamp glowing on the kitchen table, the lit candles on the mantel, and Jason sitting with his hands folded on his Bible—she walked onto the porch, closed the door, and patted a nervous Blue. Jason was right, the hound did appear excessively vigilant this morning. "Watch over them, boy."

CHAPTER SIX

A rough, wet puppy tongue disrupted LuAnn's forced afternoon nap. As she opened her eyes to pet the persistent Huck, frames from a dream scrolled through her mind. She'd been walking hand-in-hand with Brad through a field of black-eyed Susans. Far in the distance loomed Christ Fellowship Church, the bell in its belfry clanging loudly, seeming to call to her. They came to a crossroads marked with an old wooden sign, the words on it unreadable. "Let's go left." Brad tugged at her arm.

"We have to keep going straight," she replied. "Can't you see the church?"

"But look." Brad pointed. "There's something shiny over there. Maybe it's"—he let go of her hand and turned to the left—"pearls."

She tried to yell, but words wouldn't form. She tried to run, but her feet wouldn't move. And all the while the distance between her and Brad grew larger and larger.

At that point, Huck's sloppy kisses saved her from the dream.

"Don't need a therapist to analyze that one," she muttered.

Huck nuzzled her arm. It was unnerving the way the pup seemed to understand her at times. She gave him a gentle nudge, and he answered by licking her ear.

"You've got exactly one week to break that habit, Huck. Tess may not appreciate—" Her warning dissolved in a laugh as cat paws began massaging the top of her head, shoving silver strands of tangled hair across her eyes. Steady kneading accompanied by a contented purr. "I'm going to miss my spa treatments, Tom." She ran her hand along the cat's sleek black and white fur. "I'm going to miss waking up to you two. But I'll be here almost every day. I promise I'll bring treats."

The cat squinted with contentment, and she was almost sure the dog grinned.

LuAnn brushed her hair and freshened her makeup, then picked up her wedding planning notebook and silver pen. She tamped down the guilt at doing nothing at three in the afternoon while her co-owners and the inn staff cleaned up after the lunch rush in the café downstairs. She'd been given orders to take a bubble bath and a nap in preparation for their "special dinner"—aka the surprise shower she wasn't supposed to know about.

There wasn't supposed to be a shower for her to know about. She'd told Tess and Janice she didn't need a bridal shower. It would be ridiculous for people to waste money on mixers and toasters and towels when she was moving into a fully equipped home. They'd finally relented, or so she'd thought, until she'd accidentally eavesdropped on Saffron and Wendy talking about helping with decorations.

She sat in her favorite chair overlooking the Ohio. Something else she would miss. The view…and the chair. She was leaving it behind. Though Brad had encouraged her to make any changes she wanted, it made no sense to crowd in more furniture.

Sensible was the name of the game. She picked up her copy of Prudence Willard's journal. Two years ago, they'd found the journal in the same room they'd found the key that fit the brass box. Prudence had worked right here in this building, housekeeper and cook by day and, often, Underground Railroad conductor by night.

LuAnn flipped to a page in 1861 where Prudence described a wedding she'd planned in just two days.

Today, Lieutenant Asher Bailey will marry his true love in front of the fireplace at Riverfront House. God has blessed us with a cloudless sky and fields ablaze with color. I have just returned from picking a basket overflowing with day lilies, black-eyed Susans, little yellow trefoil blossoms, moth mullein, butterfly weed, Queen Anne's lace, chicory, and prairie rose. Elizabeth has polished the candelabras and baked a lovely sponge. I have taken in my wedding dress and added a bit of ivory lace, and blue ribbon that matches the fabric of the skirt, to the collar and sleeves, hoping to freshen its appearance, but I am sure the necklace Z insists she borrow and the glow in Salome's eyes as she looks at Asher in his dress blue uniform, shall more than suffice. It will be a simple wedding, but every- thing they need.

"A simple wedding, but everything they need" had become LuAnn's motto for their ceremony. She closed her eyes and imagined being that long-ago bride. No florist, bakery, or caterers involved. No lists, no stress, yet she would have been surrounded by the natural beauty of wildflowers and candle-light. And a something-borrowed-something-blue dress that swished when she walked.

In keeping with her motto, LuAnn had planned a simple church wedding and kept changes to Brad's house to a minimum. Her husband-to-be was not quite so frugal, insisting on a honeymoon that seemed too extravagant...yet thrilled her to her history-loving toes. She smiled as she opened her notebook and pulled out the brochure she used as a bookmark—*Castles Along the Rhine—eight days from Amsterdam to Basel.* They would end their trip with three days in Paris.

As always, since the day Brad had proposed, she thanked God for giving her the desires her heart hadn't dared envision. This wasn't the first time she'd been in love, nor the first wedding she'd planned. After one romance ended in betrayal and the other with her standing graveside two weeks before the date of the wedding she'd spent a year planning, she'd decided God meant for her to be single. She'd never dreamed of falling in love in her sixties, never imagined she could feel this kind of happiness again.

She picked up her pen, but her phone buzzed before she wrote the first word. Tess.

"Hey Lu, there's some...thing down here for you. From Grant and Wendy and Saffron. It's a pre-wedding gift, just for you. I think you might want to come down and open it. Now."

A shower gift? From Wendy and Saffron...and their dad? Guys weren't invited, were they? "Okay. I'm going to do my nails and then I'll be down."

"You should come down here first."

What was a *pre*-wedding gift anyway? "Okay...but what's the rush? So they dropped off a toaster or set of towels, why—"

"They didn't actually drop it off."

"UPS?" It was too late in the day for a Post Office delivery.

"Nope."

"FedEx? Carrier pigeon?"

"Just come look."

What was that tone in Tess's voice? She'd made it sound urgent, yet...

Oh. So this was how they were going to surprise her. "Okay. I'll be right down."

"Th...it...will be waiting by the fireplace." Tess seemed to be stifling a laugh before she hung up.

LuAnn had assumed the shower would be tonight. Maybe it was now. Maybe they'd decorated while she napped. Maybe Winnie had been busy baking a cake and the guests had assembled in the café and were all waiting to jump up and surprise her.

LuAnn smiled, slid her phone in her pocket, and headed out of her apartment and into the living space she shared with Tess and Janice. She paused with her hand on the door, suddenly hit by a wave of nostalgia.

Two years ago, almost to the day, the three of them had made an appointment to look at the inn...just for fun. LuAnn was in the process of moving back to Marietta after retiring from thirty-five years of teaching English and History in an inner-city high school in West Virginia. Her mother had just passed away. She'd felt a bit lost, untethered, wondering what life after work was supposed to look like, when she'd set out for a day of house hunting with her two best friends. She'd had in mind a small, two-bedroom bungalow. And then...the handsome Realtor appeared on the scene and turned her well-planned future upside down with two words.

Though it had taken her over a year to fully admit it, Bradley Grimes, with his blue eyes, poetry, and knowledge of history, had disarmed her from day one. Why else would a sensible, list-making woman get weak-kneed when a man said, "Who knows what fascinating secrets this old place holds, ladies?" When he'd added, "It's been empty for quite a while. Sitting here with all this potential. What a waste, don't you agree?" LuAnn was rendered powerless. Who could resist a historical building with "secrets" and "potential"? And those blue eyes.

She was going to miss this place. Though she'd still be working here five days a week, it wouldn't be the same. Sharing space with her old college roommates had been healing for all of them. Tess had been widowed for four years when they bought the inn, Janice for only a little over a year. This time of laughter, of talk and prayer and shared meals and solving mysteries, had made them all stronger and given them renewed purpose. As with so many of life's adventures, she had to leave something behind in order to experience something new.

She opened the door, closed it softly behind her, and walked down the stairs with a strange mix of dread and anticipation. She heard talking, but it stopped the minute a board creaked under her feet on the second-floor landing. She paused a moment, composing her expression, checking her body language, making sure she could make her entrance into a room full of friends yelling "Surprise!" with a convincing look of true astonishment.

The café was empty. No streamers. No paper wedding bells. No people.

A wrapped package sat on the coffee table in the lobby. White paper embossed with pink roses, tied up with a massive silver bow, a small white envelope tucked beneath the ribbon. The box was about five inches high and eighteen square. Its size gave no clue to its contents.

LuAnn jumped at the sound of rustling papers. A woman she didn't recognize sat reading in one of the wing-backed chairs in front of the fireplace. A man with a thin moustache and a bit of salt-and-pepper at his temples occupied the other.

The café was closed, and they weren't expecting any new guests tonight. Had they checked in while she was napping? It wasn't unheard of for someone to walk in and ask if they had vacancies. She held out her hand to the man. "Hello. I'm LuAnn Sherrill, one of the owners. Has someone helped you?" Helped them do what, she wasn't sure. Maybe they'd hoped for a tour of the inn. She could accommodate that.

"Good afternoon." The man took her hand. His were soft, and his voice high and formal-sounding, with just a touch of an accent. British? Australian? "Sean Wolfe, with an *e*. Pleasure to meet you."

The woman lowered her book and smiled. Deep red lipstick framed bright white teeth. Sleek black hair with a bluish tint framed her face. Smile lines crinkled at the corners of her eyes. She looked like a woman who could find humor in just about anything. She reached toward LuAnn with red-nailed fingers. "Erica Garrett. Nice to meet you. And, yes, Tess checked us in, and Janice showed us to our rooms." The woman's eyes danced. Startling eyes…bright teal with flakes of metallic gold. A person needed a prescription from an optometrist to get eyes that color. "We're looking forward to our time in Marietta," she said. "We'll be here until Friday."

Why hadn't Tess mentioned on the phone that there were guests lounging in front of the gift she was supposed to retrieve? "I hope you enjoy your stay."

"Oh, we will." The woman's smile appeared smug.

LuAnn picked up the package. "Nice to meet you both." She stepped around the coffee table.

"You'll want to open that here," Sean said. Though worded like a command, amusement danced in his voice. His moustache, a space shaved in the middle like Clark Gable's in *Gone with the Wind*, rose on one side.

"I will?"

"Yes." Erica pointed a finger at the box. "It will all make sense when you open it."

LuAnn looked toward the café, straining to hear voices in the kitchen. Tess must be in there. Maybe Janice too. Though these strangers seemed friendly enough, she would have felt better with a familiar face in sight. With a hesitant step back, she positioned herself in front of the love seat and lowered onto the cushion, box on her lap. She slipped the card out from under the ribbon. Her name was written on the front in pink calligraphy.

The card was blank on the front. Inside, in Grant's bold printing that was so much like Brad's, were two short sentences.

Please enjoy these gifts. They will record every special moment for you to keep forever.

Love,

Grant, Wendy, and Saffron

A camera. It had to be. Grant, a photographer, often talked about "capturing the moment." A camera would be the perfect gift from a photographer. But the note said "they." More than one camera? Journals, maybe. Everyone knew her passion for a blank book. She pulled the ribbon off one corner, and the bow slid onto the love seat. Though still not sure what these two people were doing here, her shoulders relaxed. Maybe they were here to show her how to use the camera. Or cameras. Excellent customer service, if that was it. She slid her finger under one flap and then the other. After loosening two more pieces of tape, the stiff paper lifted off.

A white box. No store name. No markings of any kind. She lifted the cover. A white photo album nestled in a bed of pink tissue paper. "Brad & LuAnn" and their wedding date was printed in gold on the cover, and taped to the front was a gold flash drive, etched with the same words. LuAnn opened the album and stared at the blank pages. "Very n-nice." *But why are you people here?* She looked at the woman, who bent and slid a black bag from beside the chair. As if choreographed, the man mirrored her actions, sliding out an even larger black bag.

Erica lifted a card from a side pocket and handed it to LuAnn. Sean did the same. "*We* are the real gift, Ms. Sherrill," he said with a smooth smile.

LuAnn read the cards. *Erica Garrett, wedding photographer. Sean Wolfe, wedding videographer.*

Oh no. "Um...that's...thoughtful of them, but I have a photographer." Oddly, she was sure the woman she'd hired had been recommended by Grant.

Erica the wedding photographer reached out and rested her fingertips on LuAnn's arm. "We're doing your *pre*-wedding pictures. We're going to be here for your entire wedding week, recording all of the pre-wedding highlights for you and your fiancé."

LuAnn forced a smile. What in the world were they going to record? Tess and Janice had everything under control. Between tonight's shower and her hair appointment next Saturday, she wasn't planning anything out of the ordinary. Brad had even less to do—pick up his tux and show up at the church by two o'clock on Saturday. "That's...nice of them. I just think it might be"—*overkill* was the word that came to mind—"boring for you."

"Wedding planning is never boring," said Sean Wolfe-with-an-*e*. "Don't you worry about us. We'll be your invisible shadows this week. You two go about doing whatever you need to do, and you won't even know we're here."

"Okay.... Well...thank you." LuAnn felt a sudden need to walk the dog. It would buy her a few minutes to consider how to politely but firmly say "No thank you." She stood. "Well, I'm off on an errand." She stepped away from the love seat. "Let Tess or Janice know if you need—"

Her two "gifts" jumped to their feet and fell in step behind her, black bags in hand.

"Um. This errand isn't wedding related."

Erica smiled a smile that could probably get her elected to any office in the country. Or sell a bridge in Brooklyn. "We're interested in *everything* you're doing this week."

LuAnn shoved her hand in her pocket and clutched her phone. "If you'll excuse me, I have a quick call to make first." She strode into the miniscule office and stabbed at a contact listed under *G*.

Voice mail.

When the message ended, she sagged against the door and forced a smile, "Hi, Grant. It's LuAnn. I just received your… gift. Very…unique. I just have a few questions about them, so if you can give me a call ASAP I'd really, really appreciate it."

CHAPTER SEVEN

LuAnn walked out of the office, ready for an awkward conversation with the two people who seemed bent on following her closer than Huck did when she had a pocketful of Yummy Bonez. After a moment of cooldown, she knew she couldn't send them packing. This really was an amazing gift. But a gift that needed boundaries.

Instead of standing by the front door where she'd left them two minutes ago, Sean and Erica were leaning on the front desk chatting with Janice, who was looking at her watch. "Have a good nap?"

"Yes. Thank you." Her phone vibrated. She pulled it out, hoping it was Grant returning her call. Or Brad. Was he in on this?

The name on the screen made her smile. Perfect timing. "Hi, Irene. I was just thinking of coming to see you." Thinking that as of one second ago. She'd far rather talk to Irene about changing the color of the kitchen than take a walk with Huck and a camera. Or two. She needed time to think about what to do about this new gift. "I'm going to go pick up the shower curtain I ordered at—"

"I need you to do something else for me. Your pastor's wife said there are some empty boxes at your church we can use.

She was going to bring them this afternoon, but she had to sit in on a meeting, so she said she'd bring them later, but I really need them now. I have all of Thelma's clothes laid out on her bed, and she wants to take a nap. In bed. And if I don't get them off her bed she's going to—"

"I'll get the boxes from the church right away and bring them over." LuAnn said goodbye and smiled at the photographers. This is where she would draw the line. If she couldn't banish them without offending Grant and his daughters, she would, as kindly as possible, let them know they were welcome to follow her to things related to the wedding. If they wanted to accompany her to the church on Friday to snap pictures of her tying bows on the pews—if she was allowed to help—or take a video at the hair salon, she could handle that. But only that. "I'll be back in a few minutes." Or hours. "I just need to run over to the church and—"

"Perfect." Erica smiled. "We'll get to see the church. Even though we aren't doing your actual wedding photographs, it would be wonderful to get some shots in the setting where you're going to get married."

Sean nodded. "Seeing the venue you've chosen for your ceremony will give us a better feel for who you are and what you like."

A thought hit. Maybe these two were simply here for today to distract her. Maybe Irene was in on it, and this was just a ploy to get her away from the inn so Wendy and Saffron could decorate the café, and she'd come home from Irene's to an inn full of people yelling "Surprise!" Or maybe the shower was going to be at the church, and this was how they were going to get her there. Ingenious.

Lord, You sure have blessed me with creative friends. She gave the paparazzi a warm smile. "Let's go."

LuAnn started the car, letting the sound of the engine cover her sigh. "How did my future brother-in-law and nieces find you?"

Erica smiled from the passenger seat of LuAnn's car. "Actually, we found them."

LuAnn waited for more of an explanation but was met with silence. "I've never heard of anyone doing 'wedding week' photos." She envisioned feeling like Meghan Markle this week, with every sneeze being caught on digital.

"Imagine what a treasure the photos and footage will be in years to come." Sean's voice sounded as though he was scooting as far forward in the back seat as his shoulder harness would allow. "Something to treasure forever."

She had to stifle a laugh at that. At her age, "forever" didn't stretch out into the far-off horizon. It wasn't like she and Brad would be sharing their pictures with grandchildren someday. "Have you done a lot of pre-wedding photos?"

"We are actually just launching this extra service," Sean said. "We may be asking you if we can use some of your pictures for our websites."

"I don't imagine most of your future clients will be in our age bracket. Hope we can do your service justice." She flicked the turn signal and turned in to the church driveway.

Paige Murphey met LuAnn in the church parking lot with cardboard boxes and a hug. "One more week. Any pre-wedding jitters?"

LuAnn glanced at the two people sitting in her car. "I do have some jitters." Two, to be exact. She stuck the boxes in the trunk of her car. "See you tomorrow." This was where Paige would come up with some reason to ask her to come into the building.

"Okay. Enjoy the rest of your day." Paige smiled and sprinted toward the back door of the church.

Only as she was turning onto the road did LuAnn realize Paige hadn't asked about the two people sitting in her car. And the two people who'd said they wanted to look at the "venue" hadn't gotten out or asked to see the inside of the church.

The car doors popped open when they arrived at the mansion. Cameras in hand, Sean and Erica stood in the driveway, cooing about the "exquisite" and "extraordinary" landscaping. LuAnn opened the trunk and waited, expecting her tagalongs to offer to help, but they were busy adjusting massive lenses. She headed to the back door, but Erica stopped her. "Please, can't we go in the front? These old houses have such stunning foyers. I want to capture it."

"Sure." LuAnn turned toward the stone pathway leading to the porch. She set the boxes down and grabbed onto the door handle. She turned the knob and opened the oak door.

"Surprise!"

A crowd of smiling, giggling women and young girls stood in the parlor, waving and clapping. LuAnn's hand flew to her mouth. Never in a million years would she have thought they could actually surprise her with a shower she already knew about. But they'd done it.

Tess and Janice, both appearing slightly breathless, stepped up and enveloped her in a group hug. Irene was next. LuAnn remembered Janice looking at her watch right before Irene called. The call, and the photographers who were apparently not actually going to shadow her for an entire week, had all been part of their plan.

They led her to the fireplace where a chair had been decorated with pink and sage-green streamers. White paper bells hung from every light fixture, and Pachelbel's Canon in D played in the background. As much as she'd argued against wanting a shower, as she looked around at all the smiling faces, tears sprang to her eyes. Something about this felt so right.

Except for the two strangers who, at the moment, were aiming their lenses at the stairway leading to the second floor rather than at her or her guests. Strange, but then again, this historied house had a mesmerizing effect on people.

As everyone quieted and settled into the circle of chairs in the parlor, LuAnn heard the back door open and close. A winded Paige, baby on hip, came rushing in. "Did they pull it off?" she asked. "Were you surprised?"

"Very." LuAnn put her hand on her chest where her heart was still hammering an erratic beat. "I had no idea." It wasn't a complete untruth. "You were in on this, weren't you?"

Paige shrugged, a mischievous look on her face. LuAnn turned to Irene. "And you. I take it Thelma's clothes are not piled on her bed. You're a conspirator, Irene."

Irene shoved her glasses up and wiped laugh tears from her eyes. "Oh, my dear, you have no idea the secrets this old lady can keep."

"She's not the only one who can keep a secret," Thelma said, straightening her lap blanket. Tess scrambled to Thelma's side, holding out a plate of frosted sugar cookies cut in the shape of a bell. "Cookie, Thelma?"

"Oh my, yes. Did Winnie make these? I remember the cookies she made for my seventy-fifth birthday. Do you remember that party, Irene? Everyone was there. The mayor even—"

"Let's save that story for later when we have more time." Irene smiled patiently. "I think Janice has a little get-to-know-you game for us."

The front door opened. "Sorry we're late." Davinia walked in, carrying a package wrapped in flowered paper. Lesley stepped in behind her, surveying the room with what appeared to be a very uneasy smile.

What were they doing here? Other than the two photographers, no inn guests had been invited. And speaking of the photographers, at that moment, Sean darted out of the room, followed quickly by Erica, who positioned herself in the dining room, just behind the arched doorway leading to the parlor with a massive camera in front of her face.

Tess didn't appear surprised to see their inn guests. In fact, there were two empty chairs in the circle.

Saffron handed her a bowl of pink and white mints, followed by a plate of cookies. LuAnn took a sugar cookie, admiring the satiny smooth icing decorated with rows of tiny, edible silver stars. She looked across the circle at Winnie, pointed to the cookie, and smiled. "These are amazing."

Winnie winked. "So are you."

LuAnn looked around the circle, once again fighting tears. Paige had taken the chair to Winnie's left. Next to her sat Maybelline, her granddaughters Belle and Natalie, then Emma, Saffron and Wendy, and Brad's cousin, Char. Tess's daughter, Lizzie, sat beside Janice's daughter, Stacy, her daughter-in-law, Zelda, and Zelda's daughter, Brin. All of the women from LuAnn's Bible study were there, some with daughters or granddaughters. No wonder they'd had to move the piano. And here she'd been questioning what Brad was up to.

Robin Rogers, who'd helped with the inn renovations and now worked for them as a regular employee, sat next to LuAnn. "Who's minding the inn?" LuAnn asked. "Everyone's here."

"Taylor voluntarily gave up his basketball game just for you."

"Good man." LuAnn turned her attention back to Davinia who, at the moment, was standing next to her daughter, plate in one hand, coffee cup in the other. In response to something Lesley said, she laughed, jarring her cup and splashing coffee onto Lesley's sleeve.

Lesley jumped up, a look of shock—and maybe pain—on her face. She reached for a napkin and began dabbing at the sleeve of her off-white sweater. Davinia seemed to be apologizing profusely, then pointed to the dining room, most likely to the door of the powder room. Lesley nodded, gave her mother a look of disbelief, and walked out of the room. Davinia then walked immediately over to Irene, bent low, and whispered something in her ear. Irene nodded, and Davinia mouthed "thank you" and walked up the stairway. She paused on the landing to straighten an old oval-framed picture of Thelma and Irene's grandfather, and continued on her way upstairs. Moments later, LuAnn recognized the squeak of the main floor powder room door. Lesley returned to her seat and looked around, seemingly confused that her mother was nowhere in sight.

When Janice handed LuAnn a cup of coffee, already clouded with just the right amount of cream, LuAnn motioned for her to bend closer. "I'm concerned about Davinia."

Janice's eyes widened. "I'm so sorry. Davinia kind of invited herself, and we just didn't quite know how to say no. If it bothers you, I can—"

"It's okay that they're here," LuAnn interrupted. Though she had no idea why a person would ask to be invited to a bridal shower for someone she'd just met. "Davinia just went upstairs. I'm guessing to use the bathroom. Would you mind checking on her?" she whispered.

"Of course. Do you think she's ill?"

"I don't know. It's just a little...odd." She refrained from voicing the question in her head. Maybe Davinia wasn't ill... but was she up to ill?

CHAPTER EIGHT

LuAnn tried to appear calm and undistracted as she waited. Finally, Janice descended the stairs with Davinia close behind her. Davinia's expression was unreadable, and LuAnn wasn't able to catch Janice's eye. All she needed was a shrug or a raised eyebrow to confirm or deny her suspicions, but Janice didn't look in her direction. When she reached the bottom, Janice clapped her hands twice. Once a teacher, always a teacher. "We're going to play Find the Guest. Tess is handing out pens and the game. What you need to do is mingle and be nosy. It's pretty self-explanatory. We'll give you a minute to look it over before we start."

LuAnn read the questions, searching for one that would conveniently lead her to Davinia.

The instructions started with "Find someone in the room who…" Below it was a list of twenty things, including:

Has a birthday in the same month as yours

Can name all 44 US presidents

Has visited all 50 states

LuAnn stood, but before she was able to take a step, Robin touched her arm. "You were a history teacher. I bet you can name all the presidents."

"I can do better than that. I can sing them."

"Awesome. Sign here." Robin held out her paper, and LuAnn signed her name.

"I want to hear it." Saffron stood in front of her, holding out her paper. She wore a plain white blouse over a navy and white striped shirt. Her hair fell to her shoulders in soft waves. Classic casual beauty, so different from the girl with the stud in her nose they'd first met two years ago.

"Okay. Here goes." LuAnn began singing to the tune of "America the Beautiful." "George Washington, John Adams, Thomas Jefferson…" She sang it the way her students had loved to hear it…at tongue-twister speed. Halfway through, she realized the entire room had grown quiet. She knew what would come next. Thirty people would line up to ask her to sign their sheets.

She was right. She signed quickly, asking each person in turn if there was anything on her sheet they could check off. All the while Erica snapped pictures, but Sean was nowhere in sight.

Davinia was one of the last to approach her. "I've been to all fifty states," she offered.

"Wow. For business or pleasure?"

"Both. My late husband was a Professor of Architectural Studies."

"Time's up!" Tess yelled. "Who has every spot filled?"

Paige raised her hand. One of the ladies from church laughed. "Not fair! She knows everyone's secrets, so she knew just who to ask."

Tess handed Paige a white canister with blue pictures of a windmill, tulips, and Dutch children wearing wooden shoes.

Paige read the label. *"Stroopwaffles?"* She turned it around. "'Waffles made from two thin layers of baked dough with a caramel syrup filling in the middle.' Yum."

"Since we can't *all*"—Tess shot a smile toward LuAnn—"go cruising on the Rhine, we thought we'd bring you all a taste of Europe."

They played three more games. The winners received French butter cookies, Belgian chocolates, and a copy of *The Ultimate German Cookbook*. Belle, the biggest loser in the scrambled word game—because she was fielding texts from her son, typing on the babysitter's phone—got the unenviable prize of German fried herring in spicy marinade. Through giggles she said, "I think I've found the kids' new messy room penalty."

When the laughter died, Janice gave a short devotional message ending with, "Life with Jesus is an adventure. Picture it as a journey. With Him, you will travel stormy seas and float on glass-like lakes, trudge up steep mountains, then gleefully slide down the other side. And I pray there will be times when, after you have walked through dark valleys"— she gestured toward LuAnn, her eyes growing misty—"you will suddenly and unexpectedly step into sunlit meadows covered in wildflowers. And through every mile, the hard times and the wonderful times, you will never be alone. He is always by your side."

Janice closed in prayer, and Tess invited everyone into the dining room where the table was now covered with serving platters of assorted cheeses and dried fruit and tiered trays laden with chicken-salad-filled croissants. Cucumber sandwiches, fruit salad, chocolate-dipped strawberries, and Winnie's scrumptious old-fashioned butterscotch cake made with five-and-a-half sticks of butter. LuAnn hugged Winnie and thanked her for what she knew had been hours of work. "How'd you do all this behind my back?"

"Well, you have been spending a good deal of time with a certain handsome Realtor lately."

LuAnn laughed, then managed to catch Janice and Tess standing next to each other and pulled them both in for a hug. "I can't believe you surprised me. I would never have dreamed you'd do something here."

"Pretty sneaky, huh?" Irene, walking past with a full plate for Thelma, winked one pale blue eye.

LuAnn turned to Janice. "What was Davinia doing upstairs?"

Tess's confused look prompted LuAnn to fill her in.

"Davinia wasn't even close to any of the bathrooms," Janice said. "I slid my shoes off on the landing so I wouldn't make any noise. When I got up there, Davinia was walking out of Leo's bedroom. She acted all confused and said she couldn't remember where the bathroom was. When I pointed it out, she went in, closed the door, and I heard it open again when I was halfway down the stairs. She wasn't even in there long enough to blow her nose."

"Weird." Tess shook her head. "Let's keep a close eye on her."

"And speaking of weird..." LuAnn tilted her head toward Erica. "Did you guys know about them?"

Janice shrugged, looking sheepish. "Saffron told us about them. Seemed like a fun idea, plus it gave us a way to get you here."

Just then, Sean descended the stairs and darted out the front door.

"What was he doing up there?" Tess asked.

LuAnn shook her head. "I have no idea." But she intended to find out.

○─────⊱◈⊰─────○

While nibbling on a croissant, LuAnn mingled with the guests standing in the dining room. Maybelline, her granddaughters, and Emma stood just inside the library, laughing and talking in hushed tones. LuAnn had caught them glancing at her more than once. The moment they noticed her, the conversation came to an abrupt halt.

"I w-was just asking Belle how rehearsals were going," Maybelline stammered.

They spent the next few minutes talking about Belle's harp solo in an upcoming concert at Marietta College. When LuAnn saw Erica sitting down to eat, she politely excused herself.

Erica, head down and hair covering the sides of her face like shiny black curtains, crumpled something in her hand and stuck it in her pocket. She popped a mint in her mouth, then took a drink of water. She looked up as LuAnn approached. A dreamy look filled her face. "I *need* this recipe. My sister is absolutely addicted to butterscotch anything, and she would love this. I want to make this for her wedding."

"I very much doubt you're ever going to get that recipe out of Winnie, our cook, but you're welcome to try." LuAnn gestured toward the camera sitting on an end table. "Getting some good shots?"

"Yes. You are so photogenic. Have you ever considered becoming a model? With baby boomers quickly becoming the largest block of consumers in this country, there will be more and more advertising directed to your demographic."

LuAnn smiled, not sure if she should thank the woman for the compliment or feel miffed at being lumped into a massive demographic. "I don't think I'll be looking at another career in the near future, but thank you. How did you get into photography?"

"Oh...I've dabbled in it since I was young." She looked down at the squares of colored light spilling across her feet. "Such an intriguing property. Did Grant and your fiancé grow up here? Must have been fun with so many places to play hide-and-seek."

"They were raised on the other side of town, but they spent a lot of time here. Actually, Brad wasn't very fond of it." LuAnn pointed to the fireplace. "He especially didn't like those faces."

Erica laughed. "I guess I can understand that, but doesn't it add to the mystery of the place?" She looked toward the stairs. "How many rooms are upstairs?"

"Five bedrooms."

"Bet they had some fun house parties back in the day. There's so much room for parking, and the dining room is huge. I heard someone mention it's going up for sale." Erica swept a graceful hand. "What does a place like this go for?"

"I haven't heard a dollar figure."

"Bet your fiancé's family is sad to see it go." Erica's lips puckered into a pout. "No one in the family wants it?"

"It will be hard on everyone, but it takes a lot of time, work, and money to keep up with an old house like this. We're hoping just the right people come along to breathe new life into it."

Erica nodded as her gaze traveled around the room.

"What's Sean up to? Did he head back to the inn?"

"He's wandering around here somewhere getting some footage of the place." She paused, as if searching for what to say next. "Since it's part of your fiancé's heritage. He asked one of the Bickerton sisters where he could go, of course."

"Of course." LuAnn gave a slow nod. "Which sister did he ask?"

"That one." Erica gestured toward Thelma, who was dozing in her chair, half-finished strawberry dangling between her fingertips.

LuAnn thought of the boxes upon boxes of family artifacts stacked in the butler's pantry and in the upstairs closets. She was looking around for someone to send to find Sean when he came out of the kitchen, camera in front of his face.

"LuAnn?" Robin interrupted LuAnn's mental interrogation of the videographer—*Who are you? What are you up to? Where were you just now? What were you doing upstairs? What did it have to do with my wedding?* "Would you mind moving back to the guest of honor chair?"

"Not at all." LuAnn nodded at Erica and went back to the streamer-covered chair.

"Now for the really fun part," Robin announced, brown eyes sparkling. "Gifts!" She pulled a notebook from under her chair. "This time, *I* get to be the list maker." Dimples formed in both cheeks. LuAnn thought back to the young woman in work boots who had surprised them all two years ago with her knowledge of construction and ability to fix just about anything.

Janice walked in, carrying a trash bag and a paper plate with a slit in it. "Save your ribbons and bows for your rehearsal bouquet."

The first gift was from Maybelline. LuAnn read the verse on the outside of the card and then the handwritten quote on the inside. "'A heart that loves is always young.'"

"Some wise Greek philosopher said that," Maybelline quipped.

Maybelline, who was nudging eighty, was living proof of that quote. Six months earlier she'd married Axel Barrett, the father of her only child. Gone was the orangey-red hair dye and the heavily caked black mascara. In the past few months, Maybelline had reverted to her real hair color...a beautiful silvery gray. Her heavy makeup was replaced with a natural radiance. It was as if being in love had eliminated her need for a mask. Still, Maybelline wasn't a person you wanted to cross. She didn't need the fiery hair to let you know she wasn't going to let anyone push her around.

As LuAnn ran her finger under the tape, she silently hoped love would always do that for her. She pulled back a layer of teal tissue paper. Expecting something kitcheny, she thought she was looking at two dish towels. One pink, one blue. She lifted the pink fabric. A T-shirt with "On Cruise Control" printed in white. Maybelline, the newly romantic, had gifted them with matching shirts.

The next few gifts followed the same theme. Gold flip-flops decorated with huge vermillion flowers, passport covers imprinted with "His" and "Hers," a gift basket filled with sunscreen, after-sun lotion, sunglasses, and a floppy straw hat. All honeymoon gifts. LuAnn looked at Janice and then Tess, hoping her smile conveyed the thought in her head. *You know me so well.*

Robin handed her another gift from the pile at her feet. The one wrapped in flowered paper. There was no card.

"That's from us," Davinia said. "Janice just invited us today, and we didn't want to come empty-handed. I hope you don't mind regifting. They said you love blank books, and I only wrote on the first page. I tore it out." Her smile seemed a bit strained.

LuAnn slid the ribbon off and ripped the tape. Beneath the paper lay a notebook. On the cover were the words *Dream Big.*

"It's lovely. Thank you." She opened it and started to read the inspirational quote on the new first page when something caught her eye. An impression in the soft, thick paper was clearly visible. A name.

Howard Bickerton.

June 7, 1861

Prudence sat next to Asher on the jiggling seat as they rode along the river. She turned to watch the first streaks of light painting a rosy glow on the horizon.

"We'll cross up ahead," Asher said, his voice low.

"So soon?" She'd assumed they'd stay on the north side of the Ohio most of the way.

"If there's any chance she escaped and she's on her own, it would be hard for her to cross the river, wouldn't it?" He lifted his hat and wiped his brow with his sleeve. The quaver in his voice displayed his lack of confidence.

"I suppose that is true." She considered adding that, even at twelve years old, she herself had known she had to cross the Ohio to be free. Her mother had sung a song to her, over and over in the days leading up to her leaving. "March 'tween dusk and dawn till you cross the Jordan safely home." Master Fitzhugh must have heard Prudence singing it while she pulled weeds behind the big house because he had stopped to listen.

The thought of the man's evil laugh made her hands tremble now as it had back then. "That's right, girl. That's your life. Work from sunup to sundown, and then you die."

But it wasn't a song about working, or crossing the Jordan into heaven. The song was a map.

"Keep the sunrise on your right, exactly like this"—her mother had raised Prudence's arm and pointed her hand at the rising sun—"and the sunset on your left. Always. You hear me? Every day. And you'll come to the river. Then you pray, and God will make a way."

You pray, and God will make a way. What she would give to hear those words one more time in her mother's voice. God had made a way for her. An old woman, wrinkled like an apple forgotten in the corner of a cellar, had appeared out of nowhere, handed her a still warm biscuit and three coins, and pointed to a riverboat, "When the boat stops in Marietta, you ask the man with the red bandana to take you to the Quakers. Tell him Old Olive said so."

When Prudence turned to hug her goodbye and thank her, the woman was gone.

Asher stopped the rig. "It's all arranged. We'll be the only ones on the ferry." He pulled a coin from his vest pocket. "He's chargin' us twenty-five cents." They waited several long, impatient minutes. Prudence felt her pulse ticking like a clock, counting off the seconds to full light...and increased danger. Finally, a man appeared. Short and stocky, with a beard so full and matted only the whites of his dark, brooding eyes showed. Could this man really be trusted?

With a jerk of his head, he motioned them onto the ferry. Prudence jumped down and walked alongside the horses, speaking calming words as Asher prodded them onto the moving platform. The moment the back wheels touched the rough boards, the ferry started off across the river. Prudence gripped the reins with one hand and spoke to the horses in a soothing voice that betrayed nothing of what she felt inside.

All the while, she kept her gaze riveted on the white-bearded man who had not uttered a single word.

Would there be bounty hunters waiting on the Virginia shore? Would they follow them the whole way? Would they take her? Yes, her skin tone had often allowed her to pass as white, but if someone looked closely beneath her bonnet, her Melungeon features could give away her heritage and her lack of protection under the laws of this new country. Though she tried to trust God, being recaptured had been a fear that hovered like a storm cloud since she'd found refuge with the Quakers.

The ferry stopped. The bearded man took Asher's coins. It was only as the ferry was pulling away that he spoke. Quiet and gravelly. "Godspeed," he said. "You'll be in my prayers."

They rode in silence. Feeling the sun's heat increasing on her back, Prudence guessed they'd been on the dirt road about two hours when Asher slowed the team. "There's a place up ahead where we can water the—"

A muffled sneeze from behind them froze Asher's words. He whirled around. Prudence stifled a gasp as she scanned the woods. Nothing. Silence. And then a sniffle. She leapt down, ripped the canvas tarp off the back of the wagon, and jumped back in shock.

"Zephaniah?"

CHAPTER NINE

LuAnn walked out of church on Sunday morning with her hand in Brad's. "What a gorgeous day." She paged her mental thesaurus for the word to describe the exact shade of blue for the cloudless dome stretched above them. "Azure but with a swath of cornflower low on the horizon." She swept her hand to encompass the tops of the row of houses across the street.

Brad squeezed her other hand. "Life with you is definitely going to be colorful," he teased. He looked to his left and then right, then over his shoulder. "Where's your paparazzi?"

"I told them Sunday was off limits." She'd been disappointed to find that her "gifted" photographers were still planning on staying until Friday, but as long as they respected "wedding-related-only" boundaries, they'd get along fine.

"Good. You cleared the afternoon, right?"

"Yes. What did I clear it for?"

"You'll see shortly, after I drop you off at the inn to change into shorts or whatever you call those short pants." He lifted his knee and made what looked like a karate chop to the middle of his calf.

"Capri pants."

"Yeah, those. And water shoes. And sunglasses. And sunscreen."

"I happen to have a lot of sunscreen. And hot-pink rhinestone sunglasses. Get it? *Rhine*stone?" She waited for the appropriate groan. "I'll save my Eiffel Tower hat for our honeymoon." She winked at him.

"Can't wait. It should go well with my flamingo shirt. The one I wear with shorts and sandals and Argyle socks."

She stopped and put her hands on her hips. "Have you heard about this new trend called a *unimoon*? The bride and groom go on separate vacations right after the wedding. Time to have fun with friends before the drudgery of marriage sets in. When I first heard about it, I thought it was ridiculous, but…"

Brad opened the car door for her. "Fine. No flamingos."

She got in and waited for him to slide behind the wheel. "No argyle socks with sandals."

"Hmmm. Have to think about that one."

They pulled out of the parking lot, and LuAnn picked up the bridal shower recap she'd started on their way to church. "And then there's Davinia. Her daughter is just the sweetest thing. They're here because Leo told them about the inn. That's kind of surprising, don't you think? I just can't picture Leo bragging up the inn. But then they just happen to show up right before the brass box goes missing? We don't know when it disappeared, do we? Was it still on the shelf when we got there for pizza? If it was, then it had to be Leo who took it. If it wasn't, it could have been anyone who toured the mansion on Thursday. And then there's the name written in that book they gave me. I bet Lesley would tell me why her mom wrote Howard Bickerton in that book and why—"

Brad pulled to the side of the road, parked, swiveled in his seat, and took her hands in his. "Breathe. Nice and slow. Good. Again. Today is a day of rest and relaxation. You and me, two people in love, enjoying the day and each other. We're not going to talk about wedding plans or lists or mysterious inn guests or things we have to turn right and left and tap on the side. Okay?"

LuAnn's shoulders sloped with her exhale. This man was good for her. "Okay. Rest and relaxation. I can do this. I'll even l-leave all my n-notebooks at home." She made a show of straining to get the words out.

"That's my girl." Brad laughed as he leaned across the seat and planted a kiss on the tip of her nose. "Now, tell me more about the fun gifts you got yesterday."

She filled the few blocks to the inn with a list of all the silly and touching things that now cluttered her fourth-floor sitting room. "Not a single toaster in sight."

"I'll toast to that." Brad stopped in front of the inn. "I'll be back to get you in about half an hour. Don't forget to breathe."

With a loud inhale, LuAnn closed the car door and walked up the inn steps.

Sean and Erica were munching on the kitchen sink cookies Tess had taken out of the freezer this morning while leaning on the front desk chatting with Brin, who was overseeing the inn today. As LuAnn got closer, she heard Brin saying, "…on the Underground Railroad. The owners found her journal hidden in a secret room in the basement, and then they found a key that opened a brass box Harry, who owns the Salvage Mall—"

She looked up and smiled at LuAnn. "They were asking if you'd found any old papers, so I thought I'd give them the whole story."

LuAnn smiled. Tight, yet still a smile.

"A brass box with a missing key, huh?" Sean's smile was almost as rigid as her own. "What an intriguing mystery. I imagine there are quite a few mysteries surrounding that old house."

"What was in the box?" Erica asked.

"Some old papers," Brin answered. "They proved that the man who had the house built was killed by—"

"Unfortunately, we don't have time at the moment to explain it all." LuAnn scooted around the end of the desk and put her arm around Brin, giving her a rather abrupt squeeze and hoping she'd play along. "Brin has sheets to fold, and I have to leave in a few minutes. Maybe we can chat later."

"That would be nice," Erica answered. "In the meantime, we're going to head over to the Campus Martius museum and see what we can learn about your fair city."

"Great idea." LuAnn waved and turned toward the stairs.

Just before they reached the first step, Sean stopped. "Is the salvage mall open on Sunday?"

"I'm afraid it's not."

"Okay. Well, have a nice day." Sean smoothed his hand over his moustache, then suddenly jerked, turning away from them.

Brin's hand flew over her mouth.

"What's wrong?"

She held up one finger as she watched Sean and Erica ascend the stairs. "Did I just see what I thought I saw?" Brin whispered, mirth dancing in her eyes.

"What do you think you saw?"

"I'm pretty sure half his moustache just moved."

"Moved?"

"Yeah. Like almost came off in his hand." She laughed. "Reminds me of my biology teacher. His fake goatee fell off while he was dissecting a frog. Fell right into the guts." She grew serious. "Was I saying something wrong when you came in? I got the feeling you were shushing me. I've been studying the history of the inn. Did I mess something up? I didn't mean to—"

"You didn't do anything wrong. I'm just not so sure what those two are doing here, so I'd just as soon not give them too much information about anything relating to the Bickerton sisters."

"From now on my lips are sealed. I'll go fold those sheets now."

"Thanks." LuAnn started up the stairs, then turned. "You're sure about the moustache?"

"Pretty sure. He turned away so fast. Guess I could have been wrong. Want me to spy on him or search his room?"

LuAnn laughed. "No, I don't want you to spy on him." *I'll do that myself.* She walked up to the fourth floor.

What were those two up to? She pondered the question while she changed clothes.

Sean and Erica were nowhere in sight when LuAnn came downstairs wearing a peach T-shirt and tan capri pants. Brin nodded toward the library. "Brad's waiting for you. He's got company." She raised an eyebrow. "Does Davinia want to buy the Bickerton mansion?" she whispered.

"I wish I knew," LuAnn whispered back. "She loves Victorian homes. Maybe she's just curious, but she's asked a lot of questions. It does make me wonder."

She walked quietly around the corner. Brad sat with a magazine on his lap. He'd apparently been hoping for a few relaxing minutes while waiting for her. In walking shoes and a baseball cap, Lesley sat clutching her purse, a look of frustration on her face. This detour probably wasn't on her day plan. Davinia's back was turned to LuAnn. She leaned toward Brad as if she were grilling him with questions.

"...did you hide? Are there secret rooms, hidden compart—" She looked over her shoulder when Brad looked up. "Good morning. We were just talking about Brad's childhood."

"I'm sorry I have to take him away from you. Do you two have plans for the day?"

Lesley seemed to be stifling a sigh. "I'd just like to wander around town and walk along the river. Mom wants to do research on—"

Davinia interrupted with a brassy-sounding laugh. "My husband couldn't visit a city without researching its history. It was always our goal to find the oldest building."

"The Ohio Company Land Office over at the Campus Martius Museum was built in 1788," Brad said. "It's been moved a few times, but it's definitely the oldest structure in

Marietta. The first law courts in the Northwest Territory convened in that building, and the first territory maps were made there."

Davinia nodded but didn't appear all that interested. "And what year was the Bickerton mansion built?"

LuAnn jumped in before he could answer. "I'm so sorry, but we have to be somewhere in a few minutes." For the second time in half an hour she said, "Maybe we can chat later," then held her hand out for Brad.

They hurried toward the front door. "Thanks for rescuing me," Brad whispered. "That woman sure can converse." He put his hand on the wrought-iron handle, then said, "Close your eyes."

LuAnn obeyed. He put his arm around her waist and guided her down the two front steps. "Okay. Open."

Brad's truck was parked parallel to the inn. In the back were two kayaks. One blue, one lime green. She'd seen the blue one in his garage. The green one was new. LuAnn grinned and hugged him. "Where are we going?"

"I thought we'd put in at the mansion and end up right here, if the current isn't too strong."

"Let's go!"

On the drive to the mansion, LuAnn was quieter than usual. She didn't think Brad had noticed until he said, "How's that relaxation going?"

She didn't have to look at him to know he was smiling. "There's just a lot going on up here." She pointed to her forehead. "Start a relaxing conversation."

"I helped set up chairs for your shower yesterday, and while I was there I did some nosing around at the house. I didn't move boxes around too much, but I think I looked in every one Thelma or Irene could get to. I checked closets and the butler's pantry. No sign of the brass box. So I called Leo. Asked him if he took it."

"Wait." LuAnn cranked her neck to stare at him. "So I'm the only one who has to stick to a relaxing topic?"

"Yep."

"And...?"

"He said, 'What would I want with that?' He sounded genuinely confused."

LuAnn turned sideways. "Did you ask him about the instructions from the trunk?"

Brad nodded. "I didn't connect it with the box. I asked him some more questions about Giana and then casually slid in the cool old box of dishes you showed me. I asked if he'd seen the card wrapped up with the serving forks."

"And...?"

"He said he was on the phone with Giana when he opened the trunk. He read the card and took pictures of it, but his mind was, and I quote, 'a hundred and fifty miles away...with my heart.'"

LuAnn squelched a gagging sound. "He seriously said that?" She couldn't help but laugh. "That boy's got it bad."

"Yep. Anyway, trusting Leo is a new thing, but I feel pretty confident he didn't take the brass box." Brad pulled into the aunts' driveway and parked. "So, does that help put some questions to rest so you can give that beautiful brain of yours the afternoon off?"

She nodded, but she was pretty sure he wasn't any more convinced than she was. Maybe Leo was telling the truth. Maybe. But if he was, that only brought up more questions.

The Muskingum River flowed smooth and still. LuAnn focused on finding her rhythm. She dipped the left end of her paddle in, then mirrored the action on the right. Dip. Skim. Dip. Sunlight glinted off the drops that fell from her paddle. She breathed in sync with the movement of her arms. Off to the right, two turtles sunned themselves on a log. The smaller one skittered into the water as they passed. The larger one, gazing out with a look of wisdom, simply blinked at them. A red-tailed hawk swooped overhead, and the woods teemed with songbirds. She spotted two orioles, a handful of goldfinches, and heard, but couldn't locate, a woodpecker sending out his Morse code message. She waved as they passed the Moore House, a foster home recently built on the property once owned by Prudence Willard and her husband. The trees hid them, but she heard the laughter of children. Happy, safe children.

She pulled up next to Brad, and he grabbed hold of the side of her kayak. "This was a good idea," she said. "I feel very tranquil."

"Phone off?"

"Yes."

"And you didn't smuggle any lists into your life vest?"

"Not a one." She closed her eyes. "You're good for me. It seems like the harder I try to keep things simple, the more tangled up I get. Did I tell you I lost my wedding shoes?"

Brad laughed. "I would marry you without shoes, you know. Maybe we should both go barefoot. A hippie wedding. That would definitely be simple."

She kept her eyes closed, imagining wearing a plain unbleached muslin dress, bare feet, wildflowers in her hair… Brad's hair down to his shoulders the way it was in pictures she'd seen of him from his college days. Bell-bottom jeans, a paisley shirt. They'd get married in the gazebo in the park they'd just passed. Janice would play the guitar and join Tess in singing "Wedding Song." She'd carry tiger lilies and—

A strange, distant buzzing sound snapped her out of the sixties. She opened her eyes and looked around, expecting to see a massive swarm of mosquitoes. Brad let go of her kayak, balanced his paddle across his lap, and pulled out his phone.

"Not fair!" she yelled, but stilled when Brad sat up straight and held his hand over the ear that didn't have the phone pressed to it.

"Aunt Thelma, it's okay. Of course I believe you. Yes, we'll be there in just a few minutes, and then we'll get it all figured out. I'm sure there's a reasonable—" Brad's gaze swiveled toward the sky. "Irene, calm down. If she has an address, we can trace it. This is good, isn't it? It's not stolen. Thieves don't leave calling cards." He pulled the phone an inch away from his ear. Irene, who'd apparently taken the phone from Thelma, was shouting loud enough for LuAnn to hear.

"Don't you think I thought of that? I called. I got this screeching sound, and a voice said, 'The number you are calling is not in service. Please check the number and try again.' I checked the number and got the same thing. So I looked it up on the Internet. There is no Iocus anything anywhere in the country. Bradley, someone stole my mother's wedding rings and...some other valuable things...and it's all Thelma's fault!"

CHAPTER TEN

I wasn't keeping secrets. I told her the rings were in the box under the airplane picture." Thelma shot a glare at Irene. "See, I'm not the only one forgetting things."

"I didn't forget anything. I assumed you meant it was in the ring box under the airplane picture in Leo's room," Irene countered.

"Well, I can't help what you assumed. I assume Leo took the box and left the note to throw us off, but it doesn't matter what I assume, because what does it matter if Leo took the box with the rings that he's supposed to have anyway? Maybe he'll finally propose, and you can stop wasting all your time worrying about a grown-up man who needs to act like a grown-up man!"

Irene gasped. "Don't you criticize my—"

"Leo doesn't have the box," Brad cut in. "I talked to him."

"And you believe—" Thelma clamped her lips tight.

LuAnn handed Thelma a cup of honey-sweetened chamomile tea, then picked up the one she'd poured for Irene and set it in front of her. Brad brought a cup of tea for LuAnn and coffee for himself. They sat in the kitchen, all four of them now with hands folded around steaming mugs.

Brad gave Thelma a tender smile. "You took your mother's rings out of the little black box and—"

"Of course. Where do thieves look for rings? In ring boxes. Am I right?"

LuAnn couldn't argue with the logic.

"And you put them in the brass box."

"Yes. I put them under a stack of old pictures, next to the medals. Who would look there for a diamond?"

Maybe no one. Maybe the rings were taken unintentionally by someone looking for pearls. Or a...deed. "Irene?" The color had drained from the little woman's face. "What's wrong?"

"Medals? The medals I borrowed from Maybelline?"

Thelma nodded. "Hidden in plain sight. How was I to know someone would take that old box?"

"Aunt Irene?" Brad reached out and placed his hand firmly on her shoulder. "Are you okay? Take a sip of tea."

"I am anything but okay." She huffed, glared at her sister, and shoved a piece of paper at him. "Thelma found this on the shelf where the brass box used to be."

Leaning close to Brad, LuAnn examined the handwritten receipt.

Attn.: Mr. Leo Bickerton
Received, one box of pictures. To be delivered upon completion of program.

Iocus Entertainment Company

111 Joy Street

Knockemstiff, Ohio

In the upper right-hand corner, a hand-drawn logo made up of lowercase letters—*i* and *e* beneath a sideways *c*—looked for all the world like a smiley face with its tongue sticking out.

Irene puffed out her cheeks then expelled a loud breath. "We've been had." She leaned back with a thud.

"Knockemstiff?" LuAnn tried to lighten the moment. "We have a thief with a sense of humor."

"Knockemstiff is a real town," Brad said dryly. "A couple of hours west of here."

LuAnn picked up her phone and typed in the fake-sounding town name. "Here's a story they say could explain the name. It says that a preacher came across two women fighting over a man and advised the women that the man was not likely to be worth their trouble and that someone should 'knock him stiff.'"

Brad reached across the table and touched Thelma's boney, thin-skinned hand. "Start from the top."

LuAnn bent and picked up her purse and pulled out a notebook.

"Hey!" Brad shook a finger at her. "You broke a rule."

"No, I didn't. This is my purse notebook. It lives in my purse. I didn't technically *bring* it, it was just there. And I didn't take it in the kayak."

"Still cheating." His lips rose slightly on the right.

"Says the man with the phone." LuAnn opened to a clean page. "I apologize for his interruption, Thelma. Keep talking."

"When did you find the receipt?" Brad asked softly. "Can you remember what day?"

Rubbing her temple, Thelma slowly nodded. "Irene was getting her hair done."

"That was Wednesday," Irene said. "My appointment was at three, right after all of you left. In fact, Davinia and her daughter were still here chatting with Thelma when I left." She looked at her sister. "Did they go back in the house after I left?"

Thelma shook her head.

"You're sure they didn't need to use the bathroom or anything?" LuAnn prompted. They'd used that trick before.

"No. We walked around a bit, and then they left."

"Anyway," Irene continued, "Thelma said that after I left, she walked into the dining room and saw this sitting on the shelf. Like this." She propped the note up like a tent. "But then she didn't think to tell me about it until today."

"I...forgot." Thelma's eyes reddened.

LuAnn touched Thelma's arm. "It's okay. We've all been forgetting things lately. It's been a busy few weeks." She finished writing down the details and turned to Irene. "Let's make a list of all the possibilities. Who knew you had your mother's rings and that you were hoping Leo was going to propose to his girlfriend?"

"Oh my..." Irene squinted, a look of hard concentration. "Leo, of course. And the ladies in my book club, because we always catch up on what our kids are doing. Bradley, Grant, Wendy, Saffron. And I might have mentioned it to the man who fixed the sink upstairs."

LuAnn was pretty sure she could read the thought scrolling through Brad's mind. *You told the plumber? Why?*

As if hearing his thoughts, Irene answered. "We were talking about things he's found in drains. Lots of rings. So I told him about the time my mother put her wedding rings on the shelf above the sink. Leo was about four at the time, and he picked them up and dropped them down the drain, and Fred had to take the pipes apart to find them. And then, of course I had to tell him I had just put those very same rings on Leo's dresser because I was hoping he would be using them soon."

Thelma shook her head. "So the plumber came back, snuck in, and stole them." Another glare at Irene.

If Irene had hackles, they would be raised. "*I* told the plumber the rings were on Leo's dresser. *You* put the rings in the brass box in the library. How in the world would the plumber know to look—"

"Well," LuAnn jumped in, feeling like a referee, "we have lots of details to go on. Irene, do you remember the name of the plumber or the company?" *And was it the one who charged you double?* That could say something about the man's character.

"I wrote him a check, so I've got the name."

"Okay." Brad finished his coffee and stood. "I'll go get your checkbook and find the name. I think that's enough for now."

"You're not going to call the police?" Thelma asked.

Brad looked at LuAnn with a "What do I say now?" look as he stepped out of the room.

"We'll do some research on our own first." LuAnn stood and picked up her half-finished tea, then put her hand on Thelma's shoulder. "You two should rest up. You've got a busy few days coming up. If you think of anything else, let us—"

"Wait!" Thelma grabbed her hand. "I bet the painter took it!"

Irene rolled her eyes. "The painter left long before Bradley and LuAnn brought Harry and Maybelline and all those people here, and the brass box was still on the shelf."

The thin skin on Thelma's forehead rippled. "But I was sure…"

As confusion clouded Thelma's face, and her voice faded in doubt, Irene's demeanor softened. "It's okay, Thelma. How about a snickerdoodle?"

LuAnn sat across from Brad at a four-top table in front of the window in the inn's café. They'd finished turkey sandwiches before beginning their research. LuAnn closed her laptop. It had only taken her two minutes to find what she was looking for. Or not find it, to be exact. "Irene is right. Not only is there no Iocus Entertainment Company anywhere in the country, but"—was it exhaustion making her suddenly want to laugh?—"'*Iocus* is Latin for 'joke.'"

Brad groaned, apparently not in the same teetering-on-hysteria mood. "Cassidy Plumbing is a legit company. They've got horrible reviews. Only a two-star rating. But no one's accusing them of stealing anything. Can't call them on Sunday unless we have a plumbing emergency." Brad tapped her left hand. "Want to drop your ring down—"

"Don't even…"

Brad set his phone down and massaged the bridge of his nose between thumb and forefinger. "Maybe we should call the police, but I just don't know if I want to put the aunts through that right now."

"How much do you think the rings are worth? Beyond sentimental value, that is. Enough to really make it worth someone risking getting caught?"

"I haven't seen them for years, but I do remember it's a big diamond." He took her left hand and pulled it toward him. "This is a half carat, and I'm guessing the one in the missing ring is at least twice this big, and there are smaller diamonds on the wedding band. Plus, the set is vintage, and as far as I can remember, in good condition."

"I bet this has nothing to do with the rings at all. I can't imagine any of the people Irene told about the rings having a motive to steal them. Irene had already given them to Leo, so he had no motive. The women in Irene's book club are all in their eighties and nineties."

"What about the plumber?" Brad pushed his coffee cup aside and slid his phone into his pocket.

"That possibility seems too far-fetched. As far as we know, no one but Thelma knew she'd moved the rings. Plus, the fake receipt mentions pictures. Nothing about rings. Thelma's having some memory glitches. What if she moved the brass box and just didn't remember, and the receipt is for something that has nothing to do with the rings?" LuAnn took a sip of coffee. "We need to find the brass box because the deed to the mansion might be in it, and I hate the way you've been stressed over that, but I don't want our wedding ruined by—"

The front door opened, and Davinia and Lesley walked in.

"Have fun exploring?" LuAnn asked.

Mother and daughter exchanged looks then both broke into smiles. "We split up," Lesley said. "We couldn't agree on what we wanted to see, so I rented a bicycle and rode along the river and ordered pizza and had a little picnic all by myself." Her smile said it all. A young wife and mom running a B&B finally getting time to herself.

"Sounds delightful," LuAnn said. "How about you, Davinia?"

"I visited your cemeteries. Might sound morbid to some, but it tells so much about the history of a place. And then I went to the Campus Martius Museum you recommended." She stepped closer to Brad and LuAnn then turned to her daughter. "Go on upstairs. I'll just be a minute." She motioned to one of the chairs at their table. "There's something I'd like to discuss with you."

"Please." Brad stood and pulled out the chair.

"Forgive me, but I consider myself a good judge of character, and there is something about those two photographers that disturbs me. Do you know them well?"

LuAnn shook her head. "No. They were a...surprise."

"I wish I could put my finger on exactly what it is. For one thing, they seem to be avoiding Lesley and me like the plague. Yesterday, at the shower, I saw a look of what I can only describe as shock on the man's face when we walked in. This morning I was coming out of my room to go down to meet Lesley for breakfast, and the woman was descending the stairs from the third floor at the same time. The moment she saw me, she immediately spun on her heel and went back up. Neither of them came down the whole time we were eating. Then, this afternoon, they were at the front desk at the museum when I walked in. I greeted them and walked up to purchase my ticket, and the man looked at his watch and said he didn't realize it was so late, and they both rushed out."

Brad rubbed the stubble on his chin. "Any chance they know you from somewhere?"

"I don't think so. I do meet a lot of people at B&B seminars and such, and my husband had acquaintances all over the country, but I think I would have remembered them. She has such striking features. Reminds me of Snow White with that dark black hair and pale skin. And his accent... I think I would have remembered meeting them."

"Anything else you think is strange?" As soon as she asked it, LuAnn wondered if she was giving away too much of her own feelings of unease about Sean and Erica.

"Well, it appeared the man at the desk at the museum had been trying to sell them some booklets, but they left without them. One was called *Ohio Early Land Ownership Records* and another was *Ohio Land and Property Genealogy*. I told the man I knew them because we were all staying at Wayfarers Inn. He said, 'Well, I suppose they're working with Mr. Grimes then.' When I asked what he meant by that, he said it really wasn't his place to talk about it."

LuAnn and Brad simply stared at each other, unspoken questions ricocheting between them. "I'm sure they're just curious about the town's history," LuAnn said. "Just like you are."

Davinia slid her purse strap off the back of the chair. "Yes. Well. Oh, one more thing. I drove past the Bickerton estate this afternoon and saw Irene cutting flowers out in the yard. She's such a sweet little lady. I told her I'd love to stay and help with their move. Lesley needs to get home to the children, but would you happen to have a vacancy for me for two more nights?"

LuAnn swallowed and took a controlled breath. "I...believe we do. Let me check." She stood. Brad did the same and leaned over, kissed her on the cheek, and said he'd talk to her tomorrow. He left, and she walked with Davinia to the front desk and scheduled her for the same room for Monday and Tuesday nights. Davinia headed upstairs, and LuAnn scanned the main floor, making sure no extra lights were left on, then trudged up to the fourth floor, feeling older than she wanted to feel six days before her wedding.

Collapsing on the love seat in their sitting room, she sighed. "Three more days."

"The aunts stressing you out?" Tess, ever on the lookout for new and healthy snacks that didn't enlarge their waistlines, set a plate of fresh-from-the-oven sweet potato chips on the coffee table and sat across from her.

"The aunts and the paparazzi and Davinia."

Janice joined them, kicking her shoes off and tucking her feet under her on the other end of the love seat. She pointed to the notebook in LuAnn's hand. "Fill us in."

She told them about Davinia peppering Brad with questions and her observations of Sean and Erica, Brad's call to Leo, Thelma finding the receipt, her question about the painter, and what Irene told the plumber.

Tess took a handful of chips and sat back. "The brass box isn't anything all that special to look at, and it's heavy to lug around. I can't imagine anyone stealing it unless they knew there was something valuable in it."

Tess sat up. "Brad thinks the code card you found with the china was talking about the brass box. So who all knew about that?"

"Leo, possibly his girlfriend, Irene, maybe Thelma, me, Brad." LuAnn lifted a finger for each name. "And…Irene said Leo took pictures. That means…" She took out her phone and tapped in Leo's name on Facebook. She scrolled through two weeks of pictures. "No pictures of the card, so that's not…" She stopped at a picture of Leo with five other people. His arm was around Giana. The group stood on either side of a large rustic sign that read, "Welcome to Paw Paw Patch B&B."

"Hey." She looked beyond the faces to a building behind the sign. A small shed, or outbuilding of some kind.

Tess and Janice leaned in as she spread her fingers to enlarge the picture. Tess gave a small gasp. "Isn't that exactly like—"

"Yep." LuAnn tapped her finger on the weather vane that topped a cupola on the small building. Wings outstretched, the soaring eagle held the handle of a six-sided lantern in its beak.

CHAPTER ELEVEN

With the Monday breakfast rush over, LuAnn had a little time to make phone calls before their weekend guests would be checking out, and the café would start to fill with the lunch crowd. She darted upstairs for a few moments of quiet.

First on her list was Pastor Ben. He'd given her a copy of a traditional order of service and asked her and Brad to make any changes they wanted. They'd given him their updated ideas two weeks ago and hadn't heard back from him yet. She called the church, chatted with the secretary for a few minutes, and was put through to Pastor Ben. She asked for his thoughts on their changes.

"Changes? The ones… Oh! Yes, it's all good. I'm sorry I didn't get back to you on that. Anything else?"

"Do I need to do anything for the rehearsal?"

"Nope. Nope. Everything's good. All pretty simple and straightforward. It's going to be a *spectacular* wedding in every way. A day to remember, I guarantee."

LuAnn wasn't sure what to make of his over-the-top enthusiasm. Simple and straightforward didn't seem to warrant "spectacular" said with so much emphasis. "Thank you."

They said goodbye, and she checked him off her list and picked up the phone to call Blooms. Once again, she talked to the same young clerk. "Katrina said to tell you she and Janice got it all figured out, and you're not to worry about a thing."

Not to worry. Not to worry. Why did those words tighten the cords at the back of her neck? She sighed. "What part of r-e-l-a-x don't you understand, Lu?" She'd promised to trust her friends, and she was checking up on them. No more.

The next person on her list was her future brother-in-law. She'd heard Brad complain that his brother wasn't the best communicator in matters that didn't concern business, but this was ridiculous. She'd called him on Saturday. Expecting to leave a message once again, she called his number. To her surprise, he answered.

"Hey, Lu, sorry. I had a crazy weekend. You had some questions about your gift?" His words danced on a layer of mirth. She could picture him holding back a belly laugh.

"Many questions. It was so…thoughtful of you. But I'm pretty sure you know we're not doing anything picture-worthy this week, and this must be costing you a fortune."

"Actually, it's not costing me a penny. They didn't tell you that? Hey, I'm pretty much the best brother a guy could ask for, but I'm not that generous. They got in touch with Wendy online and offered to do it for free. I knew Brad would be thrilled." This time he didn't hold back the laugh.

"Uh-huh. Well, as it turns out, I'm the one who is…thrilled. They apparently want to film my every pre-wedding breath."

"Hey, I'm sorry. They're really that annoying? Saffron mentioned they were all over the house and grounds at the shower. Not sure what that was about. I figured I was bringing business to the inn, and they'd record some fun moments for you two. If they're bugging you, just kick 'em out."

"Okay. At least I know I won't be hurting your feelings if I tell them to back off."

Grant laughed again. "Not at all."

They said goodbye, and LuAnn felt a bit of tension leave her shoulders. Without needing to worry about offending Brad's family, she wouldn't have to put up with Sean and Erica crossing any more lines. She closed her notebook and went to the closet for a sweater. Though the outside thermometer hovered around eighty and it wasn't even noon, the kitchen temperature was in the sixties today. Keeping Winnie comfortable while she chopped and diced and stirred soup in front of Big Red, their vintage replica stove, was the priority. The rest of the staff could layer up if they got chilly. She opened the closet door, reached for her tan sweater...and froze.

Her wedding shoes were back on the shelf. Which meant she hadn't simply mislaid them. Someone had taken them and then returned them. She took one down. The towel was still stuffed inside. She looked at the bottoms. No dirt or scratches or any sign they'd been worn.

Buttoning her sweater, she walked out of her room and down the hall. Tess was just coming in with Huck on his leash. She pressed her sleeve against her forehead. "Getting hot out there."

"Mm-hmm." LuAnn stared at Tess's feet. Nope, too big. Not that she didn't already know that. The three had never been able to share shoes.

"You all right?" Tess asked.

"Yeah. I think." LuAnn sank her hands into the pockets of her sweater. "Did you borrow my wedding shoes?"

"Me? Your shoes would never fit me."

"I know, but... They were gone for a couple of days. And now they're back."

"Huh. Weird." Tess filled Huck's water bowl. "Did you taste Winnie's avocado soup? It's amazing. Chilled lemon basil avocado. It didn't sound good when she first talked about it, but it's divine. I was thinking we should get out those little cups we used for mints at that baby shower we did last month and offer samples because people might be reluctant to try a cold soup even though it's perfect on a day like today. What do you think?"

"I think you're acting weird."

"Me? You're the one I'm concerned about. You're stressing, aren't you? It's all going to come together perfectly, exactly like you've always dreamed. Okay?"

LuAnn gave her best version of a smile, then walked out, massaging the back of her neck.

LuAnn greeted lunch regulars as she poured coffee. Emma and Belle, who'd become friends after finding out they were both assets in discovering who was hunting for a ruby-crusted Civil War decoder hidden under the stairs at the inn, were chatting a mile a minute. Harry was enjoying his second bowl of avocado soup while poring over a stack of old yellowed papers. Part of his job description, LuAnn assumed. Several guests had the MTDC 10 percent off coupons torn from the back of the new brochures, now available at the Visitor Center and area attractions. This was the first LuAnn had seen them, and she couldn't wait to tell Brad the Marietta Tourism Development Coalition was already having an impact.

Tess seated the paparazzi at a table for two against the wall. They were both armed with cameras. That must get tiresome, LuAnn thought, especially when you'd offered to record a week's worth of fun pre-wedding moments for free and then there weren't any. She considered avoiding them altogether, but it was her table—she was supposed to take their order.

Erica tugged at her bangs. Sean looked up and smoothed his moustache when she approached. LuAnn tried to look nonchalant as she studied it. Perfectly straight. They said "Hi," at the same time.

LuAnn asked if they wanted coffee then told them what was on the menu for the day. "The beef barley soup should really be called a stew, it's so thick. If you want something cool and light on a hot day, I recommend the lemon avocado soup. I just had a bowl myself, and it's absolutely addictive."

They ordered a bowl of each. Before LuAnn could walk away, Erica said, "What are we doing after the café closes?"

We? LuAnn blinked. She should have been prepared for this. "Nothing wedding-related. Just helping the Bickerton sisters pack up. They're moving this week."

"Sounds fun," Erica said. "Will Brad be there?"

"Yes." The moment she'd said it, she realized she should have been more vague. "Unless he needs to show a house, of course."

"Wonderful. It will be a great chance to capture the two of you working together. We'll be ready."

Capture. That was exactly the word to explain how she felt. Captured. Now was the time to send them packing. And yet…if she did, she'd never find out what they were really up to. Knowing she could tell them to leave at any moment gave her the strength to tolerate them a bit longer. She shaped her lips into a smile. "Great. See you then."

Lesley came down alone around one, explaining that her mom had skipped lunch to "do some research." She was still lingering over coffee when the crowd had thinned enough for LuAnn to take a break. After topping off Lesley's cup and setting a fresh cream pitcher on her table, LuAnn asked if she could join her for a minute. "We're always looking for opportunities to chat with our guests," she explained.

"I would love that." Lesley smiled, the worried look on her face diminishing.

"Have you enjoyed your stay?"

"Yes." Her tone lacked enthusiasm. "It's just…" She shrugged. "The mother-daughter relationship can be…trying."

LuAnn nodded. "My mother's been gone two years. I miss her every day, but how well I remember those tense moments. Even in my sixties there were times I felt I was still trying to prove to her I was a competent adult who could make my own decisions."

Her admission was met with laughter. "You do understand. When Mom sets her mind to something, there's no stopping her. I've benefitted from that many times, but it's also caused me some major headaches."

"And she lives with you and your family?"

"More like we live with her. She owns the B&B. My husband and I are working, and I do mean working, to pay it off, and then it will be ours. Please don't tell her, but Kurt calls us indentured servants."

LuAnn couldn't help but laugh. "Winnie said you raise all of your own produce and animals."

"Most of it. It's our claim to fame, but it's hard on the kids. We homeschool, and we're up at five thirty every morning, getting chores done before we start lessons. They're learning a good work ethic, but I sometimes wonder if we put too much responsibility on them. Anyway, we really do love it."

"I saw a picture online. Do you know that you have the exact same weather vane as the one at the Bickerton mansion?"

"Yes. I couldn't believe that. When Brad said it was a one-of-a-kind, I was going to say something, but Mom shushed me. That whole mom thing again. She can be so wonderful. This trip was her idea. She paid for everything and got me my own room." Lesley sighed and closed her eyes for a moment. "Heavenly. I never get time to myself. The problem is, now I feel obligated to do whatever she wants to do. I absolutely love old houses. Traveling with my dad was amazing. I learned so much. But at this time in my life, I just want to chill. I suppose that sounds harsh."

"Not at all." LuAnn offered an understanding smile. Though she'd never had children of her own, she could empathize with a frazzled mom. "Did your dad pick up that weather vane on his travels?"

"Yes. It was one of his most prized possessions. You know how copper turns green? He would never allow that to happen. So now that's one of my jobs, polishing the eagle."

"Do you know anything about its history?"

Lesley nodded. "I thought it was a one-of-a-kind. It came off a house owned and built by an architect in London in the early 1800s. I can't remember his name. He was very involved in freeing slaves in Britain. Brad was right about the symbolism. That's exactly the way my dad described it. I'm guessing the same architect designed the Bickerton mansion, don't you think?"

"I imagine. Just seems like a strange coincidence that Leo would happen to stay at your B&B."

"I know, right? That was such a fun weekend. As you well know, guests can be...trying. But the Fontaines were wonderful. Giana is just the sweetest thing, and so is her sister, Gwen, and they all have this zany sense of humor. I haven't laughed so much in a long time. And they're all so gifted. They were there on one of our talent show nights."

"Oh?"

"They acted out the Pyramus and Thisbe scene from *A Midsummer Night's Dream*. Had all of our guests in stitches."

"Leo mentioned their involvement in theater." How was she going to guide the conversation to Davinia's interest in the Bickerton house? She decided to just jump in. "Leo must have described the mansion in glowing terms to pique your mother's interest."

"Oh, he did. He told us all about the imaginary games he played with the statues in the yard. It actually made me feel kind of sorry for him, growing up as an only child."

LuAnn sat back, folding her arms across her waist. "I haven't heard those stories."

"You'll have to get him to tell you. He pretended his room was a pirate ship and there were treasure maps and letters from the king hidden in secret compartments in it." Lesley laughed. "I'm pretty sure he never found any treasure." Her expression grew serious. "Can I ask a personal question? Please tell me if it's something you don't want to answer."

LuAnn nodded, inviting her question even though she had no idea where this would lead.

"Why won't the house go to Leo when his mother and aunt move?"

"Well…that's complicated." And why was Leo talking about that to people he didn't even know? She wasn't sure she wanted to tell a near stranger about the missing deed. "You heard the story about the imposter, the man who killed the real owner and assumed his identity? The property never legally belonged to Irene and Thelma's ancestors. But that won't affect them. The sale of the estate will assure they'll be taken care of for the rest of their lives."

"And Leo?"

How should she answer that? Clearly Leo had made a favorable impression on Lesley, and LuAnn wouldn't cast a shadow on his hopefully reforming character. "Well, my fiancé and his brother are—"

The front door opened, and she was quite literally saved by the bell as a group of eight women wearing red hats swooped in the door on a wave of laughter. The café's harvest table was already set up for them, but extra hands would be needed to take their orders. LuAnn smiled at Lesley. "I'm afraid my break is over." She stood, then hesitated for a moment. "Can I ask *you* a personal question?"

"Sure."

"Is your mother interested in buying the Bickerton mansion?"

Lesley's face pinched, and she let out a long sigh. "I wish I knew what my mother is interested in." With that, Lesley stood, laid a twenty-dollar bill on the table, and walked briskly toward the stairs.

A moment later, a flush-faced young man in a UPS uniform lumbered in, carrying a box half as tall as he was. LuAnn jumped up to hold the door for him. Janice, who'd been filling salt shakers, came to help.

LuAnn glanced down at the top of the enormous package. It was addressed to Winnie, with a return address in Indianapolis. "Victorian Repro. Wonder what that is."

"Where do you want it? It's kind of heavy." The delivery man eyed the stairway, likely hoping they wouldn't ask him to carry it to the fourth floor.

LuAnn pointed toward the kitchen. "If you wouldn't mind taking it into the kitchen, that would be wonderful."

"I'll get the door." Janice almost sprinted ahead of them to the kitchen door. "Winnie, you have a delivery from Indianapolis."

Winnie walked out of the pantry. "Wonderful. Just set it there." She pointed to the corner of the kitchen. As she thanked the young man, she shoved the box against the wall between Big Red and a crate of potatoes.

"Are you redecorating, Winnie?" LuAnn couldn't imagine what Winnie would be ordering for her house from what appeared to be a company that made Victorian reproductions.

"Workin' on a little something," Winnie answered. "Right now we gotta get food out to the Red Hatters. Somebody get the squash rolls out of the oven. You know how those ladies love their bread. And take 'em some extra butter too."

Janice stepped in front of Big Red, shoved the box closer to the wall with her foot, and slid her hands into oven mitts. "Happy to, Winnie!" she said through a smile as fake as the silk roses on the windowsill.

Weird was the word for the day. But best not to ask too many questions. It hadn't occurred to her until just now that Winnie could have ordered a wedding gift to be sent to the inn. LuAnn walked out, order pad in hand, and headed for the Red Hatters.

"Excuse me." Harry's scarecrow form stepped toward her. "I'm sorry to bother you, LuAnn, but I just found something I think you might be interested in." He handed her a faded, tattered-edged page. Actually, part of a page. The top half was torn off. "I was sorting through some old plat maps from the 1800s, and I found this." He pointed to a spot on the map.

It took LuAnn a moment to orient. Rectangles filled with names written in pale, thin script filled the triangle of land created by the confluence of the Muskingum and Ohio rivers. But one rectangle, the one just above Harry's fingertip, was different. On this one, someone had printed over the original fine lettering. On the lot that once read *Bickerton*, darker block letters written with a fountain pen now said *IMPOSTER!*

June 7, 1861

"We can't turn back." Asher raised his hands for the second time and let them fall to his sides. "If we don't get to Deborah in the next three days..."

Prudence stroked Zephaniah's head as the boy clung to her, sobbing. Why had he not listened when she told him not to run away? In truth, it was her fault he was here. She had told him that if things got too difficult, he could always come to her house. And he had... "We must take him home. It is far too dangerous for—"

"No!" Zephaniah wrenched away from her. "I will not go back. They are not my parents, and they hate me. Leave me here. I will walk to New York and get on a ship going to England. I will find my brother."

Prudence shook her head. The boy had no knowledge of how to survive on his own. And Asher was right. The clock was ticking for Deborah. "'Tis true." She lowered her voice to a husky whisper as she looked at Asher, no longer with pleading in her eyes. "Maybe he will be an asset. A couple traveling with a child may come under less suspicion."

"Let us pray you are right." Asher gave a sigh of resignation and held out his hand, introducing himself to the boy. "And you are?"

"Zephaniah Bickerton. My father is the real Mr. Howard Bickerton. I promise I won't get in your way. I can build a fire, and I know how to tie seven kinds of knots, and I'm not scared of the dark or bears."

For the first time since they'd left Marietta, Asher smiled. "I believe you will be a great asset, Mr. Bickerton."

They watered the horses and let them graze. While Asher and Zephaniah tended them, Prudence spread a blanket under a willow tree and set out bread and cheese. When they joined her on the blanket, sweat beaded on Zephaniah's upper lip, but he was smiling widely at being asked to help. He pulled a loaf of rhubarb bread from his cumbersome sack. "I took this without asking, but Cook knows I am the only one who likes it," he said. "Cook spoils me." A sad smile touched his eyes. "So it wasn't really stealing, was it?"

Prudence raised one brow. "It would have been better to ask, but I am quite sure Cook would understand. Let us ask

God to bless it." She bowed her head and, as was the Quaker way, offered a silent blessing. As they ate, she explained the purpose of their journey to Zephaniah. "We are on a very important mission to rescue a woman in danger. Since thee is now part of our team, thee must understand this is very serious. Someone could lose their life if any of us say or do the wrong thing. It is like a play. We each have our part." She gestured toward Asher. "This is thy father, Mr. Miller, and I am Mrs. Miller, thy mother. What name should we call thee?"

"Can I be Matthew, like my brother?"

Prudence nodded. "Matthew is a good name." She wrapped the remaining bread in a tea towel. "Let us be on our way, Matthew Miller, and let us pray God will give his angels charge over us."

CHAPTER TWELVE

J ust leave those." Irene gestured toward a set of green Depression glasses on the top shelf of her built-in china cabinet. "I won't have room for them, and they match the kitchen. They should stay with the house."

LuAnn stood on the counter, poised to grab the first glass. "Are you sure? These are beautiful."

Erica snapped a picture. Not a flattering angle.

"They are," Irene answered. "I remember you admiring them the first time you visited."

"Maybe you'd like to sell them, or give them to someone." *Like me.*

Irene's cotton candy waves bounced as she shook her head. "Can't think about that now. I have a strategy. The only things I want to pack today are the things we're taking with us. The rest we can worry about later."

"Okay." LuAnn gripped the edge of the cupboard as she lowered herself to the floor. "You're the boss."

Irene laughed. "And don't you forget it."

Sean aimed his massive lens at Irene. "Mrs. Martin, you've lived in this house all your life, right?"

"Right." Irene didn't smile for the camera. Her distrust of this man wasn't even remotely disguised.

"It was your great-grandparents who originally lived here, I understand."

"Your understanding is correct." Irene looked at LuAnn and pointed to the cupboard to the left of the one that held the Depression glass. "I want that bud vase. Daddy gave it to us for our twenty-fifth wedding anniversary. The rest of them can go to Goodwill."

LuAnn smiled at her. *Way to deflect, Irene.* Erica took a picture. Sean kept videoing.

The sound of the front door opening and closing carried toward them. LuAnn looked at Irene. "Are you expecting any front door people?"

"Nope. And front door people usually ring the doorbell. Grant and Brad and Saffron are the only people I'm expecting." Irene stressed *only* as she looked pointedly at the paparazzi before she walked into the dining room. "Oh! Hello?"

LuAnn crawled down from the counter and followed Irene, wondering who had both startled Irene and caused the question mark at the end of her greeting. She sensed Sean and Erica hovering close behind.

Davinia stood in the parlor wearing faded jeans, a baggy T-shirt, and a baseball cap. The look was so incongruous with the meticulous way she'd dressed up to this point that LuAnn had to do a double take.

"I'm ready to work."

LuAnn bent toward Irene, grateful the little woman still had excellent hearing. While keeping a semblance of a smile in place and moving her lips as little as possible, she whispered, "You weren't expecting her?"

Irene shook her head. "Come in. Always nice to have an extra pair of hands. LuAnn and I are working in the kitchen."

"Then I'll head upstairs. I'll pack up your bathrooms, and I have a hanger bar for my rental car, so I'll get one of your clothes closets next."

Irene looked up at LuAnn. Her expression seemed to be asking the same questions that were echoing in LuAnn's head. *Who does that? Who offers to help a virtual stranger move and then announces what she's going to do instead of asking how she can help?*

"I think it would be fun if we all worked together." LuAnn beckoned Davinia into the kitchen. "Irene has a plan."

"Oh, I've moved more than a dozen times in my life." Davinia brushed off LuAnn's suggestion with a dismissive wave of her hand. "I've got quite the knack for it."

LuAnn opened her mouth, but Irene beat her to it. "I'm sure you do. What was your name again?"

Davinia shot a quick glance at LuAnn before giving her name. LuAnn had all she could do not to respond with a reproving look. Maybe this was an occasion for holding her tongue, but she chose not to. She addressed her question to Irene. "I thought you two had a conversation yesterday while you were cutting flowers?"

Irene's eyes narrowed behind her glasses. "I did cut some hydrangeas to take to a friend, but I didn't talk to you." She cast an accusing gaze at Davinia.

Davinia's face flushed as she looked at LuAnn. "Maybe I didn't actually talk to Irene. I drove past, and seeing her made me think it would be nice to stay and help."

"Well, Davinia," Irene said, drawing herself up to her full four-foot-eight, "I appreciate your offer of help, but this is still my house, so we're going to do things my way. How's that sound?"

Davinia stretched her stiff lips over her perfect teeth. "That sounds...like fun."

When LuAnn turned back to the kitchen, Sean and Erica were gone. She spotted them outside, taking pictures of flowers.

For the next hour, Irene pointed, and LuAnn and a rather sullen Davinia wrapped dishes and filled boxes marked *CM* for Countryside Manor, or *G* for Goodwill. There was nothing wishy-washy about Irene's decision-making processes. She'd clearly thought it all out ahead of time.

LuAnn pulled a teapot from the back of one of the top cupboards above the stove. It was covered in a thin layer of greasy dust. It wasn't until she held it in both hands that she realized what she was looking at. "Irene! Look. This matches the...other set." She'd caught herself before blurting out too much in front of Davinia. She set the teapot securely on a shelf, then lowered herself onto a step stool. "I think I'll just go pack it away with the others."

Thankfully, Irene gave an understanding nod. "Good idea. In fact, you haven't had a chance to repack that box, have you?" Her eyes twinkled.

"No. I'll get to that right away." She lifted the pot, wondered for a moment if she should leave Irene alone with the seemingly manipulative Davinia, and decided the little woman could hold her own.

Padding quietly past Thelma, who appeared to be reading but was in fact softly snoring, LuAnn walked up the stairs to the second floor. After the palpable tension in the kitchen, the peacefulness of the empty floor embraced her. She allowed a moment of stepping back in time, imagining gaslights casting flickering shadows across the polished oak railing.

She took the long way around, passing first Leo's room, then Thelma's, Irene's, the guest room, and the master. The colors they'd chosen for each room were inviting. Selfishly, colors that appealed to her. Though Victorians loved opulence and vivid tones, she'd used more subdued colors. "Rose brocade" and "mulberry silk" for Thelma's room, and "patchwork plum" with cream trim for Irene's. Leo's room, smaller than the others, had an entire wall of built-in cupboards of various sizes. Irene had explained that this had originally been designed for little Zephaniah, who would have been four at the time he was supposed to have moved into the house with his father. To offset the rich golden woodwork, LuAnn had chosen "majolica green" with off-white trim for Leo's room.

They'd decided not to touch the guest room, the one Brad had often stayed in before he was married, and again after his wife died, and he couldn't face going home. He had painted it dark brown on the bottom and tan above a cream-colored chair rail. It had a decidedly masculine feel to it, and LuAnn could picture the new owners claiming it for a study, adding a massive antique desk, a leather chair trimmed with brass studs and floor-to-ceiling shelves filled with thick leather-bound books.

For the master bedroom she'd chosen "peacock plume," a shade of green with hints of blue just slightly darker than the seafoam used in the adjoining bathroom. This room had elaborately carved eight-inch molding around the ceiling. This, plus the wide baseboards and trim around the windows, had been painted white.

The room was an oasis. Had the lure of unpacking the trunk not beckoned her, she may have succumbed to lingering, stretched out on the white, scalloped-edge quilt.

She wished for a moment that the house had looked like this when Brad was little. With light flooding in every window through lace curtains or sheer panels, he may have come to love the Bickerton mansion.

Walking up the narrow stairs, she thought of the feet that had trod these steps more than a century and a half earlier. Had Prudence ever seen the inside of this house? It was likely she would have if the real Howard Bickerton had lived. They'd planned on working together to provide a safe haven for escaped slaves heading north. But after her shock at discovering the deceit, had she kept her distance from the Bickertons... all but the little boy she called Z? Entries in her journal showed her tenderness for the poor orphan forced to go along with a lie. Had she ever tried to help Zephaniah? Because of a letter Brad's cousin Char had shown them, they knew Zephaniah's older brother had finally come for him in 1866, after the war. A long time for a child to wait.

LuAnn set the teapot on the floor then knelt in front of the trunk. Something small bit into her knee. She raised up and found a small oval-shaped white pill. Even before she read the brand name stamped on it, she guessed what it was. Her mother had taken them with every meal for years because of lactose intolerance.

But who…? She'd knelt in this exact spot twice in the past week. Wouldn't she or Brad have seen it? Neither Thelma nor Irene took them. The way Leo had scarfed down pizza on Friday night, she was pretty sure that wasn't his issue either.

Who had been up here since Friday night? One of the bridal shower attendees? Two came to mind right away. Sean the wandering videographer. And Davinia.

LuAnn unpacked every dish, stacking each one carefully in an empty cardboard box. When the trunk was empty except for a pile of powdery wood shavings, she went downstairs to get a paper bag, a dustpan, and some newspaper. She found Irene and Davinia leaning against the counter chatting amiably.

Irene smiled when LuAnn walked in. "I've lived in a Victorian house all my life, but this woman knows way, way, way more about them than I do. She was just telling me about the Wedding Cake House in Kennebunk, Maine. It was completely restored in the 1980s, and then, in 2005, the owners opened it to the public as a fundraiser for Hurricane Katrina relief. It made me think we should have done that when we had that flooding a few years ago. I never thought of charging people to come to..."

As Irene chattered on, LuAnn gathered the things she needed. When Irene came up for air, LuAnn held up the dustpan and said she'd be back down in a few minutes. She was halfway into the dining room when she heard Davinia say, "If you change your mind about selling, I could help you set something up."

LuAnn paused, considering marching back into the kitchen, but decided against it. She would mention it to Brad, make him aware in case Irene started talking about keeping the house. That was a complication Brad didn't need. She headed back to the attic and scraped most of the sawdust out of the trunk. If she could lift one end, she could get the rest of it. As she grabbed onto a leather handle, she suddenly realized what she was doing.

What if *this* was the thing with the false bottom? She grabbed her phone and tapped on Brad's name.

He answered her call with, "Hey, Beautiful, I'm almost there."

"Good. Hurry."

"Something wrong?"

"No. I just have a crazy thought."

His laugh rumbled through the phone. "One of the things I love about you. I'll see you in a couple of minutes."

While she waited, she tapped on the bottom of the trunk. It did sound hollow, but so did the sides. And she couldn't find anything to turn to the right or the left. She felt along the inside, running her hand along the cloth that covered the bottom and sides.

She heard Brad's footsteps and rose to greet him. He opened his arms, and she stepped into them, talking into his shoulder. "Do you still have the instructions for opening the thing with the deed and M's pearls?"

"Hi to you too. And yes. I stuck it in my wallet."

She told him her crazy idea. Together, they hefted the trunk onto one end.

"I don't see anything to turn," Brad said. "But it wasn't a crazy thought."

She scooped out the rest of the dust, and they eased the trunk back down. LuAnn sighed. "I love a good mystery to solve as much as the next person, but why this week? And why so many? Who took the box, and why, and what are Davinia and the paparazzi up to? None of them has a really good reason for hanging around." She handed Brad a stack of newspapers. "Let's wrap each dish separately. I don't know where these are going, but they're going to have to get moved."

Brad seemed to hesitate a moment, then opened a newspaper and began wrapping cups. LuAnn set a stack of dinner plates in the bottom of the trunk. She brushed the cloth lining of the lid as she pulled her hand away. Something crinkled. She'd checked the bottom and sides. Why hadn't she thought to check the top? She touched the cloth again. It wasn't adhered to the side. Had she heard the crunch of old, disintegrating glue? Running her hand along the line where the cloth met a strip of leather held in place with brass tacks, she realized the entire arched top panel was loose.

"There's something behind this." Using just her fingertips, she gently pulled the cloth away from the top. Brad's shoulder pressed against hers as she pulled out a large envelope.

"Whoa." It was more of an exhale than a word as Brad ran his finger along the words inscribed on the front.

Last Will and Testimony of Howard Z. Bickerton

LuAnn felt her pulse quicken as she unwound the string holding the envelope closed. "Would this still hold up in court?" She lifted the flap. "If he bequeathed everything to—"

The envelope was empty.

"Another dead end." Brad sighed. "Well, now we know he had a will. If we—"

A door slammed below. Followed by a scream.

They scrambled for the door and ran down to the second floor.

CHAPTER THIRTEEN

The second floor was empty. LuAnn darted into the master bedroom, then Irene's room, as Brad checked the rooms on the other side of the stairway. "Irene? Davinia?"

"I'm right here." Irene gripped the railing as she ascended. Her other hand flattened on her chest. "Did you scream?"

"No. I thought it was you."

LuAnn peered behind Irene. "Where is Davinia?"

"She said she was going to get more boxes from the parlor."

Brad walked out of Thelma's room. "The scream was too loud to have come from downstairs. She has to be here somewhere." He strode into Leo's room. "Two minutes, and I'm calling 911."

"I'm in here."

The voice, clearly Davinia's, sounded small and weak. LuAnn had the sense it wasn't because the woman was hurt in any way other than her pride. LuAnn hurried into Leo's room, Irene right behind her.

A knock sounded from the wall of cupboards. "I know where she is." Brad laughed and stepped to the middle cupboard. The bottom of the door was about two feet off the ground. The door was about four feet wide and five high. He opened it, but it was empty. "When you're facing the door, feel for a notch on your right," he called to Davinia. "That panel slides back and you can crawl to the other side."

A scramble was followed by a grating sound, and then Davinia appeared in the open middle door on her hands and knees, flashlight held in her mouth.

"What in the world?" Irene slid around LuAnn and stood at the foot of the twin bed, hands on hips. "What are you doing in there?" Full-blown indignation tightened her words.

One foot thrust out of the cupboard, then the other. Brad held out his hand and told her to watch her head. Davinia was not a petite person. It took some maneuvering to get her out. What had possessed her to wedge herself in a cupboard in the first place?

When the disheveled woman stood in front of them, LuAnn realized she and Brad had both mirrored Irene's arms-akimbo stance. It was the body language a parent or teacher takes with a wayward child. The three stood in silence, waiting for an answer to Irene's question.

Davinia smoothed her hair. "I was just...curious."

Her accusers continued to wait for more of an explanation.

"Leo told us about this room and its secret compartments, and I just..." She shrugged, smiling like a child who'd been caught taking a bite of her sister's ice cream.

LuAnn forced her shoulders to relax a bit. Was this really just a matter of overactive curiosity? "What were you looking for?"

"Oh, you know...history. And I did find something, actually." She leaned into the empty cupboard and pointed her flashlight toward the outside wall. "Numbers."

LuAnn's skin prickled. Another code?

Brad opened the end cupboard. "My first grade girlfriend's phone number," he said, pointing at a row of numbers separated by dashes. "Grant and I used to play in here." He winked at LuAnn. "Don't worry, I was over her by 1961."

"You better be right about that. Maybe I should scratch out that number just in case." LuAnn nudged his arm, then played with the glass handle on the end door. "The door didn't just get stuck. This is made to lock when it's shut. If the handle is original, who would put this in a kids' room?"

Brad rubbed his chin. "Someone who wanted to protect his kids."

"By locking them in a cupboard?"

"You're right." Brad shook his head. "I remember Irene and Thelma's mother telling us how to get out if we got stuck inside. She said it was made…" He shook his head. "That doesn't make sense."

"To keep the pirates from getting the children," Irene said. All eyes turned toward her. "That's what my mother told us when we were little."

The room fell quiet. Davinia headed toward the door. She hadn't made eye contact with anyone since being released from her predicament. "I suppose I should be going."

LuAnn thought of mentioning that even though it was six hours after check-out time at the inn, she wouldn't charge her extra if she wanted to leave today.

"What time should I return to help you tomorrow?"

Irene looked incredulous. "I'm not sure I…we'll…"

"Anybody home?" Grant's voice carried up the stairs.

"Up here!" LuAnn yelled.

Grant and Saffron joined them in the small room.

"What's everyone doing in here?" Grant asked. He looked at the open cupboard. "Looking for the secret tunnel?"

Davinia's eyes sparked. "So it's real?"

Grant shook his head. "I think it was all a figment of Thelma's fertile imagination, but it made for some fun when we were kids, right?" He looked at Brad.

"We used to pretend we'd find secret passageways that led us to pirates' treasure."

Grant peered into the cupboard. "Do you remember Thelma telling that creepy story about pirates who hid pearls in this room and put a curse on them? She said any child who found the pearls and didn't give them to an adult would be turned into wood and become one of the faces on the fireplaces."

"Ew." LuAnn shuddered. "Who says things like that to a child?"

"I remember that." Brad looked as though he'd just experienced a light bulb moment. "That might be why this place freaked me out so much. I remember asking my Sunday school teacher if pirate curses were real, and she said no."

Grant laughed. "Thelma had a lot of stories. Do you remember the one that was like Cinderella only she made it about us? I think it was supposed to make us stop fighting."

"Wow." Brad sat on the end of Leo's bed. "I haven't thought of that in decades. Two brothers got in a fight, and one ran away and found a princess who put a magic spell on the other brother and said if he was ever mean to his brother again she would turn him into a poor orphan living in the woods all by himself with no food."

"Why in the world would someone tell scary stories like that to little children?" Davinia addressed the question to Irene.

Irene waved it away. "Thelma was just repeating stories our parents told us, passed down from our grandparents."

Davinia's question was a valid one. Why would an adult deliberately scare a child? Unless they were stories based on truth.

Were "M's" pearls hidden in these walls?

Davinia left, and Sean and Erica soon wandered back into the house. To LuAnn's surprise, Sean pitched in and helped Brad and Grant carry Goodwill boxes out to the truck Grant had rented. Erica stood in the hallway getting "some great black-and-whites" of Irene, Saffron, LuAnn, and a now wide-awake Thelma tackling Thelma's bedroom.

LuAnn picked up a framed black-and-white picture of a man, a woman, and a little girl and held it up to Thelma. "Are these your parents?"

"Yes. That was taken before Irene was born. We had such happy times back then. I remember that day. The photographer came here to the house, and we had to sit so still for such a long time, but I was a good girl, and I didn't squirm or cry, so after it was over, we all changed clothes and had a picnic down by the river. Just Mama and Papa and me."

Thelma appeared to have transported back to that long-ago day. The cadence of her voice and her choice of words sounded like a five-year-old girl. "We were so happy..." Her words drifted off, and she seemed to be lost in the past.

LuAnn picked up a milk glass vase. When she'd redecorated Thelma's room, she'd filled the vase with silk flowers that coordinated with the curtains and the bed quilt.

Thelma blinked back to the present. "I like that. I do wish I could take this whole room with me," she said wistfully. "You did a lovely job, LuAnn."

"I'm so glad you like it." LuAnn held up a bottle of perfume, and Thelma pointed to the trash bag hanging from the closet door handle. "You know I'd be happy to come and decorate your room at Countryside. We'll take this quilt and the curtains and get the same color paint."

"That would be delightful. It might help ease the pain a bit." Thelma sat in a white wicker rocker beside a small table with a Tiffany lamp. Next to the lamp sat a notebook and pen.

"Do you still journal, Thelma?"

"Not as much as I used to." She pointed at a row of white boxes on the top shelf of her open closet marked *Journals*, followed by a range of years. "Thank you for organizing all of them. Did you read them?"

"No. I would never do that." Though she had been sorely tempted when she'd been readying the room for the painter and found stacks upon stacks of notebooks, each labeled with a year beginning in 1938. "I do admit I would be fascinated to read the thoughts of a young woman in the thirties and forties. Would you consider having them scanned and printed?"

Thelma's eyes flashed. "Absolutely not! Those are for my eyes only, and when I die they must be burned."

Saffron knelt beside Thelma and took her hand. "You know, Aunt Thelma, the lessons you've learned throughout life might really benefit younger generations. I started keeping a diary when I was ten, and I hope someday my daughter or granddaughter will read them and learn from my mistakes."

Thelma stared at her, tired eyes seeming to grow sadder. "Well, maybe if I'd been allowed to marry"—she cast an accusing look at Irene—"so I could have a daughter and a granddaughter, I would have had some life lessons they could learn from. As it stands, they are filled with the whinings of a bitter woman and a lot of dry old family history."

A mixture of empathy and intrigue filled LuAnn. How she'd love to get her hands on some "dry old family history" of the Bickertons. But, at the moment, Thelma's bitter heart was the thing that needed attention. She knelt next to Saffron and took Thelma's other hand. "Life can be hard for those of us who've been disappointed in love."

Thelma nodded. "But you're getting your chance now, aren't you?" Her tone wasn't bitter, only wistful.

"I am." The starch went out of LuAnn's planned pep talk. "But up until this point I had to force myself to look at all the ways God had filled my life with good things. I determined a long time ago to start each day with gratitude." She tapped the notebook sitting next to Thelma. "A few months after my fiancé died, Tess and

Janice gave me a thankfulness journal. Every day I had to write down five things I was grateful for. It turned my thinking around, forced me to look at all the light in my life instead of the dark."

Tears gathered above Thelma's lower lashes. She blinked, and they coursed down lined cheeks.

Saffron grabbed a tissue from the box on the bottom shelf of the small table and pressed it into Thelma's hand. Thelma dabbed her eyes and cheeks. "I wonder if it's too late for me to start looking at the light. Papa always said we were his night and day girls. Irene is the positive one, but then, things have always gone her way."

"Thelma, that's not true, and you know it." Irene stood with a blouse on a hanger in each hand. "You know you were Mama's favorite."

"And what did that count for when you were Papa's?" Thelma's shoulders sagged. "If I wanted a cat and you wanted a dog, we got a dog. If you wanted chicken but I wanted meat loaf, we had chicken. Mama and I said we should go to Virginia Beach and walk on the boardwalk. You said we should go to Ocean City, so of course we went to Maryland." She closed her eyes. "And those were the small things."

LuAnn knew Thelma was referring to Fred. She'd always wondered how it came about that Irene married the man Thelma had been in love with. But now was not the time to ask. "Thelma, I've heard from Brad and Grant and Leo that you are a wonderful storyteller. Tell me the story about the pearls and the pirate curse." She was treading on thin ice, taking the risk that she'd be unearthing memories of Stuart Dawson's

143

deathbed confession, but there was a chance she'd learn something. And it was definitely interrupting the sisters' conflict, putting them in separate corners of the ring for a bit.

Thelma smiled. "Those are stories my father told me. I think his father told them to him. He said a long, long time ago pirates came on a big ship and saw our house and decided it would be the perfect place to hide their treasure. So they crept up from the river in the dark of night and climbed the trellis until they got to the nursery." She pointed toward the wall. Leo's room was on the other side. "They snuck in through the window without waking the little boys who were sleeping there and hid their treasure chest. They also hid secret codes telling how to open the treasure chest, but they said it could only be opened by a grown-up. If a child found the treasure chest, he must give it to an adult because if a child opened it, he would be instantly turned to wood and become one of the children on the fireplaces."

A small chill raised goose bumps on LuAnn's arms. Grant was right. Creepy. "They said there was a story about two brothers who were fighting."

Thelma nodded. "Once upon a time there were two little boys, a good boy and a bad one, and they had a fight, and the bad one ran away."

LuAnn cringed. Labeling a child "good" or "bad" bristled every teacher fiber in her body.

"He went on a long adventure to rescue a princess, and when he came back the princess put a magic spell on everyone in the family, and from then on they had to be nice to him all the time, or they wouldn't ever get the pirate treasure. But if they found the treasure chest full of pearls and then found the key to it, they could be rich, and they could send the bad boy far, far away over the ocean and never, ever have to see him again."

"And did they ever find it? In the story, I mean?"

Thelma's faraway look returned. "I don't think so. When my father told us the story, he said we should keep looking for treasure because the story just might be true."

June 7, 1861

They neared Millwood as the sun was slipping behind the trees. Asher pulled the buckboard under a massive oak and stopped the team. "We'll make camp here. I'll stand watch."

"We will take turns, Asher." Prudence felt her spine stiffen with resolve. "I will fix us a meal, and then thee will take the first watch, and I will take the second."

Asher's hand slid to the gun in his holster. "Thank you, ma'am, but I don't think—"

"God will protect us while thee sleeps, Asher." She said it with all the sternness she could muster.

To her surprise, Asher nodded. "Have to have a cold supper. Can't risk a fire." He jumped down and began tending the horses.

"Let us fix another picnic, Matthew." She spoke quietly to Zephaniah, not wanting to scare him, yet sensing the danger around them. The man, or men, who had taken Deborah, knew Asher would be coming from Marietta. Knew he'd be carrying eight hundred dollars. It took little imagination to picture two men engaging in this evil together and one attempting to outsmart the other by taking the money before they reached the tavern. Was someone, even now, watching their every move?

They ate another meal of bread and cheese washed down with water from a spring Asher found just yards from their campsite. As she cocooned Zephaniah in one of the two blankets she'd brought as a bedroll, she thanked God for a warm night with just the right amount of breeze ruffling the oak leaf canopy above them. She stroked Zephaniah's forehead, fighting back tears as she thought of Jason tucking Moses into his bed. Since his birth, she experienced more fear than ever before when she was called away on a night mission. As the boy snuggled in her blanket closed his eyes, she recited a verse that had been a comfort on many rescue missions. "'For the LORD your God is he that goeth with you, to fight for you against your enemies, to save you.'"

Zephaniah's eyes fluttered open. "Are we in real big danger, Miss Prudence?"

"God will protect us, son. He is faithful to—"

A branch snapped. A curse word cut the air. Asher gasped. "Run, Pru! Run!"

CHAPTER FOURTEEN

After a night of waking repeatedly with a list of clues scrolling through her head, LuAnn opened her eyes on Tuesday morning feeling like she'd spent the last seven hours in a wrestling match with her pillow and the sheet that wound around her left leg like seaweed. The other leg was now uncovered, thanks to the corner of the sheet clamped firmly in the jaws of a playful puppy growling and prancing on the floor. Tom, on the other hand, sprawled across one of LuAnn's decorative pillows, seeming as reluctant as she was to start the day.

"Did I keep you awake, Tom?" LuAnn nuzzled her face against the cat's soft fur. Only four more days to wake to her fur babies, and then... She tried to imagine waking up in Brad's house. Would he serve her coffee in the morning? Would she serve him? And she had to stop calling it Brad's house. "Our house. It's going to be *our* house."

Huck stopped tugging and tipped his head to one side. LuAnn freed her leg and swung her feet over the side of the bed, then bent down and scratched Huck's head. "Thank you for always listening when I talk my thoughts." Would Brad understand her need to talk to herself? Maybe that was a habit she could break.

She threw on a T-shirt and a pair of stretchy pants and put her hair in a ponytail. "Go get your leash, Huck." The dog ran to his toy box and pulled out his retractable leash. His entire body wagged at the prospect of a walk.

The hallway lights were still dimmed, and all was quiet at the inn…except for a muffled voice coming from Davinia's room. A pale glow seeped beneath the door to Apples and Cinnamon. With a twinge of guilt, LuAnn stepped closer.

"I'm almost sure of it. No, I don't have proof yet, but I'm close. I just need a little more time. Once I find it, I'll figure out who to ask, and the spread is ours!"

Davinia said a quick goodbye, and LuAnn backed away from the door and scurried down the steps with Huck at her heels.

What was that all about? What did she mean by "spread"? People talked about homes that way, said things like "Nice spread you've got here." Was Davinia talking about the Bickerton estate? Had she been looking for the deed in Leo's room? If so, how would that help her take ownership of "the spread"? Or was she looking for something that would ensure she'd get a good price for it? What could that be?

Questions clambered in her brain as LuAnn walked out into the heavy June air. The western sky was a dark, gun-metal gray. She usually loved watching thunderclouds gather and roll over the Ohio. It always gave her a sense of God's power. Today it seemed to stir up unrest inside her. She thought of a passage from the book of Job and made a mental note to look it up when she got back.

She led Huck along the riverbank, trying to pray as she walked, but finding her mind as roiling as the surface of the river turned choppy by the rising wind. She pulled out her phone. Brad would be up. She called him and relayed everything she'd heard.

"I can't think of anything she'd find that could undermine the sale of the house," he said. "I'm sure it's nothing to worry about."

Unconvinced, she told him she loved him and hoped he'd have a good day, and then said goodbye and trudged up the bank, across the road, and into the inn.

By the time she'd finished showering and dressing, raindrops were pelting the old, wavy glass of her bedroom windows. The weather matched her mood. She sat in her favorite chair overlooking the river and looked up the Job passage in the concordance in the back of her Bible. "At this my heart pounds and leaps from its place. Listen! Listen to the roar of his voice, to the rumbling that comes from his mouth. He unleashes his lightning beneath the whole heaven and sends it to the ends of the earth. After that comes the sound of his roar; he thunders with his majestic voice. When his voice resounds, he holds nothing back. God's voice thunders in marvelous ways; he does great things beyond our understanding."

A shard of jagged white split the pewter sky across the river, followed almost immediately by a crack of thunder that rattled the windows. As she gazed at the display of God's might, she made a valiant attempt to surrender her worries. "You are powerful enough to bend the trees and stir the waters, Lord. You are certainly strong enough to handle whatever is going on with whoever is doing what here." The sentence almost made her laugh, but the vague, confusing words summed up how she was looking at Davinia and Lesley and Erica and Sean Wolfe-with-an-*e* and Leo. Who was after what and why?

She pulled out her current Clues & Suspects list and wrote down everything she'd heard while eavesdropping outside Apples & Cinnamon.

The breakfast crowd was light, likely due to the deluge that hadn't stopped for two hours. Around eight o'clock, Tess and Janice shooed LuAnn out of the café, telling her to go do relaxing "bride things." Unfortunately, they'd said it within earshot of Sean and Erica.

LuAnn was in no mood to be followed or interviewed but decided to use the situation as an opportunity to turn the tables. This time, she was going to be the one asking the questions. She smiled sweetly at her camera crew. "I'm going to stop in at the caterers and then go for my final dress fitting." Finally, she had things on her to-do list that actually came under the pre-wedding category. Not that she was actually supposed to be checking in with the caterers. But she had something to drop off, and it seemed silly to ask her already busy friends to do it. And it wasn't like she was going to make changes to anything Tess and Janice had already done.

The three of them scurried to her car. LuAnn wore a rain jacket. Sean held an umbrella over Erica who clutched her hair as if afraid it might shrink if it got wet. They both sat in the backseat, making LuAnn feel she should be wearing a chauffeur's cap. As she turned onto Ohio Street, she framed her questions. Yesterday, on the way home from the aunts' house, they'd babbled about the beauty of the Bickerton landscaping and the "amazing" footage and still shots they'd gotten, leaving her no opening to ask why they'd darted outside and stayed there until Davinia left.

After a deep breath, she plunged in. "I get the impression you two have met Davinia Richards before."

"Who?" Sean asked. "Oh, the blond woman staying at the inn?"

LuAnn almost laughed at his clumsy attempt at sounding ignorant. They'd been at the inn for four days. Not much of a chance he was that clueless.

"Seems like you're both avoiding her." Maybe a little of Tess's confrontation skills were finally rubbing off on her.

Erica's brittle laugh filled the car. "We're trying to be unobtrusive. Seemed like there were too many people in the house yesterday, and a little conflict added to the mix. Irene wasn't expecting her, was she?"

LuAnn parked in front of Delish Catering and blatantly ignored Erica's question. "I'm just dropping something off here." All she needed to do was hand them the imprinted napkins that had come in the mail two days ago. Barb, the owner, had said she could just leave them at the church when she came for rehearsal on Friday, but it never hurt to get things done early.

In spite of feeling ridiculous, LuAnn didn't say a word when both back car doors opened simultaneously. How did celebrities do this? *Just go on with your day and try to block out the shadows behind you?* She opened the glass door and was tempted, for a moment, to let it shut without holding it open for Erica. But she didn't.

She recognized the young man at the counter. Barb's college-age grandson. She greeted Adam, reminded him who she was, and handed him the plastic-wrapped napkins. He stared down at the imprint. "But it's silver. Isn't it sup—"

"LuAnn! Hi!" Barb whirled around the corner on stilettos. LuAnn marveled that a woman close to seventy who spent all day on her feet could, and would want to, wear such torture devices on her feet. "Thank you for bringing these in. Four more days, huh?" She looked at Adam and pointed to the archway she'd just walked through. "Can you go take the crème puffs for the Johnson shower out of the freezer, please?"

Adam left, and Barb's shoulders relaxed.

"Four more days. Anything else you need from me?"

"Nope. Just need you to relax and not worry about the details. It's all taken care of." Barb grinned. Erica snapped a picture.

As they walked out, LuAnn realized she'd lost count of the number of people who'd told her not to worry. Which made her worry.

Next, they walked into a place where she finally didn't feel quite so foolish entering with an entourage. She would, indeed, enjoy pictures of her dress fitting in years to come.

The interior of Marie Rose Designs, named for Marie Antoinette's dressmaker, Marie-Jeanne Rose Bertin, felt otherworldly. A hushed oasis of crystal chandeliers, opulent furnishings, and clerks who spoke with thick, sometimes believable, French accents.

Sean and Erica sat on a purple velvet settee while LuAnn followed Collette, her personal designer, into a dressing room where her dress hung on a padded satin hanger. Collette closed the door, leaving LuAnn alone with a dress that was nothing like the full-skirted princess gown Janice had designed and sewn for her for the wedding that never happened. How she'd loved that dress, and how it had hurt to let it go. She'd given it to an organization that surprised low-income women with beautiful weddings. Though she could have seen pictures of an ecstatic young bride wearing her dress, she'd chosen not to.

Fingering the lace on the cap sleeve of this much simpler dress, she thanked God again for making possible something she never thought would happen. Were there occasional glints of sadness that she'd never have the fairytale wedding of her dreams? If she was honest, yes. But a little thankfulness was a quick remedy. *Lord, I never thought I'd be here. Thank You.*

She slipped into the dress and then put on the shoes that had disappeared and mysteriously reappeared. She smiled at her reflection. Would Brad like what he saw? She'd seen pictures of his first wedding. Stephanie's dress had been elaborate, with a train fit for Buckingham Palace. Would this ceremony, with its simple trimmings, seem "less than"?

No. Thoughts like that would never do. Brad called her "Beautiful." She couldn't allow doubt to undermine her joy. She brushed her hair over her shoulders, put on a dab of lipstick, smiled at her reflection, and walked out.

The paparazzi responded with appropriate exclamations. And pictures. LuAnn stepped onto the round, raised platform and waited for Collette, an ample-figured woman, to ask why she hadn't been eating. Collette didn't disappoint. "Oh, *mon chéri*! You are shrinking. One must keep a little padding for the curves, no?"

In truth, LuAnn hadn't felt her appetite diminish at all since she'd first tried on the dress. But the stress of the past few weeks must be ramping her metabolism. She opened her mouth to apologize for causing Collette extra work, then decided against it.

"I will take a nip here and a tuck there and ze dress will be perfect," Collette said around the pins in her mouth. "Such a… spare design, but that is good, no? It does not need to be a wedding dress. You can wear it for many other things."

Odd way to put it. *It does not need to be a wedding dress?* Keeping her arms raised like a ballerina in second position, LuAnn turned with tiny, mincing steps under Collette's direction until she faced the settee. Erica had set her camera down and was frantically searching for something in her purse. She pulled out her phone, grimaced at Sean, and darted out the door. She stood in front of the window, partially obscured by the silver lettering spelling out Marie Rose. LuAnn watched her expressions change like a storm moving across the horizon. From worry to what appeared to be a forced smile. Erica seemed flustered, the way people act when they are trying too hard to come across as happy, relaxed, and normal.

"Now go, take zis off carefully, and hang it on ze hanger." Collette held out a hand with rings on all five fingers and helped LuAnn off the platform.

As she was heading to the dressing room, LuAnn noticed something lying on the champagne-colored carpeting next to Erica's open purse. She bent and picked it up. A contact lens blister pack. As she stretched to set it on the settee, she got a glimpse of the contact through the clear back. Not an unnatural teal color.

The contact lens was pale blue.

CHAPTER FIFTEEN

The Inn Crowd gathered on the patio behind Wayfarers Inn at five o'clock on Tuesday for what Tess had called "a little housekeeping stuff." In an hour, Robin would be there to watch the front desk, and they'd all be headed in different directions. Janice to take her grandson, Larry, to Over the Moon for pizza, Tess to her God's Weigh healthy eating meeting, and LuAnn to what she hoped would be a stress-free dinner with Brad, sans paparazzi.

LuAnn took a sip of the made-from-scratch raspberry lemonade Janice had brought out and nodded her approval. "How much work would it be for us to add this to our summer menu?"

Janice held up her right hand, supported at the wrist by her left. "I think I have carpal tunnel syndrome from squeezing enough lemons for one pitcher. If we got an electric squeezer, we could do it."

"Done." Tess tapped the side of her glass with a pen. "I'll fit it into the budget. People will come just for this. And speaking of budget—and business in general—we have a happy problem to talk about."

"Bring on the happy problems." LuAnn opened her *Everything* notebook to a blank page. This was the spiral she kept in a drawer in the café kitchen. Anything that popped in her head or was suggested by a guest or staff member went in this book first, and then onto its proper list in the right notebook.

"Remember Todd and Gail Baxter, the Honeymoon Suite couple who were here in October?"

LuAnn nodded. "Missionaries to somewhere in Africa, right?"

"Nigeria." Tess picked up a folded paper. "We got an email from Gail today. They'll be home again this fall and want to host a two-day meeting here, with four other couples on furlough, the third weekend in October."

"Wonderful!" LuAnn raised her glass.

"Wonderful they want to return, yes, but I had to say no. We're booked to capacity on the dates they need. That's the weekend of the Sheffield-Brown wedding. They reserved every room for the bridal party and parents. Since internet is spotty for them, I told Gail we'd try to find another option."

"Butterfly Farms B&B?" LuAnn suggested.

"That's peak color week," Tess said. "I'd be surprised if they had openings. Where else could we send them? It needs to be someplace quiet and restful."

"Someplace with character," Janice added. "With scenic views."

LuAnn's thoughts went immediately to the Bickerton estate and the cornucopia of color that had burgeoned on the grounds last fall. The crowning glory was a two-century-old sugar maple that seemed to be lit from within by golden lanterns when the sun shone on its rich orange leaves. She'd pictured weddings beneath that tree. It would be the perfect setting for missionary R&R.

And missionary R&R would be the perfect purpose for the estate…

"Lu? Hey! Come back to us."

Tess's words broke through just as a thought struck with perfect clarity.

"Where were you?" Janice asked. "What era?"

LuAnn blinked hard and took a sip of lemonade. "Oddly for me, I was in the future."

Janice smiled. "Seems the right place for a bride-to-be." She leaned forward. "What were you thinking about?"

LuAnn crossed her arms across her waist, trying to tamp down the adrenaline rush. "I don't know why no one has thought of this before. Wouldn't the mansion make an absolutely perfect retreat center?"

Tess nibbled on her bottom lip. "Hmm. It would, wouldn't it?"

"Something to think about," Janice added.

LuAnn picked up her phone. "I'm calling Pastor Ben."

"About…" Janice prodded.

"About the church buying the mansion. Or maybe forming a parachurch organization to purchase it. It would take financial backers, but look how generous people were when we raised money for the Moore House. I hate bothering him at home, but this is time sensitive. We need to talk to the missions committee and then get the word out to other churches to see if—"

"Lu…" A note of warning edged Tess's voice. She glanced at Janice and then back at LuAnn. "I think you're forgetting someone."

"Don't you worry, I'm including both of you. Think about it. The three of us alone have so many connections from our years of teaching and being involved in various ministries." She focused on Janice. "You know so many retired pastors, and I'm sure you still have connections with missionary boards. Wouldn't it be fun to be involved in helping raise money for keeping the house a historic landmark that would benefit the community?"

"I'm not talking about us. I'm talking about your fiancé."

"Oh. Of course. I wouldn't be able to do a thing…I mean, he'd have to be totally on board."

"It's a good idea, Lu." Janice seemed to be treading lightly, as if not saying what she really wanted to say. "But is this the time to be thinking about it?"

"I agree," Tess added. "It does sound exciting, but maybe you should table it for now. Wait until a while after your honeymoon to jump into something new."

"What if Grant finds a buyer while we're gone? If I started making contacts today, I could be following up while we're in Eur—"

"No!" The shout came in stereo.

Tess shook a finger at her. "You are absolutely *not* going to be on your devices doing any kind of work on your honeymoon."

"You have one mission next week," Janice added. "And only one. You focus on Brad. That's it. Got it?"

"But finding a buyer for—"

"Zip!" Tess ran her thumb and forefinger across her lips. "None of that. Brad's the Realtor. Let him handle it. I'm sure *he's* not going to be thinking about work on his honeymoon. Nothing can be done without the deed, anyway."

"If the church was interested, Brad would just have to get his attorney to look into it. People do sell properties without deeds. This would be such a perfect solution for everyone. Thelma and Irene would be thrilled, and think of the ministry opportunities it would open up for the church." She turned a page in her notebook...only to have it snatched out of her hands by Tess.

"This couldn't be any more perfect." LuAnn rested her forearms on the white linen tablecloth on the *Valley Gem* sternwheeler. She stared out at the lights of Marietta as the boat neared the dock.

"It is pretty perfect." Candlelight reflected in Brad's eyes. Those incredible blue eyes that had captured her the moment they'd met.

Brad had chosen the ribeye steak with bourbon cream sauce, and she'd savored the Tuscan garlic salmon with grilled asparagus. The meal had ended with warm caramel bread pudding and coffee. They'd spent the last two hours learning more about each other, talking about childhood memories and what they'd dreamed of being when they grew up. LuAnn had reached out and laid her hand over his when he talked about wanting a "bunch of kids." Sadly, that dream hadn't come to pass for him and Stephanie.

"Will a dinner cruise on the Ohio still sound romantic after we've spent a week on the Rhine?" she asked.

"As long as I'm with you, it will." His mouth lifted a bit at one corner. One of the things she loved about him—his ability to say something tender without making it sound too corny. That easy smile kept it real.

"Thank you for tonight," she said. "We needed some time away from all the distractions. I'm sorry my brain hasn't always been totally present lately."

"You've got a lot going on. Dare I bring up the topic of your suspicious guests? Or would that ruin the evening?"

LuAnn gave a sigh of contentment. "I don't know if anything could ruin this night. And I'm beginning to think the most suspicious thing about three of our guests is me."

He raised an eyebrow in amusement. "Do you want to explain that?"

"The wedding rings are missing. The brass box is missing. Whatever medals Irene was talking about are missing. Sean and Erica and Davinia keep doing weird things. But I don't think all of those things are tied together. Sean and Erica weren't even here on Wednesday, and if any of them had taken the rings or the box, doesn't it seem logical they would have absconded with them? Why are they still here? The one who's not here is Leo. But Leo had no reason to essentially steal from himself. The rings are his, and the box has been right under his nose for two years."

Brad rubbed his chin. "Leo's not the only one who left. What about Davinia's daughter?"

LuAnn gave a small start. "Lesley? No. She's as sweet as…" Her voice trailed off when she thought of other "sweet" guests whose deceptions had shocked her. "Wow. When will I ever learn to not be so gullible?"

"And here you thought you were overly suspicious. Nothing wrong with being a trusting person, you know."

"Unless you're trying to solve a mystery. Then it just works against you. I need to work on my cynicism." She feigned a scowl. "So how do we find out if Lesley is the culprit, or one of them? Probably wouldn't work to just come right out and ask her mother if her daughter is a thief." She thought of Davinia stuck in the cupboard. "And the two of them may be working together. Maybe Lesley pilfered the box and ran, and Davinia is still here searching for more."

LuAnn rubbed the back of her neck. "Lesley confided that her relationship with her mom is strained. They operate their B&B together, and Lesley and her husband are buying it from Davinia. It's easy to imagine they'd want to find a new venture for Davinia that's a nice, call-before-you-come-to-visit distance away, like the Bickerton mansion. Or maybe it's Davinia who wants to buy it. She's a walking encyclopedia on Victorian houses."

Furrows creased Brad's forehead. "You told her it's not for sale yet, right?"

"Well…no. I didn't want to discourage her." She gave him her sweetest smile. "Until now."

"Something about that smile terrifies me. What are you thinking?"

She laid out her ideas. "It would provide jobs in the area. Housecleaners, groundskeepers, a cook. Think of the people in MTDC who'd love to get involved. When it wasn't booked for retreats, it could be rented out for weddings or craft fairs or corporate events. And if it really took off, there's enough land to add another building. Can't you imagine a separate meeting house with a fireplace and—"

Brad held up one hand. "Whoa. You haven't mentioned this to Ben yet, have you?"

"No. I wanted to write up a business plan first. I think I can have something on paper by tomorrow. I know we won't get an answer immediately, but at least we can start the ball rolling, and they can be talking about it while we're gone. Would they need any zoning changes or variances or—"

Again, Brad held up his hand. He took a swig of now cold coffee. "You do remember we're getting married in four days, right?"

"Of course. And wouldn't it be wonderful if you knew you had a potential buyer before then? You'd be so much more relaxed."

"Do I seem not relaxed? It seems to me I'm not the one who's worried about getting the house sold." His head tipped ever so slightly to one side. That gesture said so much more than his words.

"I'm only trying to help. I thought you'd be happy if you and Grant didn't have to go through all the work of making up spec sheets and planning open houses and everything else you do. And how would you feel if Grant made the sale while you were gone? You and I have put more work into getting the house ready than he—" She closed her mouth. "I'm sorry. I just want everything to be—"

"Perfect." His hand closed around hers. "And you want everyone to be happy. Two of your most endearing qualities, but not this week, okay? For once in your life, you need to sit back and be a little selfish. Or do this for me. I want a happy, relaxed wife who can be thoroughly present in the moment on Saturday." Those blue eyes took on a puppy dog look. "Please? For me?"

She held back an army of "But..." and "What if...?" statements and simply nodded. She would do what he asked. She would table all ideas for the future of the mansion and simply focus on who did what, when, and why. She'd make a phone call to Lesley. And she'd call Giana...just to get to know a future shirttail relative who might know if her boyfriend had absconded with the brass box.

She could do that and still be "in the moment" and totally relaxed, couldn't she?

Of course she could.

CHAPTER SIXTEEN

LuAnn waited until the time on her phone changed to six fifteen. Lesley had said they were up at five thirty every morning. Hopefully, she'd given her time to feed her kids. Would she be willing, and able, to talk while doing chores? LuAnn pressed the number on the website.

"Paw Paw Patch B&B. May I make a reservation for you?"

LuAnn smiled. Not a bad way to answer the phone. "Hi Lesley, this is LuAnn Sherrill at Wayfarers Inn."

"Good morning, LuAnn. Is my mom behaving herself?"

About that… "Your mom is fine. I was wondering if you had a few minutes to chat."

"Sure. Okay if I put you on speakerphone while I milk a goat?"

Now that was a first. "I don't mind at all."

"What can I do for you? You know, I was thinking it would be fun to stay in touch and share some inside tips on B&B ownership."

"I'd like that." *But first I need to find out if you stole something.* "For now, I won't keep you. I just have a quick question. You know the brass box that Harry pointed out in the library at the Bickerton mansion?"

"Yes. Beautiful piece."

"Well, it's gone missing. We think it's possible one of the Bickerton sisters packed it away or forgot where she put it, but I wanted to ask you if you might have heard anyone talking about it. It's likely it disappeared the same day Brad gave that group a tour."

"Oh! I sure hope you don't think either of us took it." The sound of milk squirting the side of a bucket emphasized her concern.

"I just wondered if you'd seen or heard anything."

"We all walked out together after the tour, didn't we? I can't remember anyone carrying a purse or bag large enough to hide that thing. Mom and I hung around in back talking to Thelma for a while about the statues. Let me think... Irene left, and a woman drove in a few minutes later. Thelma said it was the painter coming to do touch-ups on the bathroom."

So Thelma had been right all along. "Thank you. That information really helps. If you think of anything else, please let me know."

"I will. And, LuAnn, don't be afraid to ask my mom to step back if she gets too...intense."

LuAnn smiled. "You and your kids—human and otherwise—have a wonderful day."

When LuAnn walked into the kitchen, Winnie was singing "Amazing Grace" over the hum of her electric knife. Both sounds stopped when she cut the last slice of homemade cinnamon bread from one loaf and reached for another.

"That sound means only one thing." LuAnn took her apron off the hook. "Stuffed French toast."

"Mm-hmm. Thorn's been asking for it. He and Beverly are going to try to be first in line this morning."

"You spoil him." Tory Thornton, handyman extraordinaire, was the first person they'd hired after deciding to purchase the inn. In two years, he'd gone from homeless to happily reunited with his wife and daughter. If the Inn Crowd ever needed confirmation they were in the right place at the right time, the man they affectionately called Thorn was proof.

"I like to think I spoil all our people. Speaking of that, think we should put it on Facebook?"

LuAnn smiled at her use of "we." Winnie wasn't fond of social media and, to LuAnn's knowledge, had never posted anything on the inn's page. "I'll do that right now." She pulled out her phone and found a picture she'd taken the last time Winnie had put the indulgent treat on their breakfast menu. A quick cut and paste and a couple of sentences describing thick slices of batter-dipped bread stuffed with sweetened cream cheese and topped with warm cherry pie filling and a generous dollop of fresh whipped cream, and she was done. "Hope you're prepared for a crowd. They'll be breaking down the doors in about fifty minutes, and I don't want to be the bad guy who has to tell anyone we've run out."

Winnie gestured at the five loaves cooling on wire racks on the counter. "I've got at least that many in the freezer. Don't think anybody's going away hungry. And in case a certain someone asks, do not tell her the secret ingredients."

"Certain someone?"

"Paw Paw Patch woman. I don't know what she's up to, but I don't need any more of her nosin' around."

"I promise I won't divulge any of your secrets." LuAnn felt privileged to know Winnie sweetened the cream cheese with coconut sugar and added a dash of orange zest to the mix. She'd never repeat this inside information to anyone. "Has she been asking for recipes?"

"Under the guise of sharing hers with me, but I'm not fooled. I don't need her biscuit recipe. She uses vegetable oil instead of butter." Winnie turned around, one hand on a hip, the other gesturing with the electric knife. "Culinary blasphemy is what that is."

LuAnn smiled at Winnie's colorful phrase. "What do you want me to start on?"

"Wash those oranges. The grater's in the dishwasher."

LuAnn brought a bowl of oranges over to the sink. A drop of water clinging to the faucet created a prism in the morning sunlight. The drop fell and another formed, then another. LuAnn cranked the handles. "Winnie, how long has this sink been leaking?" As she asked, a plan began sparking in her head like embers about to burst into flames. A plumbing emergency! Well, a plumbing excuse anyway.

"Just a few days. Wanna ask Thorn about it?"

"We don't want to interrupt their breakfast date with shop talk. But don't worry, I'll take care of it." She finished zesting the oranges, then beat a dozen eggs. When she had a moment to get away, she looked for a website or Facebook page for Cassidy Plumbing but found neither. How did the man expect to attract business? A search produced his phone number. She waited through six rings, expecting voice mail with each one.

"Cassidy. Whatcha need?"

Oh my. Another interesting way to answer the phone. Not quite as inviting as Lesley's. "Hello. Mr. Cassidy?"

"Call me Butch."

Seriously? "Okay. Butch. This is LuAnn Sherrill at Wayfarers Inn on Ohio Street."

"Yep. Know where it is. You're the one marrying one of the Grimes brothers, right?"

"Yes. Brad. Did he call you?"

"Nope." He laughed. "Sounds like you two got communication issues even before you tie the knot. Me and my wife couldn't get nothin' straight. Maybe that's why she left me." Again, the laugh.

LuAnn cleared her throat. "I was wondering if you might have time to come and look at our kitchen sink at the inn…today."

"What's wrong with it?"

"The faucet is leaking."

"I'm just over on Second finishing up a tub job. The Grimes brothers' aunts paid me real good for a job I did for them. Guess I owe the family a little extra." He laughed, one of those inside joke kind of sounds. "Be there in a bit."

"Thank you." LuAnn slid her phone into her apron pocket, wishing she'd told him to come after nine. What would Thorn

169

say about her hiring someone to do the kind of work he did for them all the time? She busied herself making coffee, then filled cream and syrup pitchers. Tess and Janice joined them, and they worked, as usual, like a finely tuned machine. At two minutes to eight LuAnn walked into the café, two pots of coffee in one hand. Davinia was already seated at a two-top, and LuAnn greeted her with more than her usual morning cheer, promising she'd return to fill her cup in moments. She turned on the OPEN sign, unlocked the front door, and was not surprised to see a line reaching all the way to the corner. The recommended ten thousand steps would be easy to come by today.

Taylor, the college student who'd started out bussing tables and was now learning the role of host, came out of the kitchen and began seating people, leaving LuAnn free to pour coffee. Harry sat at his favorite table in the corner by the window. Once again, a file folder sat on the table next to the cup LuAnn filled with regular coffee. "I found something you and Brad will be interested in," he said, tapping the folder. "Let me know when you've got a minute." He turned to his left, looking directly at Davinia. "Maybe later, when things quiet down. I'll be here for a while."

"Do I get a hint?"

Harry stroked his chin. "I found the other half of that plat map." A teasing smile accompanied the shooing motion he made with his hand. "I don't want to keep you from your work."

After sending a look of mock exasperation at him, LuAnn stepped over to Davinia's table and filled a white ironstone mug. "What are your plans for the day?"

Davinia looked up through tired eyes. "Well, I know I might not be welcome, but I was wondering if you need any help moving the Bickerton women. And if I might be…allowed to help."

LuAnn blinked, no idea how to respond. She'd assumed Davinia would be checking out this morning. "Well… Why?"

It was Davinia's turn to blink in surprise.

"I'm sorry. I just can't help but wonder why—" A high-pitched laugh followed by a child's squeal drew her attention to the front door. Two young women were attempting to corral three toddlers as Taylor pointed to a table. LuAnn turned back to Davinia. This wasn't the time to try figuring out the woman's intentions. She took a quick breath. "You mentioned you had a clothes pole in your car. I'm going to be emptying their closets today, and that would really help."

The contours of Davinia's cheeks smoothed as if LuAnn's invitation had given her an instant face-lift. "I have a few things to do this morning, and then I can go over and get started."

LuAnn cringed inwardly. She should have been clearer. "I work until about three. Enjoy your day and we can—"

"I don't mind going early. You have so much on your plate right now with the wedding. I'll go help the sisters, and then there will be a lot less work for you to worry about."

Before she could think of a way to dissuade Davinia, Janice approached with her order pad. She looked at LuAnn and said, "In case you haven't noticed, there's a handsome silver-haired man patiently waiting at table two."

Brad sat with his chin resting on folded hands. Crinkles formed at the corners of those blue eyes when she smiled at him. Three days! Her heart made a soft thud as it skipped a beat and then resumed ticking at a faster pace. She excused herself and walked over to him. "Coffee, sir?"

"Sweetened with a good-morning kiss?"

She bent and kissed him, marveling once again at being sixty-five and about to become "Mrs." She remembered a conversation they'd had not long after their first kiss. She'd started to explain that it might take her a while to get used to showing affection in public. She'd said, "Kissing a man for the first time in thirty years is…" but hadn't been able to finish the statement, partly because she couldn't find the words, and partly because he'd simply kissed her again. In Jeremiah's Coffee House, in front of God and everybody. And then he'd laughed and said her shyness was adorable.

"I'm showing two houses this morning and then heading over to the aunts'." Brad wrapped his hands around his coffee mug. "I'm taking a load to Goodwill first and then moving their dressers and Thelma's rocker. Any chance you can get away a little early? I'd like to get them settled at Countryside before supper, and I think it would help the transition if you were along."

"Absolutely. The girls keep telling me I should take the whole week off, but I don't know what I'd do with my time."

"You'd primp and relax." He winked at her. "Think you could meet me over there about one?"

"I can do that. Robin's offered to fill in anytime. I'll give her a call." This would give Davinia less time to go searching for pirate treasure—or whatever it was she was hoping to do. She nodded toward Harry. "You might want to go join Harry.

He found something he thought we'd be interested in." With a glance at Davinia she added, "Though he sounded like he didn't want to share it in present company."

"Intriguing. I'll go talk to him."

Tess set a plate of French toast in front of Brad just as Taylor seated Thorn and Beverly. LuAnn blew a discreet kiss Brad's way and went off to greet them. She'd just brought Beverly's tea to their table when Thorn, whose military training had him always taking a seat facing the door, looked up and scowled. "What's he doing here?"

A giant man in a stained white T-shirt stood at the front desk, carrying an equally giant scarred yellow toolbox.

LuAnn cringed. "I called him. The sink in the kitchen is leaking, and I didn't want to bother—"

"You don't want him, Lu." Thorn's voice lowered. "Cassidy does shoddy work and charges way too much."

"I know."

"You know?" His eyes widened. "So you're purposely hiring bad workmanship at an exorbitant price when I'm sitting right here willing to do it for stuffed French toast?"

"Yes. Now you're catching on."

Thorn's rich laugh rolled across the café. "What's going on?"

"We've got a little mystery on our hands. I need to talk to Butch"—she winced as she said the name—"Cassidy to find out if he knows anything."

"Anytime I'm around you three I go home laughing. Okay, just know I'm going to go in and fix it right when he's done."

"I'm counting on it."

June 7, 1861

"Zeph—Matthew! Wake up!" Prudence yanked the blanket off the boy with one hand as she shook his shoulder with the other. "We must leave. Now!" Her insistent whisper barely carried over a sudden gust of wind.

Zephaniah's wild eyes scanned her face. He bolted up. "My bag!" Fluttering moonlit shadows made his movements appear to jerk as he frantically patted the ground. "My box!"

"Here!" She handed him the heavy canvas bag. Why had he brought the cumbersome brass box?

They leapt to their feet, Prudence gripping Zephaniah's shirt, and ran toward the river. Instinctively, she was drawn to the willows that had shielded her last night when she washed up. She tugged Zephaniah under the overhang of thin branches that danced in the wind. The swish of their narrow leaves camouflaged all other sound. Where was Asher? Was he still—

Father, protect him, and us, by Thy mighty right hand.

They waited, Prudence holding the trembling boy in her arms. "'The LORD is my rock, and my fortress, and my deliverer; my God, my strength, in whom I will trust...'" She repeated the verse over and over until she heard Asher's voice above the wind.

"Pru! Are you all right?" His voice shook as he drew closer.

"We are unharmed." She ushered Zephaniah into the open. "What happened? Is thee hurt?"

"No." Asher sank to the ground. "They snuck up on me. Didn't even have time to draw my gun. One held me down while the other"—his voice cracked—"found the money." He covered his face with his hands.

Prudence stood, frozen in place. The money was gone. They had nothing to bargain with. What would happen to Deborah now?

Zephaniah pulled away from her. She felt him fumbling with something in his bag. After a minute, he stood. "Use these." He held up a loop of something that glowed with a soft luster in the moonlight.

A string of pearls.

CHAPTER SEVENTEEN

On her way to meet the plumber at the front desk, LuAnn was startled to see that Davinia had moved to a different table. She was now sitting face-to-face with the two people LuAnn had been sure were avoiding her.

She didn't have time to ponder that situation. She approached the desk with her host smile in place. "Mr. Cassidy, would you mind following me around to our back entrance?" She didn't stop to shake his hand. "I wanted to talk to you about something before you look at the sink."

The burly man in the stained white T-shirt lumbered after her, his massive dented toolbox banging against his thigh as he walked. She pointed toward a small round table with two chairs near the corner of the building.

Butch dwarfed the wrought-iron ice cream parlor chair. LuAnn sat across from him. "You mentioned doing some work for the Bickerton sisters."

"Yep." He laughed as his large head swiveled from side to side. "What a kick. Don't they remind you of the sisters in *Arsenic and Old Lace*?"

The comparison had crossed her mind a time or two, especially recently, as Thelma's clarity occasionally faded. But now was not the time to discuss their likeness to two wacky homicidal characters in a offbeat comedy written in the thirties. "Irene said she told you about her mother's wedding rings."

"Irene's the short one, right? What a funny little lady. She sure does talk, doesn't she? And the other one…she's losing it, huh? Happened to my ma at the last. One minute she's all there, the next she's back swinging on a tire in her head like she's five. Kinda sad."

"You talked to Thelma too?"

"Yep. She showed me all sorts of old stuff. That radio alone could bring in a pretty penny. My brother dabbles in antiques, and he said he seen one like it not long ago that fetched about four hundred dollars."

"They do have an interesting collection. What else did she show you?"

"There was an old bugle, a wedding dress, and a metal box that looked mighty old. My brother said that might be a one-of-a-kind, maybe from Asia judging by the designs I described to him. Have you had it appraised?"

LuAnn's gut clenched. "No."

"I got his card here somewhere." Butch pulled out a bulging wallet and selected a dog-eared card. "Guess I've carried this around for a good long while." He straightened the bent corner before handing it to her. "I asked my brother to look into what the rings were worth. He's got connections. Big chunk of ice, huh? And being that old…"

"Irene showed you the rings?"

"Thelma showed them to me. They were in the metal box. Just sittin' out on a shelf like that wasn't a very safe place, I told her."

LuAnn fingered the shabby business card. The face on the picture looked like a mug shot. "Not a very safe place at all."

After Butch left, leaving a sputtering Winnie in his wake—"We don't need him when we've got Thorn!"—but no bill, LuAnn went out to fill coffee cups. Tess walked past her with four plates of French toast lining one arm and two on the other. LuAnn reached out and touched her shoulder. "Can we have a powwow if things slow down in a bit?"

"You got it."

Coffee carafes in hand, LuAnn made her rounds. Brad had moved his plate to Harry's table, and the two were engaged in an animated discussion. But the file folder was still closed. As she neared, she realized they were arguing the strengths and weaknesses of the Ohio University Bobcats pitchers, past and present. She topped off their coffee, resting her hand on Brad's shoulder as she did, but didn't interrupt. The men lingered until Sean, Erica, and Davinia finished their breakfasts and got up and walked out the front door. Together.

Harry motioned her over. "Got a minute?"

She looked around the café as she cleared their plates. Only three tables still occupied. This was the lull before the lunch rush. "Is this something Tess and Janice can hear?"

"Sure."

"Why don't we move to the office? I'll go get them." She carried the plates into the kitchen and asked her two best friends to join them.

When they gathered in the office, Harry spread out several sheets of paper, photocopies of book pages. He handed Brad a copy of the torn plat map he'd shown LuAnn. "I've always loved old things, but as I'm getting older myself, I'm more interested in the stories they have to tell." He smiled at LuAnn. "I get your wish for a time machine." His eyes widened for a fraction of a second, and Janice coughed, as if her coffee had gone down the wrong way.

Brad swallowed hard, his Adam's apple dipping and rising. LuAnn's gaze swept the circle of clearly uncomfortable people. What was going on?

"'Imposter,'" Brad read. "Interesting. Any idea who wrote that?"

Harry grabbed another paper and held it out for all of them to see. "Here's the other half."

LuAnn leaned close to Brad to read the words scrawled at the top of the map next to the title, "Marietta, 1888."

Prudence,
Don't you think enough time has passed for you to finally set the record straight? Shan't we teach our grandchildren the real history?

Asher Bailey

Janice sighed. "Prudence died in 1888. I wonder if she saw this." LuAnn shared her wistfulness. Prudence's journal writings had made her come alive in their minds, made her seem like someone they'd actually known. Prudence Willard had become an honorary member of the Inn Crowd.

"The name Asher Bailey sounded familiar," Harry said, "so I went digging around in all those files Maybelline is hoarding. Turns out Major Asher John Bailey was a decorated Civil War hero. He married an escaped slave in 1861. I found a note about their wedding in a diary kept by a Quaker minister. There's no record of it, of course, but I gotta wonder if your Prudence was involved in the woman's escape."

Brad tapped on the word *imposter*. "He knew about Stuart Dawson taking Howard Bickerton's identity."

LuAnn nodded. "I wonder when he learned about it and if he ever did anything about it after Prudence was gone." If he had, if Stuart Dawson had been exposed as a fraud, what impact would that have had on Zephaniah or his older brother Matthew, the true heirs to the Bickerton estate? And wouldn't there be some record of that somewhere? And if he had, Irene and Thelma and the two generations before them would not have grown up on the plat of land labeled *Imposter!*

They knew, from an old letter Brad's cousin Charlotte had shown them, that Matthew had come to the States in 1866 looking for Zephaniah and discovered the deception. They didn't know what he had done with the information.

As they all sat digesting what they'd just learned, Harry stuck the papers back in the folder. "I'll leave these with you. I'll keep snooping around, see if I find anything else. And speaking of snooping, two of your guests—the guy has a moustache like Charlie Chan and the woman has the strangest eyes I've ever seen…"

"Sean and Erica," LuAnn supplied.

"They stopped in on Saturday with a ton of questions about the brass box. I had a feeling they were up to something, so I didn't tell them anything." He stared at Brad and then LuAnn, clearly waiting for them to fill in the blanks in his information.

LuAnn got a barely perceptible nod from Brad. "The box has been missing for a few days. It's possible one of the sisters packed it away and can't remember where, but it seems—"

"Like a pretty strange coincidence that I'd go and stick my foot in my mouth by talkin' about it in front of strangers and then it goes missing."

"Irene?" LuAnn called for the third time. She'd gone through the main floor of the Bickerton mansion without finding either of the sisters. Now she stood at the bottom of the steps. No sound came from upstairs. She called again as she walked up, then circled around the stairway, peeking into each room. No sign of them. Had Brad changed his mind and taken them to Countryside Manor earlier than planned?

A thud sounded overhead. What were they doing in the attic? And why had they closed the door?

She opened the attic door, and then, just before stepping onto the creaky stairs, slipped her shoes off, closed the door silently, and tiptoed up. When she got to the top, she crouched, listening to whispered voices. A lot of voices.

"Let's get a shot of you two opening that wardrobe again."

Sean? What was he doing here?

"Did you play up here when you were little, Thelma?" This from Davinia. Had their three main suspects joined forces? For what? What were they after?

"Oh, yes. Scared us silly, but when we found the pirates' shaft, how could we not? Spent most of my childhood looking for the secret compartment where they hid the pearls."

"Did you ever find anything?" Erica asked. "Secret papers or names on walls or anything?"

"Lots of papers. I remember showing one to Father. Don't know what it was, but he snatched it out of my hand like it was on fire and asked if I'd found other papers." Thelma giggled like a five-year-old. "I never, ever told him. I took some and hid them up here. Don't remember where though."

Had Thelma been the one to hide the clue card in the box of china? Did she have a copy of Howard Bickerton's Last Will and Testament, or was it still hiding somewhere up here? And what was the pirates' shaft? It made perfect sense that Howard, who planned on taking an active role in hiding and shuttling runaway slaves on their journey to freedom, would create secret passages in his home like the ones they'd found at the inn.

LuAnn crouched lower, listening.

"Are there secret compartments up here?" Davinia asked. "Did you ever find a plaque with a man's picture on it? Maybe in a strange place where you wouldn't expect someone to hang a picture?"

What was that all about? So Davinia was after something specific. A picture of Howard Bickerton? Or Stuart Dawson?

"Now that you mention it," Thelma said, "there was a picture. It was stuck to the wall in the closet in my father's study. I remember calling it a picture of a bumpy grumpy man."

Davinia gasped.

Thelma laughed. "That does sound funny, doesn't it? I thought it was so strange that he had a picture hanging in the closet..." Thelma's words trailed off. "There is no closet in that room, is there?" Her voice rose barely above a whisper and sounded like a sad little girl.

"Maybe there was at one time," Irene answered, her voice soft. "The back parlor used to be Papa's study. Mama never liked that room. It has shelves on one wall that were filled with books, and my mother said they soaked up the smell of his cigars and made the room reek like an old ham." She chuckled. "Mama had a way with words. After Papa passed, she turned the study into a formal parlor."

"I'll have to take a closer look at that room," Davinia said. "I love bookshelves."

Even empty ones? The sense of repressed excitement in Davinia's voice triggered more questions. LuAnn massaged her temple. Time to intervene. She took one step up and stopped.

"Lu? Irene? Where are you?" Brad's voice echoed from the second floor.

Gripping the railing, she padded down the steps, opened the door, and pressed one finger to her lips as she stepped out of the stairwell and closed the door, not letting the latch click. Taking him by the hand, she led him into the master bedroom.

"You look good in this room," he teased. "The color suits you." He grew serious when she didn't respond. "What's going on? Where are the aunts?"

"In the attic," she whispered, and then began peppering him with questions. "Are there secret passages in this house? Are there ways someone could sneak in when the doors are locked? Do you know anything about a bronze plaque with Howard's face on it? Could Thelma have told—"

"Whoa." He put his hands on her shoulders. "Slow down. The aunts are in the attic? Why? I didn't even think Thelma could still climb those stairs."

"The aunts are in the attic with Sean and Erica and Davinia."

"I thought you said Davinia said Sean and Erica ducked out anytime she was around."

"I did. And I've seen them do it. This morning they sat with their backs to her, but the next thing I knew, the three of them were sitting together looking all conspiratorial like they were comparing notes on everything they've learned about us. And now they're up there taking pictures. And do you know anything about some papers Thelma found when she was a kid that must have been important because her father demanded to see all of them but she wouldn't give them to him and then she hid some in the attic but she can't remember where and now those people are up there snooping around and they just might find Howard's will or the deed and who knows what they might do with—"

Brad's finger landed softly on her moving lips. "Breathe," he whispered. "How about we go up and talk to them. Okay?"

She gave a slow nod, silently thanking him for corralling her runaway thoughts.

This man sure was good for her.

Sean's video camera swiveled toward them as LuAnn and Brad stepped into the attic. "Here comes the happy couple now!" Erica's too-bright voice ricocheted off the rafters. "Here, stand in this shaft of light. I want to get some black-and-whites." She told them how to stand, where to look. "Lower your head, put your right hand here, your left there, now smile..."

Erica Garrett was a gifted distractor. As they posed, Davinia excused the rest of them with, "Come on people, back to work." Taking Thelma's arm, she supported her down the stairs.

"Wonderful. Perfect. These might be the absolute best pictures of all the ones I've taken of you. Even the ones you didn't know I was taking." She winked, then put the lens cap back on her camera. "Guess I'd better make myself useful."

Just before Erica bent to pick up her bag, LuAnn noticed a smudge on her index finger. Burgundy. She squinted for a better look. Burgundy velvet fibers.

Had she found the cloth that held the code card by accident? Out of curiosity? Or had she known what she was looking for?

CHAPTER EIGHTEEN

It was almost two thirty by the time LuAnn finally found a way to talk to Davinia alone. Brad had returned the U-Haul truck and was now loading boxes of the sisters' seasonal clothing and Christmas decorations in the back seat of his car. These would go into storage at Countryside Manor. He'd handed Irene two glasses of lemonade and told her to join Thelma on the front porch swing. "One last time," he'd said with a mysterious wink. LuAnn had tried to decipher the unspoken message but couldn't. Some shared experience she hadn't heard about, likely. When things calmed down she'd remember to ask him about his lemonade wink.

Sean carried a box out to Brad's car. Erica took pictures. Carrying the last bundle of hanging clothes to the back door behind Davinia, who had proven to be an invaluable help, LuAnn said, "This is everything. Mind if I ride over with you?"

"N-not at all."

LuAnn pretended not to notice her hesitation. She asked Sean if he would mind driving her car back to the inn and tossed him the keys, then followed Davinia out to her car. They slid hangers onto the clothes bar. "What a great invention. I had one back in college, but it was much clunkier."

"This one retracts to fit in a suitcase. My husband and I did a lot of flying and a lot of rental cars. Being a somewhat full-figured woman, I like structured pieces. Can't just throw a T-shirt into a duffel like I imagine you can, and I'm not a fan of ironing. I try to buy things that the wrinkles shake out of when I hang them." Davinia crowded the last of her bundle onto the bar, slammed the driver's side back door, and got behind the wheel.

"Wish we could do that to our skin at this age." LuAnn got in the passenger side and shut the door as Davinia laughed.

"Isn't that the truth? But I'll be happy if I can have the kind of inner beauty and spunk Irene Bickerton has when I get to my nineties. She and Thelma sure are contrasts, aren't they?"

"From what Brad says, Thelma has always been a bit more serious, but it sounds like she was quite the fanciful storyteller when she was younger. You probably heard some of her stories today."

"We did. What do you know about a pirate shaft?"

"Nothing." She'd never heard about it until eavesdropping in the stairwell. "I was surprised to see you with Sean and Erica."

Davinia smiled. "Not as surprised as I was. It turns out they stayed at our B&B a while ago." She slowed the car as they approached a stop sign and glanced at LuAnn. "I'm not a person who asks for advice often, but can I ask you something? You've made some huge changes in your life in the past two years, and you're about to make another one. How did you know you were doing the right thing?"

"I prayed."

"And…?" Davinia tapped a finger on the steering wheel.

"And God gave me peace. Not that there weren't fearful moments along the way. Moving to Marietta, putting most of my savings into the inn…sometimes I felt like I was stepping off a cliff. But I knew the Lord would catch me if I fell."

Davinia nodded. "I haven't given religion much thought for years. Maybe now's the time. I need some direction, need to make some changes. Living with my daughter and her family is not working. I'm afraid our relationship will be strained to the breaking point if something doesn't change soon."

"What are your options?"

"Move out. Get my own place. Find a job, and people to do things with." Davinia shrugged. "I don't have close friends like you do. Since my husband passed, I've been kind of lost."

LuAnn said a short, silent, one-word prayer. *Help.* "At the risk of sounding like a broken record, my answer to that is the same. Pray. God has a plan for each of us if we're willing to let Him direct us."

"I admire your faith." Davinia's tone was wistful. "Leo's girlfriend talked like that too."

"I can't wait to meet her."

"She's such a delight. I'd put her and her family up there in our top ten guests. I'm hoping they come back for a visit. With Leo, of course. It's interesting to know he grew up hearing his aunt tell stories. He's quite the storyteller himself."

"Pirate stories, huh?"

"Among other things. The way he described all of you and the inn and this house"—she nodded toward the mansion as they backed out of the drive—"made me want to visit Marietta and see it all firsthand. So much history and beauty."

"Did he tell you the story behind the brass box that Harry pointed out?"

"Yes. I wish my husband was around to hear that. How you found the key, and the salvage guy remembered an entry about a locked box. Fascinating."

LuAnn sucked in a steadying breath. "Did Leo mention the code, or instructions, he found in the attic that might be for that box?"

"A code? No, do tell. But you already opened it, right? Leo said you found papers that proved what Brad told us on the tour about the murder."

"Yes." Now where to go? She was pretty sure Davinia was telling the truth about the code. That still didn't mean she or her daughter hadn't taken the brass box. Or the rings. Or both. She wanted to believe Lesley, but it was still possible. Maybe she'd made up the story about the painter returning just to make them suspect someone else. "We found some instructions and don't know what they're for. Probably something that hasn't been around for decades."

"Interesting. What do you know about the man who had the house built? Did he design it himself?"

Davinia was good at redirecting the course of a conversation. "I don't know." LuAnn wracked her brain for things they'd learned from Prudence's diary or other sources. "He had it built for his family while he was still in England. He had a wife and two sons, but his wife died before they came to America and his eleven-year-old son left home and refused to come with him."

"Mr. Bickerton sailed across the ocean without his son? At that age?" Davinia's eyes bulged.

"I know. It does seem incomprehensible, but the boy was staying with an uncle, and it was a different time. Howard Bickerton moved here only about twenty years after Dickens published *Oliver Twist*. England had passed some child labor laws by then, but that only meant kids couldn't work in mines or factories until they were nine or ten. Even though the Bickertons were an affluent family, I'm sure Howard viewed his eleven-year-old son very differently than we would today." LuAnn shook her head. "Sorry, the history teacher in me gets a little chatty."

"Don't apologize. Your knowledge is fascinating. I wish my husband could have met you."

Davinia chatted about houses she had visited with her husband. Homes designed by Frank Lloyd Wright, Oscar Niemeyer, Frank Gehry, and others. As they neared Countryside Manor she stopped talking, appearing very contemplative. "My husband used to say old houses absorb the dispositions of the people who have lived in them, creating their own unique personalities."

"I like that."

"The Bickerton house sure has personality. Must be so hard for the people who grew up there to think about leaving."

"For Thelma especially, and I'm surprised how hard it seems for Leo. Irene is handling it well. This was actually her idea. Brad and his brother wanted to hire in-home help, but she said it was time someone else filled the house with memories." LuAnn had questioned her on this decision so many times as they'd talked about room colors and ways to update the house without losing its historic integrity. Every time she'd said, "Are you sure you don't want to stay here?" Irene had answered with her usual quick wit—"Sure as God made little green apples."

"It will be important to the Bickerton sisters that the house ends up in good hands. I've been thinking it would make a lovely retreat center."

Davinia's face brightened. "That's a wonderful idea."

LuAnn sat in silence for a moment. While she'd love to see the church catch her vision for the mansion, now that she'd had a little time to process, she realized that was a long shot. She was warming to Davinia and her love of Victorian houses. Maybe Davinia was exactly who she said she was, a woman who'd lost her husband and was looking for a new purpose, new meaning in life. It wouldn't be breaking her promise to Brad to talk about her vision, would it? She took a deep breath and smiled at Davinia.

"As you well know, a B&B needs to be open most of the time to accommodate referrals and keep regular patrons happy, but a retreat center is different. You could probably make enough hosting a couple of events a month, leaving lots of free time in between. And properties listed in the National

Register of Historic Places or the National Register of Historic Districts are eligible for a twenty percent tax credit. If you qualify, the state may offer tax credits as high as thirty percent for privately owned historic properties."

Davinia laughed. Not the desired response. "You are going to be the perfect wife for a Realtor. Do you plan on working with him?"

"I haven't thought about it." Had Brad? But that wasn't what they were talking about right now. Had nothing she'd said in her high-speed elevator pitch impacted Davinia? "You're interested in the mansion, aren't you?"

"Definitely. Old houses and their stories have been such a part of my life since—Oh! Am I interested in buying it? No. I'm sorry if I gave that impression." She grimaced. "I can see why you'd think that. It's kind of weird that a stranger would just want to hang around like I have been, and my daughter says I ask way too many questions. The house fascinates me, and I won't say I wouldn't love to have a place like that, but I couldn't afford it, and I'm too old for the work it would take to run it."

Then why are you just hanging around like you have been?

"Isn't this just as cozy as can be?" Irene's voice registered higher than usual as they walked into Thelma's bedroom at Countryside Manor. Her upbeat chatter had started the moment they stepped onto a porch lined with wooden platform rockers.

"Can't you just see us enjoying the morning sun out here, Thelma?" Her optimism had seemed genuine until now.

The room was beautiful, decorated just as LuAnn had fixed up Thelma's room at the mansion. Thelma walked in, ran her hand along the quilt that covered the bed, and walked to her chair in the corner, next to a table with her favorite books and reading glasses. She sat in the chair, her face expressionless. Brad, Grant, Wendy, Saffron, Irene, and LuAnn stood by the door, collectively holding their breath. Thelma rocked, paused, rocked again. Was she actually present in the moment, or had she drifted back to "swinging on a tire in her head like she's five," as Butch had so aptly described? They waited, at least a full minute, and then a smile. "Feels like home," Thelma said. And they all exhaled.

Irene's room was next. She was silent as they entered. The room was arranged just the way she'd wanted. Bed, dresser, reading chair, TV. Was she just now realizing how small her world had become? LuAnn's eyes smarted as she thought of the sacrifice this woman had made for her sister. She could have chosen to send Thelma here alone, or could have opted for an apartment with more room but farther away from her sister.

"Very nice." Irene's voice was flat. She adjusted a picture on the wall that didn't need adjusting, probably giving herself time to put on a good front. She turned to face her entourage. "I think I'll be very happy—" Her face suddenly lit with what LuAnn could only describe as pure joy. No longer looking at them, her gaze focused over Brad's shoulder. Was she experiencing a tire swing moment like Thelma?

Brad turned around, giving them full view of the doorway…and the man who stood there, holding a bouquet of flowers. Leo.

Irene pushed through the crowd and wrapped her arms around her son. "I was hoping you'd come."

"Couldn't let you move in without us, Mom."

Who was this man, and what had he done with Irene's self-absorbed son? Wait…

"Us?" Irene and Brad asked at the same time.

Leo stepped back, held out his hand, and an arm reached out to him. With a grin unlike LuAnn had ever seen, Leo pulled a young woman into his arms. "Mom, this is Giana. Giana, this is my mom and my sort of cousins Brad and Grant, and Grant's daughters, Wendy and Saffron, and Brad's soon-to-be-wife, LuAnn."

Giana was as adorable as Leo had described her. Her smile lit the room. "Hi, everyone." Bending, she encircled Irene in her arms. "I feel like I already know you from all of our talks." She turned to LuAnn. "We just had to come early for so many reasons. I couldn't imagine my mom moving without me being there, and Brad and Grant are the closest thing to brothers Leo has, so I wanted time to get to know you, because we're kind of going to be sisters, right?"

"R-right." LuAnn returned Giana's embrace.

"I called your inn before we left and talked to Tess, and she said my room is open, so here we are! I absolutely love old buildings. I can't wait to see your inn and Leo's house."

Leo's house. Not that it wasn't still his home, for the moment. She'd just never heard anyone refer to the mansion that way. She smiled at Giana. Vivacious, bubbly, and seemingly completely genuine. Once again, LuAnn prayed she was wrong, that Giana had no ulterior motives, and there was a simple explanation for "I know the clock is ticking...my Mom won't be a problem..."

June 8, 1861

After a fitful night under the willows far from where Asher had been attacked, they started on the final few miles to Millwood. Every rock that spit out from beneath the wheels of the wagon caused Zephaniah to jump.

Prudence had never asked the boy how he'd learned about his father's death. When he had first come to the inn, she was the only one he would talk to, and then only in one or two words in answer to questions. Slowly, patiently, she had drawn him out, made him feel safe. She had thought prodding him for details, asking him to relive the moment, might only deepen the pain of his grief. He talked, on occasion, about his father "disappearing," but now she wondered... had he seen Stuart Dawson shoot his father? The horror of that possibility made her recoil.

"Zeph, thee does not need to do this. The pearls belonged to thy mother and—"

"No." He shook his head. "Mama would want me to do it. I can't remember what she looked like, but I remember one thing. When she tucked me in at night, she said, 'Always do what is right.'" He looked up at her. "It was wrong that I ran away, wasn't it?"

Prudence sent up a quick plea for wisdom. The answer to that question required a Solomon. "Have they hurt thee?"

"No. They pretend I am not there. They don't talk to me. Except for Rom. We are friends now, I think."

"May I ask why thee left? Did something happen?"

He took a long shuddering breath. "They asked Cook to leave. She burned the potatoes, and Mister said she was too old to see or hear. Cook is the one who takes care of me. I eat with her, and she sometimes sneaks upstairs and reads to me when I go to bed. When they said she had to leave, I snuck out of my bedchamber the secret way and I came to your house and I heard you and Mr. Jason talking about leaving early in the morning so I waited and hid in the wagon."

They fell silent as they pulled into Millwood. Asher stopped the wagon in front of the tavern. They had talked about this, choosing not to hide but to act as normal as possible. A family traveling, stopping for breakfast. Prudence reminded Zephaniah what to call them and not to react if she introduced him as Matthew.

The tavern was dark inside and smelled of old grease and alcohol. Two men slouched over pints at a rough-hewn table in the corner. A portly man wearing a filthy apron was the only other person. Asher walked up to him and asked for Joe. The man nodded toward a back door.

"Wait here," Asher said.

"Take 'em with you. I'm not gonna play nanny."

Prudence gripped Zephaniah's hand and followed Asher. *Father, protect us.*

A man sat on an overturned crate in the back room. Daylight showed through cracks where chinking had fallen out. Another man leaned against the bars of what appeared to be a jail cell. Prudence stifled a gasp as she spotted Deborah curled in a corner of the cell, knees to chest.

The seated man held out one meaty, scarred hand. "Le' me count it."

Asher's shoulder rose and fell. "Money's gone. Somebody stole it."

The other man laughed, coarse and threatening. "Then what're you doin' here?"

"I have something else."

A click reverberated off the ceiling as the standing man pulled back the hammer on his pistol. "Don't know who to shoot first. You or her." He swung around and pointed the barrel at Deborah's face.

"Take these." Asher held out the string of pearls. They reflected the light of a single kerosene lamp on a cluttered table.

The seated man spat on the packed dirt floor. "Not a chance." His hand slid over a silver pistol sitting next to the lamp. "Probably paste."

"Let me look at them." The standing man released the safety and stepped forward, holding out his hand. "Hmm. Used to work for a swindler who sold fakes. Had a whole roomful of women making little glass bubbles and filling them with dissolved fish scales. True tale." He held the string in both filthy-nailed hands and bit down on a pearl with his yellowed teeth. "Ouch." He rubbed his jaw. "I will take these, and you can take that off our hands." He nodded behind him where Deborah had managed to stand, clinging to the bars. "I find out this ain't real..." His reddened eyes sought out Zephaniah. "I'll come find you. Make no mistake. I'll come find all of you."

CHAPTER NINETEEN

B est crab cakes I've had in my life." Giana dabbed her mouth with a cloth napkin. They sat at an outdoor table at Boat House Barbeque, Brad and LuAnn on one side, Leo and Giana across from them, and Grant and Saffron on the ends. "One big happy family" was the phrase that ran through LuAnn's head. This was nice. If only she could turn off the recording of the video call that looped through her brain.

Giana had been asking everyone get-to-know-you questions since their entrees arrived. It seemed impossible that this caring, outgoing woman had an agenda that might hurt Irene. Was this all an act? She did, after all, come from a theatrical family. Had she simply put on the sweet Giana persona the way she might don a costume for a performance? Was she after money? The mansion? The pearls? Was Leo in on it, or was she using him?

"How did you two meet?" LuAnn directed the question at Giana, who giggled.

But it was Leo who answered. "That was the night that changed my life."

"We met in the ER," Giana added. "After one of the worst hailstorms we've ever had in our area, the power had been out for nine hours. I haven't worked the ER for years, but I got called in to cover because there were power lines down, and people couldn't get to work. And there was this cute guy in bed five, out cold." She grinned at Leo.

"I was at the casino when the lights went out. I learned later that it took less than a minute for generators to kick in, but in those few seconds I got clocked by a guy who stole my chips. I woke up, and there was this angel praying over me. I was sure I'd died and couldn't believe I was waking up in heaven. I couldn't open my eyes, but she was praying for my eternal soul, and right there and then I knew I had one more chance to do things right. So I prayed along with her."

Giana looked at Brad and Grant and then LuAnn, her eyes dancing. "He woke up and said, 'I'm sorry for everything I've done, and whoever you are, please say you'll go out with me.'"

LuAnn felt confusion build in her head like a thick fog. So much for her theory that Giana had found out who Leo was, assumed he was the heir to a fortune, and somehow manipulated him into falling in love with her. *Lord, forgive me once again for jumping to wrong conclusions.* "What an amazing story."

Giana nodded. "And it just keeps getting better and better. Now it's your turn. Leo told me how you met, but I want to hear your first impressions. Love at first sight?"

Brad nodded. LuAnn laughed.

Grant added his own laughter. "Brad was lovestruck. Never would admit it, but I could always tell when he'd been around LuAnn. His brains were a little scrambled the next day. We probably lost a few sales because his head was somewhere in the stratosphere."

"This is going to be interesting." Giana pointed at Brad. "You first."

"I'll admit it now. I was... I don't know what the word is. Bedazzled, flummoxed? I don't actually believe in love at first sight, but I was sure of something all right. A little bit gut-punched because I never expected to feel anything for anyone after my wife passed. But here was this beautiful woman with a passion for literature and history... Yep, bedazzled." He put his arm around LuAnn. "But I had the distinct feeling she was gun-shy, so I knew I had to be cautious. We took our time getting to know each other."

"Friendship is a perfect foundation for marriage," Saffron said with a wisdom beyond her years.

Giana turned her finger on LuAnn. "Were you really gun-shy?"

LuAnn nodded. "Yep. I'd been hurt before, and this silver-haired, silver-tongued poet seemed just a little too good to be true. I figured he was just trying to make a sale." She smiled at him. "Not that I was totally immune to those blue eyes."

"I overheard her best friends teasing her about me, so I knew it was just a matter of time. If they were on my side, I figured she had to give in and see my charms before long."

Their server came with a dessert menu. The interruption gave LuAnn time to strategize how she was going to find out more about Giana. "Leo and Davinia have both painted glowing pictures of your family," she said. "They sound like a lot of fun."

"They are. We used to have our own traveling theater group. We performed in churches and schools from New York to Chicago. My sister and I are Irish twins, thirteen months apart. Up until college, when Gwen decided to get her nose fixed, people outside of our family had trouble telling us apart. That was perfect for theater. We put on *Parent Trap* and the *Princess and the Pauper*."

"Like Mary Kate and Ashley," Saffron said. "What fun."

"Yep. We were the Olsen twins of the Fontaine Theater Company. We took advantage of looking alike at other times too. Gwen had a lot of stomach issues when we were younger. It took the doctors a long time to figure it out. She was terrified of doctors and needles, but I was the kid who loved to watch those little test tubes fill and—" She stopped when Leo groaned. "Sorry, I forget where I am sometimes. Not everyone grew up thinking phlebotomists are superheroes." She winked at Leo. "Anyway, I was destined to be a nurse, I guess. Where was I? Oh yeah, a couple of times when Gwen was supposed to walk over to the clinic after school, I went instead. We were probably in fourth and fifth grade then. Too young to realize the consequences of the lab testing my blood instead of hers."

"Is your sister okay now?" Wendy asked.

Giana nodded. "Once they figured out she was lacking some essential enzymes, she was fine. Thanks for asking."

LuAnn was warming to Giana by the minute. But she couldn't let her objectivity get clouded by feelings. "And you have a brother?"

"Thomas. He's a little more serious than Gwen and me. He majored in Shakespearean drama in college. We're constantly working on him to loosen up." Gwen rested her fork on her plate with a satisfied sigh. "I want to hear all about the wedding. LuAnn, I'll ask you about your gown when Brad's not around, but what can you tell me? What are your colors?"

"Dusty rose and kind of a muted green, like eucalyptus leaves."

"Sounds pretty. How many attendants?"

"Two each. Tess and Janice and Grant and Leo."

The questions continued on the way to their cars. As they started to say their goodbyes, Giana asked for a tour of the mansion. "Leo gave me a video tour, but I bet it's beautiful all lit up at night."

Grant, Wendy, and Saffron begged out of the tour since Saffron had to be at work early. LuAnn looked at Brad, who answered with a smile that seemed to say "Why not?" She wondered what it would feel like for Leo, and even Brad, to walk into an empty house with no one there to greet them.

Brad had set a timer on three lights, two downstairs and one up, all in rooms that faced the road. They were set to go off at ten, but just before they turned into the drive, a bright flash ricocheted off the oak tree in front of Leo's window. Seconds later, as they drove in the drive, the light in Leo's room went out. It was eight minutes after nine.

"Guess I need to tweak that one," Brad said.

They parked then walked in through the kitchen. Brad opened the door and let LuAnn walk in first. They'd left a light on over the stove, and the soft glow seemed to welcome them. "This is my second favorite room," she said as Giana stepped in, and Leo turned on the light above the table.

"I can see why." Her eyes were wide as her gaze traveled around the room. "What's your first favorite?"

"The master upstairs. It's huge, and there's a view of the yard leading to the riverbank."

Giana ran her fingertips along the countertop. "And you and Brad don't want to live here?"

LuAnn cast a glance at Brad, who was deep in a conversation with Leo about changing out the light switch covers. "Brad's never been a big fan of the house. Besides, there are way too many rooms for two people."

"But think what you could do with it. It has so much potential. The library alone…" She turned quickly back toward the stove. "When Leo gave me a video tour, I just fell in love with it."

LuAnn almost laughed when she said "potential"—one of the words that had captured her heart when they'd first looked at the inn. "I'll have to tell you my dreams for this place when we have time. I'm working on finding a buyer that will catch the vision."

The look of shock on Giana's face was exactly what she'd been looking for—clear indication that Giana had other plans for the estate.

Brad took LuAnn's arm, startling her as she was trying to decide what to say next. They walked together into the dining room, then stepped aside for Leo to conduct the tour. They stood back and watched Giana as she entered the library, her face alight with awe.

"Something's not right," LuAnn whispered. "Has Leo said anything about you selling the house out from under them?"

"Not a word. Leo's not the type to settle down in one place."

"But if he's getting married... Maybe Giana wants it." Sensing Brad's frustration with the direction of the conversation, she batted her eyes at him. "A man will do anything for the woman he loves."

Brad grinned. "Yes, he will. But Leo hasn't had a single objection that I've heard."

"Well...good." She didn't want to end the day on a low note, filled with her probably fanciful suspicions.

"I heard what you said to Giana about finding a buyer." His voice was tight, slightly strained. "Davinia?"

"Davinia isn't interested."

He stepped in front of her. She looked up into blue eyes filled with distrust. "Did you talk to Ben?"

"No! I told you I wouldn't. I won't talk to Ben until after we get back. I was just baiting Giana. I wanted to see her reaction. She was shocked, which makes me think she and Leo have a plan for getting the house. I overheard them talking last week about needing to find some papers and the clock ticking and how whatever they were doing might hurt Irene. I can't just sit back and not do whatever—"

"We have a buyer."

"What? Who? When did that happen?"

"Irene wants to keep it quiet until we know if the other party can make it work. I promised her I wouldn't share any details with anyone."

"Oh. Well. That's good news." She tried to brush aside an irrational feeling of being left out. "Is it a family with children or someone interested in—"

He bent and kissed her. "No details."

Leo and Giana walked out of the library and into the front parlor hand in hand. "Leo says you picked out all the colors. I love your taste, LuAnn. I wish I had that gift."

"Don't believe her," Leo said. "She painted the pediatric chemo room at her hospital. It's amazing."

Giana blushed. "That's different. I painted a safari mural. That's not the same as interior design."

"Let's look at the back parlor and then head upstairs," Brad said.

Giana commented on everything from the chandelier in the foyer to the stained-glass squares above the front door.

"Wait." LuAnn grabbed Brad's sleeve and held her arm out in front of Giana. To her knowledge, she'd been the last one to leave the house when they'd left with the aunts. She'd leaned against the square newel post while Irene and Thelma said their goodbyes, one room at a time. They'd gone into the back parlor and stayed there for at least fifteen minutes, reminiscing about where their father's desk had once been and how their mother had turned it into a formal sitting room when he was gone. When they'd walked out, LuAnn had gone in and shut off the old bronze floor lamp in the corner by the fireplace.

The door was closed, and light shone beneath it. "You didn't set a timer in there, did you?" she whispered.

Brad shook his head.

"Were Grant and Saffron planning on coming back here after dinner?"

"Not that I know of. Why?"

"All of the doors were op—"

A loud groan, like the sound of resistant metal hinges, came from behind the door. A heavy slam followed.

CHAPTER TWENTY

"Irene hired a cleaning lady. It's probably her," Brad whispered.

"At this time of night?" Leo answered, his hushed voice bouncing off the tiled floor in the foyer.

Brad gripped the door handle. "Stand back." He pushed LuAnn gently but firmly behind him.

"Maybe we should call the police," she said. "If there's a burglar—"

"There's nothing in there to steal."

"*They* don't know that." She reached for her purse, but she'd left it in the car. The top of Brad's phone stuck out of his back pocket. At the slightest hint of danger to him, she could lunge and grab it.

"Who's there?" Brad called, turning the knob an inch to the right.

Silence. He eased the door open. The floor lamp glowed. The rest of the room was exactly as LuAnn had left it, empty except for a tapestry-covered mission-style chair and ottoman. "What made that sound?" she asked, looking first at Brad and then at Leo.

"No clue," Brad said.

Leo began running his hand along the left edge of the bookshelf. "What if Thelma's stories were true?"

Giana clung to his elbow. "The pirate stories?"

Leo knocked on the back of the shelf. "This side of the room would be right below the cupboards in my room, right?"

Brad nodded. "Yes." His voice sounded distant, as if floating on a long-ago memory. "The boy who got in a fight with his brother snuck out of the house in the middle of the night through a secret passageway, the same one the pirates used to sneak in to hide their treasure."

Goose bumps rippled along LuAnn's arms. "It makes sense that Howard would have put in secret rooms or passages since he planned on helping with the Underground Railroad, but wouldn't one of you have found something when you were playing in the cupboards?"

"What's on the other side of this wall?" Giana asked.

Brad scratched his head. "The porch."

"A storage cabinet." Leo's answer overlapped Brad's.

Brad looked at him like he'd lost a few screws. "This is just to the left of the chimney."

"Behind that old metal trellis is a storage cabinet. I found the handle when I was about eight. My grandma caught me before I got it open and told me that's where they kept the weed killer, and it was highly poisonous. Now I wonder. And why would you have a trellis on a porch anyway?"

"I never questioned that. I suppose you could put a potted plant underneath it. But you're right," Brad agreed, "it is kind of weird. Let's go out and take a look."

"Wait." LuAnn pointed along the edge of the bookshelf where it met the outside wall. "Have you ever seen shelves like this?" The bottom board was a little over a foot wide. Each successive shelf was about two inches shorter than the one below it. The top board, a foot from the box beam ceiling, would only have been wide enough for knickknacks.

Brad gave a slow nod. "Like stairs."

"There were always big books on the bottom and smaller ones up higher," Leo said, tapping a shelf.

LuAnn's gaze latched on the square of ceiling plaster framed by dark oak beams. "If these are stairs, could that be a trap door like the ones in the ladder at the inn?"

Resting one foot on the bottom shelf, Brad reached up and tested the others. "Seems sturdy enough."

"One way to find out." Leo hoisted himself up, one step at a time until his head was just below the ceiling. Leaning against the shelves, he pressed against the panel with both hands.

The white square slid away.

Brad stepped close to the bottom of the shelf, shining his phone's flashlight into the dark abyss above the trapdoor. "What can you see?"

As he scrambled up, Leo's laugh sounded like that of a little boy. "I'm in one of the cupboards in my room. Man, I could have used this escape route in high school."

Brad stepped back to let Giana follow Leo. "This is so cool!" she called down when her feet disappeared above the ceiling.

LuAnn stared into the dark abyss above them. Had Howard Bickerton designed it to hide runaway slaves, or as a way to protect his children in the event someone found out he was involved in helping people to freedom? Did the imposter know about it? She could imagine him sitting here, smoking a pipe with his feet propped on a desk built for another man, a man of integrity. Did he jump at every sound, afraid someone had figured out his entire life was a lie?

"Where are you, Lu?" Brad waved a hand in front of her face.

She blinked. "I was in 1857." She turned in a slow circle. "The inn tunnel makes sense. Prudence brought people across the river and through the tunnel to the little room in the basement." Brad knew all of this, of course, but detailing it out loud helped her think it through. "All this trapdoor does is let someone go from this room to the one above it and vice versa. That doesn't seem useful for the same purpose."

"Unless..." Brad rapped his knuckles on the back of the bookcase.

Picking up on his thoughts, LuAnn stared at the wide vertical board that divided the two sides of the bookcase and then at the shape of the shelves. "Why would the shelves be rounded on the ends?"

"Decoration?"

"Or utilitarian." She examined the ends of each board. On the third from the bottom, she let out a squeal. A raised wood rectangle jiggled under her fingers. It was her turn to tell Brad to stand back. She pressed the wood bar.

The left edge of the bookcase sprang open. She grabbed it and swung it toward her. The same sound they'd heard minutes earlier—a groaning metal hinge—echoed through the nearly empty space as the shelf pivoted, stopping when it stood perpendicular to the wall. On the back side was the wrought-iron trellis. As Leo had described, one scroll of black iron was actually a well-disguised door handle.

"Whoa." Brad stepped out onto the porch. "This is crazy. How is it possible I never knew about this?"

"Maybe the aunts don't know about it. Maybe Thelma's stories are a mishmash of truth and legend. I'm guessing there were no pirates and no little boy who was saved by a princess, but the secret passage is— Look." Recessed in the eight-inch-thick wall that framed the opening was a brass plaque bolted to the wall. She touched the raised bronze face of a "bumpy grumpy man," and read the inscription.

Designed by

Alfred Weathersby, Architect

London, England 1856

"This is what Davinia was looking for." But why? LuAnn took Brad's hand and joined him on the porch. As she did, something fluttered near her feet. A tiny piece of something white stuck to the edge of the door. She pulled it off the wood and looked at three blue letters—*L-a-c*—knowing instantly what it was.

"Got a clue, Sherlock?"

"Actually, yes." She handed it to him.

He examined the small corner of a silver-lined pouch. "What is it?"

"Remember the pill I found in the attic? They come in separate little packets like this."

LuAnn collapsed into a chair in the fourth-floor gathering room. Tess brought her a cup of tea. "You, sister, look exhausted. You are taking the next two days off. No arguments."

Janice joined them, plopping down on the love seat. "You have tomorrow to finish packing and doing any last-minute stuff, and then we are all taking Friday off."

"What?"

Her two friends smiled like Cheshire cats. Tess handed her a pamphlet. "Spa day."

"The Inn Crowd is scheduled for seaweed wraps, mud facials, Himalayan sea salt scrubs, and manis and pedis at nine on Friday morning," Janice added.

"Who's going to be here? And I already have an appointment for a manicure and—"

"No, you don't." Tess grinned even wider, if that were possible. "Trust us. We've taken care of everything. Brin and Taylor and Robin have the café covered. All you have to do is show up."

Janice shook her head. "You don't even have to do that. We'll come get you and escort you out of the building, and you won't have to make another decision until rehearsal."

"You guys are—"

"Wonderful?" Tess supplied, while Janice said "Amazing."

"Yes. All of the above. What did I ever do to deserve such wonderfully amazing, albeit sneaky, friends?"

"Sneaky? Us?" Tess laughed.

"You put up with us all these years, that's what you did." Janice tucked her feet beneath her. "How did the aunts handle the move?"

"I'll tell you about that in a minute." LuAnn sat up, her tiredness pushed aside by the anticipation of her best friends' reactions. "We found a secret door at the mansion."

Tess and Janice didn't disappoint. Tess said, "Seriously?" over Janice's loud, "What?" LuAnn showed the video Brad had taken of her reenacting the door opening. "This old trellis completely camouflages the door from the porch. If you pull on that curly cue, it opens from the outside."

"How did you find it?" Tess asked.

"That's the creepy part. Someone was in the parlor. We heard them leave."

"Who?" Janice posed the obvious question.

LuAnn shook her head. "I have ideas, of course. I'm guessing Davinia, or Sean and/or Erica."

Tess and Janice exchanged looks. "What time was that?" Tess asked.

"We got there at nine."

Janice shrugged. "The three of them came back here around nine thirty. Davinia was humming to herself and asking if we had fresh decaf, but Sean and Erica acted really spooked. Sean said they'd gotten a call about a new job and had to leave immediately."

"A wedding photography emergency?" LuAnn wasn't buying it.

"They were packed and out the door in ten minutes, if that," Tess added. "They literally ran down the stairs. Spooked is the right word."

LuAnn pinched the bridge of her nose. She pointed to her phone with her other hand. "Look in my pictures. I overheard Davinia asking Thelma if she'd ever found a plaque hanging in a strange place. I think that bronze plaque is what Davinia has been searching for. No idea why. I suppose the house is worth a lot more, to some people anyway, now that we know who designed it. She says she's not interested in buying it, but my guess is she's planning to give us a low-ball offer when she knows it's worth way more. Maybe she's just going to turn around and resell it."

"That's rather cynical, Lu." Janice's chastisements were always done in a soft, sweet voice.

"We don't have any proof yet that Davinia was the one you heard."

Tess's comment reminded LuAnn of the "clue" in her back pocket. "Have you noticed any of our suspects avoiding dairy or taking pills before they start to eat?"

Janice shook her head. "Winnie mentioned that Davinia uses vegetable oil instead of butter in her biscuits. That doesn't mean anything, I guess."

"Why did you want to know?" Tess asked.

She pulled the evidence out and handed it to them. "I found a little white tablet in the attic that would have come in one of these, and this was stuck between the wall and the secret door."

"So our thief, or one of our snoopers anyway, is lactose intolerant," Janice said.

"I don't know if that's going to prove anything though." Tess chewed on her bottom lip. "The three of them came back to the inn together. If they were the ones who escaped through the secret door, this only proves that one of them was there."

"True." LuAnn rubbed the back of her neck. "We already know they're snoopers." She flopped against the back of the chair.

"We need to give the clues and suspects part of our brains a rest," Janice said. "Tell us about the big move. Was it emotional?"

"A little. They both got a little teary saying goodbye to the house. So did I, for that matter. Thelma seems to like her new surroundings much better than we could have hoped. Irene wasn't so sure, but then Leo showed up with Giana."

"Isn't she just the sweetest thing?" Janice smiled. "I can see why Leo's changing. She's like this ray of sunshine."

"Yeah. Maybe." LuAnn still couldn't put her misgivings into words.

"You don't sound so sure. What happened?"

"Nothing today. She was absolutely charming. We went out to dinner, and she was gracious and funny and interesting. But I overheard something a few days ago." She told them about Leo promising Giana he would look for "both documents."

"Maybe the papers Leo was looking for are things he needs to get a marriage license," Tess suggested.

Janice shook her head. "All you need in Ohio is a photo ID and proof of your social security number."

"What do you think they could be up to? Trying to get the house?" Tess asked.

"That's the most likely, isn't it?"

Tess stood and stretched. "As long as we can't seem to get away from clues and suspects, I have to show you something." With that, she got up and left the room. In moments she was back. She laid her copy of Prudence's journal on the coffee table. "We need to hire someone to type this up. With a digital copy we could search for words or dates."

"So true," Janice said. "What were you searching for this time?"

"Asher Bailey."

LuAnn had read Prudence's words about planning the wedding so many times, she was sure there were no surprises about Asher in these pages.

Tess opened the journal to a page marked with a hot-pink sticky note. "When Harry said his name was Asher John, it got me wondering. Prudence refers to his full name when talking about the wedding, but I think he's also AJ."

"Prudence and her use of initials." Janice scooted forward to lean in closer to the journal. "'Z' and 'C' and all the others. I don't remember an AJ."

"A couple of entries before the wedding. June 6, 1861." She turned the journal so it faced Janice and LuAnn. "She may have disguised his name before their mission."

They read in silence.

I stand on the riverbank and gaze at land that has now become foreign soil. Our country is rent in two, and hatred gathers like thunderheads. Yet, in the midst of fear and turmoil, love and hope still flourish...like a daisy pushing through parched, cracked earth. It is with hope, and because of love, that AJ and I will set out before the sunrise declares a new day. Father, guide our quest, protect the one we search for.

"So you think Prudence and Asher helped free the slave he married?" Janice asked.

"Maybe. But that's not the really interesting part. She has an entry between this one and the wedding." She flipped the page and began to read. "'Arrived home with Deborah last night. Never in my wildest dreams could I have imagined the homecoming that awaited us—'"

A loud knock at the door froze them all.

"Lu? Tess? Anybody up?"

"Brad?" Janice's forehead wrinkled.

LuAnn jumped up and opened the door, her heart slamming against her ribcage.

Brad stood in the fourth-floor hallway with a remorseful-looking Davinia beside him, staring at the floor and holding out her cell phone.

CHAPTER TWENTY-ONE

Caught her coming out of the hidden door." A vein on Brad's temple pulsed in time to the words he shoved through gritted teeth. "I went back to find a way to lock it from the inside, and there she was. Should have called the police, but—"

"I can explain. I'm sorry. I never should have... Just give me a chance to explain. Please."

LuAnn opened the door all the way and stood back as they walked in. Tess told them to sit at the kitchen table, then went to get a folding chair from her room. LuAnn read Tess's thoughts. *Don't get too comfy, lady.*

Unfortunately, Janice's offer to make "a nice pot of jasmine tea" pretty much ruined the interrogation atmosphere.

They sat. And waited. The intense hue of Davinia's flushed face lightened some as she took two slow breaths, exhaling through pursed lips. "I was looking for a picture. A plaque. I knew it would be hidden. That's why I was...in the cupboard. I called. Last week I called and asked one of the sisters if I could come and search for something I thought might be hidden in their house. She told me there were no more secrets. She said she almost went to the grave with them and then someone found the key, and now she had to move."

Brad cringed. They all knew which sister she'd talked to.

So Davinia had asked permission to look at the house, and when she didn't get it, she just broke in? LuAnn was pretty sure a vein was popping out on her forehead to match Brad's. "What made you think there was a hidden picture? Did Leo tell you it was there?"

"No. He showed us pictures of the house. When I saw the weather vane and the faces on the fireplace, I knew it had to be an Alfred Weathersby house. The faces are his children. It's one of his trademarks, along with secret compartments and hidden doors." She tapped her phone. "My daughter doesn't know about this, so I couldn't talk about it when she was here and then…I don't know, the hunt just kind of took on a life of its own. And then I recognized Sean, and we had something in common because they were looking for something too, and Erica offered to take pictures for my feature and—"

"What were they looking for?" Brad asked.

"I don't know. They just kept saying they had an amazing plan for the house, and everyone would love it."

"Feature?" LuAnn prodded.

Davinia set her phone on the table. "I've been freelancing for *Victorian Living* magazine for many years. A good friend of mine is the assistant editor. She said if I could get an exclusive, something sensational, and write my own spread, her boss would consider hiring me full-time. That way I could support myself enough to move out and let my daughter and son-in-law have the Paw Paw Patch. Like I said,

I need to move on. As you can imagine, I can be a bit difficult to live with."

I can imagine. LuAnn offered up a quick prayer of confession and a request for an understanding heart.

Davinia pointed to the magazine cover pictured on her phone. "My husband was a huge Alfred Weathersby fan. We lived in London for a year, and I thought we'd seen all of the Weathersby homes. I wrote an article about him for *VL* several years ago. When I found out there was a Weathersby house here in the states, well, you can imagine how I felt. I know I should have asked your permission to look, but I was afraid you'd all turn me away like the Bickerton sister—I guess that was Thelma—did and, well, this felt like completing my husband's legacy. Like a way to honor him. Does that make sense?"

It did make sense. It hadn't been the right thing to do, but it did make sense. LuAnn felt her indignation dissipating. Most of it, anyway. But there was one thing she had to find out before she could get beyond what Davinia had done. "Do you or your daughter have the brass box?"

"The brass...no! I would never... Lesley said you called her and asked her about that." Her gaze dropped to the table. "I can see why you'd think I might take something, but, no. And my daughter would never, ever..."

LuAnn nodded. "I had to ask." Not that she'd expect a thief to immediately confess, but Davinia's shock at being accused seemed genuine. LuAnn looked to Brad for a clue as to what to do next.

"You want to write a story about the house?" he asked. The question seemed hard to voice. *Giving grace rarely comes easy,* LuAnn thought.

"Yes." Davinia appeared to be holding her breath.

Brad sighed and rubbed his eyes. "I should say no, considering the way you went about this, but I can't see how it would hurt. As long as Lu and I and my brother get a chance to read it before it goes to—"

"Thank you!" Davinia jumped out of her chair and wrapped her arms around Brad's shoulders. "Thank you. Thank you. I know I don't deserve this. It was a horrible, dishonest thing to do and I just… I'm so sorry. I've never done anything like this before, and I promise I will do the estate justice. I think we could time it so it would help you sell it. It's an online magazine, so it's easier to add things than it would be for print. I will make it shine in all its Weathersby glory." She straightened, picked up her phone, and walked to the door. Before walking out, she flashed a triumphant smile. "Not only will you sell it, but I can just about guarantee there will be a bidding war, and you'll make enough money to keep those sisters living in luxury for the rest of their days." With that, she left.

As LuAnn watched her go, she suddenly started laughing. "I didn't see that one coming."

She turned back to Brad. "Too bad you already have a buyer."

"You do?" Janice was wide-eyed, her gaze lasering Brad.

"Don't ask," LuAnn said. "Client-Realtor privacy."

Janice gave a slow nod. "Congratulations. I can't wait to see what the new owner does with it."

"Me too," Brad said. "Me too."

One more day. LuAnn stared out at the river as she smoothed the covers on her bed. Huck attacked a throw rug like a wolf pouncing on its prey, then shook it and growled with playful fierceness. Tom stretched and yawned on the bed he hadn't left even while LuAnn tugged and rearranged the quilt.

Tears stung her eyes as she opened the closet, now half-filled with the boxes she'd spent most of yesterday packing, and picked out a spa day outfit. How could a person be so happy and so sad all at the same time?

After showering and dressing, she sat down with her Bible and prayer journal. Paging through the journal, she stared at names of inn guests. People who had enriched her life over the past two years. Would she still feel as invested in them when the inn was simply a place to work? She'd felt such a sense of purpose since moving back to Marietta. Would all that change? And what would happen when Brad decided to retire? He'd brought up the subject several times in the past few months. Would he expect her to quit working here? She couldn't imagine living a life of idle leisure. Would that be a source of conflict for them?

Her mother's voice broke into her stream of worry. "Do not be anxious for tomorrow. Sufficient for the day is its own trouble." She smiled. *Yes, Mother.*

When she felt "prayed up and read up," another one of her mother's expressions, she opened her laptop to check messages. She started with business emails, hoping, as she did every morning, to read gushing thank-yous and glowing ratings from past guests. After deleting ads and things she needed to unsubscribe from, there were three emails worth reading this morning. The first was from a guest saying she had heard about the dog show they'd hosted in April and wondered if she could bring her three Pomeranians when she came to stay. LuAnn made a note to answer with a polite "While we are all dog lovers and have our own inn mascot, the dog show was a special, one-time event, and we need to be sensitive to our other guests who may…"

The second message made her smile. Elliott MacIntosh, the metal detecting Realtor they'd secretly dubbed Santa Claus, was coming back for a visit and wondered if she had any recommendations for places where "we might find other historical artifacts buried in the rich Marietta soil that might lead us to another delightful mystery of murder and mayhem." She sent off a quick message to Tess, who'd be thrilled at Elliott's use of "we," as she'd been the one to find the slave tag back in October that had led them on a race to find gold buried before the Civil War.

The third email made her sit up straight in her chair. Had she recognized the address, she would have read this one first.

Dearest LuAnn,

I am so sorry we were unable to finish recording the exciting moments of your wedding week. A family emergency arose, and I needed to return home. Here are several of your photographs. I will continue editing the rest and send them when they are ready. Sean plans to send your video soon. We had a wonderful stay at your charming inn and will recommend it to others. May your marriage be richly blessed.

Sincerely,
Erica Garrett

A family emergency? Hadn't Tess and Janice said they'd left because of a job opportunity? Not that it surprised her. She knew they'd left because of fear they'd been seen escaping through the secret door. Or because they'd already found what they were searching for.

Lord, help me focus on fun today and not on the what-ifs. Whatever is in the brass box, we didn't know about it before it was stolen, so it's not actually a loss to anyone. If the deed to the house was in it, and we've lost that, well, we're no worse off than we were before. So I need to just leave this all in Your hands and enjoy this day.

As if on cue, there was a rap at her door, and Tess called out, "Up and at 'em, Lu!"

"Come on in."

Tess plopped on her bed and scooped Tom onto her lap. Then she faced LuAnn. "How are we going to get along without you?"

"How do we live without you?" Janice stood in the doorway, singing her own version of a LeAnn Rimes song from the early nineties. Tess joined in, clutching both hands to her heart.

These friends… Just moments ago, LuAnn had been on the verge of getting misty-eyed over the thought of leaving, and now her eyes brimmed with laugh tears as she joined in the corny, though beautifully harmonized, mockery of a love song.

When the song came to a clumsy end with a drawn out "How do we liiiiive?" Janice beckoned with her hand. "Time to go de-stress."

LuAnn picked up her sweater and purse and said goodbye to Tom and Huck. "You guys are going to spoil them when I'm gone, aren't you?"

"Absolutely," Janice assured. "But stop talking about it like you're riding off into the sunset. It's not like you're going far."

"First stop, breakfast," Tess said. She led the way downstairs. The café was full, with several people waiting near the door.

"Have fun!" Robin called as she balanced a tray of plates. In the kitchen, Winnie handed Tess a picnic basket and Janice a large thermos. With a wink at LuAnn, she said, "Relax and enjoy, ladies," and turned back to Big Red.

They got in Tess's car and drove to Muskingum Park. Winnie had thought of everything. Tess spread a tablecloth over a picnic table near the river. "Couldn't have asked for a more perfect day," she said as Janice took pans of still-warm cinnamon rolls and ham-and-Swiss quiche out of the basket. A bottle of orange juice, a container of fresh fruit, and mugs for the coffee created a picture-perfect setting.

"Since my paparazzi have thankfully gone AWOL, I guess I'll have to take my own pictures." LuAnn reached for her phone, but it wasn't in her back pocket. "Left it in my purse, I guess. I'm going to run and get it." She took the keys Tess held out. "Don't touch anything till I get back." She ran to the car. As she opened the passenger door, two women came out of the attorney's office across the street. They were laughing as they headed toward a van parked on the street. Each wore a bright pink sweatshirt with the hood up.

LuAnn stared. Was that Giana? She couldn't be sure.

The other woman dropped the hood when she reached the sidewalk. What in the world? "Lesley?" LuAnn waved and raised her voice. "Lesley!"

The women didn't even glance up before getting in the van and driving away.

June 10, 1861

Prudence tucked stray hairs up into her bun as they turned onto to the dirt road leading to their farm. Her pulse did a little dance of anticipation...and fear. Her heart was near to bursting with hope, but all could still go wrong. Asher had rehearsed his lines the way an actor readies for the stage. Would their audience be receptive?

Only if they felt they had no other choice.

She had prayed for Zephaniah since the day his sad face first appeared at Riverfront House, prayed for someone to love him and care for him as their own. Yesterday, as she had listened to Deborah and Zephaniah talking, singing, and telling stories, it was if the heavens had opened and God had spoken in an audible voice. She had whispered her plan to Asher and been relieved at his enthusiastic agreement. When she told Deborah, the poor woman broke down in tears.

Now, as they approached the farm, Deborah asked, "You sure we gonna be safe?"

"I am sure." She was not as confident on the inside as she sounded, but she smiled for the sake of the people in her care. When they'd gotten a safe distance from Millwood, they'd stopped, and Asher sent a telegram to the Millwood sheriff, reporting the theft. Next, he sent two more messages. One to Jason, telling them they were safe and when they hoped to arrive home, and then one to a fellow soldier at Camp Putnam.

As the house came into view, Salome was the first to come running, wrapping her arms around her mother and sobbing, then flinging herself at Asher, who lifted her off the ground, swung her around, and whispered something in her ear. Salome's answer was a resounding "Yes and yes!" born on a sob. Moses was next, running on his chubby little legs. Never had Prudence been so overjoyed to see her son. She clung to him, and Jason wrapped them both in his strong arms.

The sound of wheels caused them all to fall silent and turn. As the Bickerton carriage approached, Asher stepped out of the shadows and stood next to Zephaniah. The carriage stopped, its shiny wheels and tasseled top out of place against the backdrop of the rail fence. Romulus jumped from the carriage before it stopped and hugged Zephaniah, who froze for a moment, then hugged him back, laughing.

When the Bickertons exited the carriage, Prudence heard Deborah take an audible breath followed by "O Lord A'mighty, sure could use some help here."

Asher, back straight, chin high, strode up to Bickerton. Asher introduced himself and shook a stunned Bickerton's hand. "First," Asher said, "I want to commend to you the actions of your son. Zephaniah singled-handedly saved this woman"—he motioned Deborah forward—"from a fate worse than death. You should be very proud of him."

"W-we are," the florid-faced man stuttered.

"Second, it has come to my attention that you are looking for a new cook. Deborah here, the mother of the woman I am soon to wed, is an accomplished cook, as is my intended Salome. They are also both experienced in caring for children. I know they would both be honored to work for you and to ensure our little hero here gets the best possible care until he reaches legal age and can assume the rights, responsibility, and property owed him under the law. Is that plan agreeable to you?" Asher held out his hand again. Bickerton stared down at it for what seemed like an eternity.

It was Charisse Bickerton who finally reached out, shook Deborah's hand, and said, "We have an agreement."

Prudence stood back, watching, her fear dissolving as the silently terrified man who called himself Howard Bickerton nodded. Asher had said nothing about knowing the truth of their deception, but, as was the nature of a life of lies, the Bickerton imposters would forever be haunted by wondering if he knew.

CHAPTER TWENTY-TWO

"You're absolutely sure it was Lesley?" Tess turned into the spa parking lot.

LuAnn looked up at a single fluffy cloud marring an azure sky. Their de-stressing day was turning into a distressing one. "Yes. But I'm not positive the other woman was Giana. She had her hood up."

"What would they be doing together?" Janice asked. "How do they know each other?"

"They met when Leo and Giana's family stayed at the Paw Paw Patch."

"What would they be doing at an attorney's office?" Tess asked.

"Contesting the ownership of the Bickerton mansion?" LuAnn tried to relax her shoulders. "Maybe Leo found the documents he was looking for. That could explain what Giana was doing, but why was she with Lesley and not Leo?"

Tess pulled into a parking spot in front of the spa. "Everybody take a deep, cleansing breath and let it out slowly. No more talk of clues and suspects for the next few hours, okay?"

LuAnn and Janice agreed.

They entered a world where music designed to induce serenity drifted around them as they changed into downy-soft robes, wrapped their hair in thick white towels, accepted frosted glasses of spring water flavored with lemon and rosemary, and reclined with cucumber slices on their eyes.

The next three hours included full-body exfoliation, mud packs, hot stone massage, a soak in a lavender-scented whirlpool bath while sipping mint-infused sparkling water, deluxe pedicures in hydro-massage chairs, and gel manicures. By the time they walked out into a perfect seventy-five-degree day and headed for lunch, LuAnn had come to a place of peace about everything concerning the Bickerton estate. It wasn't her job to answer all the questions or solve all the mysteries. All that mattered right now was Brad and their wedding and a beautiful future. Nothing was going to mar that.

In the dining room of the graceful Buckley House, a Victorian built in 1879, they started with an appetizer of seafood phyllo baskets. The puff pastry stuffed with curry cream cheese, peppers, onions, and shrimp, scallops, and lobster topped with lobster bisque sauce was delicious. "Heavenly," LuAnn exclaimed, wondering if she'd have room for the eggplant parmigiana she'd ordered. "I am thoroughly spoiled."

"Then we achieved our goal," Tess said.

Janice took a bite of puff pastry and gave a contented sigh. "You royally pampered us before our weddings."

LuAnn laughed. "As I recall, I took you out for breakfast at IHOP the day of your wedding, and we had cheese fondue at my apartment the day before Tess's. I couldn't afford anything more back then."

"Ah, the good old poverty days. It was the thought that..." Tess's eyes opened wide as she stared at something over LuAnn's right shoulder. In a split second, she recovered from whatever had surprised her and began babbling about why fondue had been so popular in the seventies, but now no one had fondue pots anymore.

LuAnn interrupted her. "Who did you see?"

"Nothing. I mean no one. I thought I recognized some... thing, but maybe it's just...." She looked past LuAnn, her eyes narrowing. Suddenly, she jumped up, threw her napkin on the table, and strode off.

LuAnn and Janice swiveled to watch Tess following a young couple out the door.

"Did you see who it was?" Janice asked LuAnn.

"No." The woman had long brown hair, the man a bit taller, but she'd only caught a glimpse from the back as they walked out. "That's odd behavior, even for Tess."

"Jeffrey knew so many people around the state. It wouldn't be the first time she's run into someone they knew from the golf course."

LuAnn nodded. "Why did she say some*thing*?"

Tess walked back in before they had time to speculate more. She sat down, winded and looking confused. "I recognized a...purse. They got in a car before I could catch up with them."

"You chased after them for a purse?" Janice scrunched her nose.

Tess nodded, still trying to catch her breath.

This was so unlike Tess. "Is it one you've been looking for?" LuAnn asked.

Tess blinked at her. "Me? No. It was orange, with a gold chain." She sighed. "I'm the one who said we couldn't talk about clues and suspects, but...it was the same purse I saw yesterday on the dresser in Erica's room."

"Well..." Janice seemed to be fumbling for something positive to say. "It's such a popular brand. I'm sure lots of women have orange purses with gold chains."

Tess shook her head, her eyes still on the door. "But not orange purses with a splotch of blue ink on the front."

"Could we run through it one more time?" LuAnn felt like a petulant child asking her pastor, fiancé, and best friends to straighten up and be serious. They acted like a bunch of third graders, giggling and whispering as she walked down the aisle carrying a paper plate festooned with ribbons from her bridal shower. She was getting a headache, and the sandals she'd bought for their honeymoon were causing a blister on the back of her heel. Not the way she wanted to feel at her wedding rehearsal. "I know it's a small ceremony, but..." Sixty-five-year-old women did not stomp their feet and cry, "But it's my *only* wedding!" so she simply stopped talking, hoping they'd get the hint.

"One more time." Pastor Ben winked at Brad. "This time will be flawless."

Why did her pastor, the man who was supposed to be the epitome of decorum, at least during the sacrament of marriage, appear to be the instigator of much of the silliness?

LuAnn turned around, walked to the back of the church followed by Tess and Janice, her two matrons of honor, and waited for the music to start again. For just a moment, she felt very alone. Even if she'd married young, she wouldn't have walked down the aisle on her father's arm. But her mother had offered to give her away. She shook off the moment of wistfulness and put on a smile as she followed Tess, who followed Janice with exaggerated pauses after each step. At the front of the church, Brad stood beaming at her while Grant and Leo seemed to struggle to keep from laughing.

Ben rushed them through their vows, then lingered over the "You may now kiss the bride" pronouncement. Leo cheered when Brad leaned in for a restrained kiss. In the front pew, Giana clapped.

"Can we go eat now?" Brad asked, loud enough for the janitor dusting in the balcony to hear.

"Yes. Let's go eat." LuAnn forced any hint of trepidation out of her voice. They'd be serious tomorrow. All would go well.

Tess and Janice were still in rare form as Brad drove the three of them back to the inn. When they came in through the kitchen, LuAnn stopped short at a sight she'd never seen in the almost two years since they'd opened. "Winnie! You're sitting down!" Of course, Winnie had often joined them for meals and meetings at the kitchen table, but to find her sitting back, legs crossed, hugging a mug of coffee as she watched the caterers prepare the rehearsal dinner was startling. Oddly, the table was draped with a tablecloth that went all the way to the floor.

"I'm just guarding my kitchen," Winnie said with a smile as her foot shoved something under the tablecloth. Her eyes never wavered from LuAnn's face. "How'd rehearsal go?"

LuAnn threw up her hands. "You've heard the expression 'herding cats'?"

Winnie laughed. "I get the picture." She pointed toward the door to the café. "Everything's ready."

"Wonderful. Leo went to pick up Irene and Thelma. We can eat as soon as they get here. I'm going to go up and change shoes." Slipping out of her sandals, LuAnn padded barefoot up the stairs, almost running into Giana coming out of her room.

What was that smell? Something sweet and eerily familiar. Something she'd smelled recently.

"LuAnn! Come see my dress." Without waiting for an answer, Giana turned and unlocked the door. "You have to tell me if it's dressy enough."

She opened the closet and pulled out a sleeveless pale blue dress. "I'm going to wear pearls and these shoes." She used her foot to point to a pair of strappy silver sandals. Next to the sandals sat a pair of running shoes, or what had once been running shoes. They were now spattered with paint. One large blob of blue-green paint was the exact shade of seafoam as the master bathroom at the mansion. LuAnn froze.

The brass box had gone missing the same day the painter had been there. What if Giana had been sneaking through the house in search of the brass box when something or someone startled her? She'd run into the bathroom to hide and kicked the paint can left by the painter and a blob of paint had spilled on her shoe...

Butterscotch! She smelled butterscotch. Giana was sucking on a piece of candy just like... She forced her attention back to the silver shoes and dress, fingering the filmy fabric of the skirt. "This is absolutely perfect. And pearls"—*Where did you get them?*—"will be just the right complement."

"Great." Giana began shutting the bifold door on one side of the closet before LuAnn withdrew her arm. "Guess we should get downstairs, huh?"

"Yep. I'm going to run up and get some comfy shoes first."

As she ran up the remaining stairs, her mind raced. Should she call Brad, tell him to come up here so she could tell him? Should she wait until after the dinner? She walked in her room, took out her phone, then shoved it back in her pocket.

"Lu?" Tess poked her head in LuAnn's bedroom door as she was standing in front of her closet, mind on a million possible scenarios while she tried to remember what she was looking for. "Hey, I just wanted to apologize for all our goofiness. I promise you tomorrow is going to be beyond your wildest dreams, and we will all behave."

"I know that." Shoes. She'd come for comfy shoes. If they didn't solve this pretty soon, she was going to be sharing a room with Thelma. "I trust you." *Even if you are an exaggerator.* Tomorrow would be lovely, but "beyond your wildest dreams" was a bit much. Shoulder to shoulder, they walked back downstairs together. She could hold her emotions and suspicions in check for two more hours, and then she and Brad were going to discuss talking to Leo about Giana's true intentions. Unless they were his too. Was it time to call the police?

Or time to tell Tess to search Giana's room? On the third-floor landing, she stopped, grasping Tess's elbow.

"What's wrong?"

"I have proof Giana was at the Bickerton house the day the box went missing," she whispered.

"Giana lives in Pittsburgh. How would she—"

"Ready, ladies?" Brad's smiling face came into view. "The servers are starting."

Tess shot LuAnn a look of question, and they followed Brad downstairs.

The café glowed with dusty-rose candles in hurricane lamps. White linen on the tables set with polished silverware brought by the caterers gave it a back-in-time feel.

The harvest table was set for seventeen. LuAnn and Brad, Tess, Janice, Grant, Saffron, Wendy, Leo, Giana, Pastor Ben and Paige, Winnie, the organist and her husband, and Brin, Robin, and Taylor, who would act as ushers. A small group. Had she been wrong to not include Tess's and Janice's grandchildren? She'd considered Larry as a junior groomsman and played with the thought of asking Harper to be a flower girl. Liam and Henry would have stolen the show as ringbearers, but the thought of the stress dressing and corralling the triplets would put on Tess's daughter made her reconsider. Now she was having second thoughts. Again.

She'd thought no one would be all that interested in the wedding of two people their age. Now that it was too late to change anything, she wondered if she'd been wrong to not make a bigger fuss. Maybe she was disappointing friends...as well as herself. The admission took her by surprise. Was it true? Was that part of the irritation she'd felt the past couple of weeks? And were Tess and Janice upset with her for not letting them have the fun of planning a huge extravaganza? All she could do now was ask them and apologize.

"Lu?" Brad whispered in her ear as he pulled out a chair for her.

She smiled and winked at him, hiding the fact that she'd been off in the land of regrets and second thoughts.

Why hadn't she made a seating chart? Tess had suggested it weeks ago, but it had seemed silly for such a small gathering. Now, when she ended up sitting between Brad and Giana, she wished she'd thought it through. But until this past week, she would have thought it would be interesting to sit next to Leo's fiancé and find out more about her.

How was she going to continue in the carefree mood set by their spa experience with questions about seafoam paint and butterscotch candy and Giana's visit to the attorney burning in her brain?

The servers set down plates of lasagna, parmesan garlic bread, and bowls of Italian salad heaped with cheese. Out of the corner of her eye, LuAnn tracked every move Giana made. "Glad I'm not lactose intolerant with this meal, aren't you?"

"Yes. My sister would be doubling up on her enzymes with a feast like this."

Enzymes. She'd mentioned that before. "Your sister"—*the one who looks like you*—"is—"

"Pastor Ben, will you bless the food please?" Brad asked.

Ben stood and prayed, then Brad thanked their guests, and Grant stood up and gave a toast. Tess and Janice followed, bringing tears to LuAnn's eyes. When tiramisu and coffee were served, Tess and Janice started talking to Ben and Paige while the organist and her husband engaged Brad and Grant by asking their thoughts on downsizing in retirement. That left LuAnn with Giana and Leo...until Leo began teasing Saffron about her new shaved-on-one-side haircut.

LuAnn scrambled for a nonthreatening topic, but Giana beat her to it. "This place is even more incredible than Leo described it. I had a few minutes to look through your memory book. I love looking at all the old photos and what it looked like before you started restorations. You've done an amazing job."

"Thank you."

"Leo says this is a ministry for you three. I love that whole idea." Giana's eyes glowed. "We'll be doing kind of the same thing in Mozambique. I'll be working at the hospital, and after Leo finishes his training we'll—"

"Mozambique?"

"He didn't tell you?" Giana looked to her right and shook her head with a laugh. "My sweet procrastinator finally got all his paperwork submitted. It took him forever to find his diplomas.

We just got word this morning that he's been accepted into a mission aviation program. He already has his private pilot's license, so half the work is done. We'll live in the city, and building relationships—like what you do here—will be part of our mission." She giggled. "Does that surprise you?"

Surprise? LuAnn was pretty sure she appeared catatonic. All she could do was manage to close her mouth and nod. "I'd heard you were a missionary. I just wouldn't have guessed Leo would…"

"I know!" Giana laughed. "We did a video call when he told his mom. You should have seen her face. She almost fainted. I was so afraid she'd be upset. We'll be gone for six months at a time, and at her age… But she was ecstatic. She said she's been praying Leo's entire life for God to get ahold of his heart." Giana put her hand on her chest. "She said she's been praying for 'the one' and she knew the first time we talked on the phone that I was it."

How was she going to bring up the paint on the shoes and the butterscotch and the brass box now?

"I just got back from Mozambique a month ago. I've got pictures." Giana pulled out her phone. As she went to touch the photo icon, something in the picture on her home screen— the family photo taken at the Paw Paw Patch B&B—grabbed LuAnn's attention.

An orange purse.

LuAnn pointed. "Is that…your sister?"

"Yes." Giana beamed. "Here, let me find that picture so you can see it better." She tapped the photo icon and scrolled until she found it, then spread her fingers to enlarge it. "These are my parents, and this is Thomas, my brother, and my sister Gwen."

LuAnn stared at the blond woman who looked so much like Giana. A rush of cold swept through her. If the woman colored her hair and changed the color of her eyes… "That purse." It was a strange thing to note when looking at a family picture. "I know someone who has one just like it."

Giana laughed. "Not just like that one, I guarantee. Gwen was refilling ink cartridges for her printer and one overflowed and… LuAnn? Are you okay?"

CHAPTER TWENTY-THREE

Lu?" Brad grabbed her hand as she stood from her chair, no idea what she was going to do next. "What's wrong?"

She was making a spectacle of herself. Not her intention. Heat crawling up the back of her neck and likely splotching her face red, she sat back down. "Something. Something's wrong here." She handed him Giana's phone, then looked from Tess to Janice in a silent plea for them to distract everyone else.

Janice jumped up. "Tess and I have a couple of songs for you." She put her hand on Tess's shoulder and received a bobblehead nod. They walked to the piano, and Janice began to play.

"What am I supposed to see here?" Brad asked. By now, Leo was leaning in, gaze bouncing from LuAnn to Brad to Giana and back.

"That purse." She jabbed her finger at the phone, then realized how ridiculous it was to be talking to Brad instead of grilling Giana. Turning to face her squarely, she said, "Your sister. She was here, wasn't she? I don't know if it was her or you, and I don't know what you two are up to, but one of you stole the brass box and the diamond rings and—"

Irene gasped. "The medals!"

"What medals?" Brad asked.

"Major Asher John Bailey's Medal of Honor and Ohio Veteran Medal. I borrowed them from Maybelline for...something."

LuAnn turned back to Giana. "I hope you still have everything that was in that box because—"

"Lu!" Brad grabbed her elbow. "What are you—"

"Wait just a minute." Leo stood, taking over the role of spectacle maker. "I'm not going to sit here while you accuse my—"

Giana whirled to face Irene. "I didn't steal it!" She threw down her napkin, stood, and ran out the front door.

The music stopped. All eyes turned on LuAnn, who turned to Leo. "Were you in on this too?"

As blank a stare as she had ever seen met her accusation. "In on what? I have no idea what you are talking about."

"Giana was at the mansion the day the brass box was stolen." LuAnn heard the bell over the front door but didn't turn around. "And then I saw her and Lesley coming out of the attorney's office. Was the deed in the box? Were you going to hide it so Brad couldn't prove the house—"

"What?" Giana stood by the door, blue eyes no longer filled with tears but wide with shock. Something else was different. It took a moment for it to register. She'd changed her blouse. And from her shoulder hung the orange purse.

The door opened again. Giana—the real Giana—stood in the doorway. And behind her stood Lesley, next to the man who'd stood on the end in the picture at the Paw Paw Patch. Her brother. Tall, thin, clean-shaven, but...

"Sean?" It was Janice who voiced it just as it dawned on LuAnn.

"Actually, Thomas." The British accent was gone.

Giana stepped forward. She reached into a massive plastic bag, pulled out the brass box, and set it on the table. She turned to Irene. "You told me you'd found a bunch of old pictures of Leo making model airplanes and pretending he could fly. Remember? You said they were in a box under the airplane picture and I could see them when I came to visit."

Irene nodded slowly. "I don't know what happened to those pictures."

"Can't leave valuable pictures in a box marked *Pictures*, Irene." Thelma rose slowly from her chair. "I put them in the brass box with the medals and the ring. For safety."

Walking toward a dazed-looking Leo, Giana said, "You told me I couldn't see those old embarrassing pictures, and I said I'd snatch them out from right under your nose. Remember?"

Leo nodded, still appearing in a stupor.

"When your mom told me she was redecorating, I posed as a painter. I walked right past you in the upstairs hall, and you never looked twice."

"Wha..."

"The pictures weren't in your room, so I had to come back. I found the box on the shelf under the airplane picture. I didn't know there was anything else in it until four days ago when I finally got around to ordering...something."

Leo's mouth dropped open. After a moment, he managed to close it. A smile teased the corners of his mouth, and he slowly shook his head. "Man, you're good." He laughed and held out his arms to her. "Come here."

"Not yet. First I need to embarrass you in front of your whole family." She turned to LuAnn. "I'm so sorry about all of this. I had no idea anyone was looking for the box, and I had no idea anything of value was in it when I took it, and I had no intension of messing with your rehearsal dinner. I promise I will apologize way better in a minute, but this is the only way I can prove why I took it." She reached back into the bag and pulled out a roll of fuzzy cloth. "Here." She handed one corner to Leo. "Hold this."

Leo did as he was told, and Giana unfurled a blanket covered in a collage of pictures of Leo as a child. A chubby little boy riding on a grocery store airplane and a little older, building airplane models and paper airplanes. In the center was the picture that hung above his dresser.

His face a deep scarlet, Leo wrapped his girlfriend in the blanket and then in his arms.

Winnie poured coffee for the circle of people sitting by the fireplace as the caterers quietly cleared the tables. Most of the guests had left. Thelma napped in a wingback chair while Leo, Giana, and Irene shared the love seat, Irene holding Giana's hand and repeating, "You're so good for my boy. An answer to prayer."

Gwen, aka Erica, poured cream in her mug, then opened a small white pouch and dumped two white tablets into her hand, just as LuAnn now realized she had seen her do at the bridal shower. "Guess it's time we tell our part of this crazy story," she said, glancing at Sean—*Thomas*—and getting a nod. She took a quick breath and faced Leo. "On our last night at the Paw Paw Patch, you and Giana went out for a walk, and Thomas and I and Mom and Dad and Lesley got to talking about your house and how sad it was that it wouldn't be in your family anymore."

Thomas leaned in, resting his hands on his knees. "We'd just been telling Lesley all about the immersive theater experience, and she said the Bickerton mansion sounded like the perfect setting for it. That got Dad talking. When he starts to get passionate about a new idea, we all know enough to stand back and get out of the way. We wanted to get more information, but we didn't want Giana to know about it. Miss Morals here would get all upset, thinking we'd be using her relationship with you to get a good deal."

"So we came up with the idea of coming here incognito," Gwen tag-teamed. "You'd told us about Brad and LuAnn getting married and LuAnn spending a lot of time at the mansion. I had a friend who'd hired a photographer to go everywhere with her the week before her wedding, so that seemed like a plausible cover. We've both taken photography courses and... Anyway, that's what brought us here. We were a little freaked out when we saw Davinia. We didn't know if we could trust her, but when she figured out who we were and told us what she was doing, it just made sense to join forces to"—Gwen pulled at her bangs, just like she had with the dark wig—"do things we had no business doing."

Gwen turned to Brad and then Irene. "Today, Lesley drove here because she's totally on board too. She wants to get her kids involved in the summers. The attorney we met with is on the Marietta Planning Commission. We were just…checking out zoning and things. I'm so sorry. That was so presumptuous. We got caught up in the idea and just got carried away."

Giana shook her head. "I can't believe you would sneak around like that." Her face lit with a sheepish grin. She looked at Irene. "You must think your son is involved with the most devious family. We really aren't—"

"What I think, my dear, is that you all did some very wrong things for all the right reasons."

"We're still very interested in buying your house. We sent our parents videos, and they're absolutely over the moon about it. We'd thought it would be perfect if Giana and Leo could live there after they…I mean, if they get married." She winked at Giana. "But now that we know their plans, I think we could easily hire—"

"They already have a buyer." LuAnn blurted the words before thinking it wasn't her place. She looked at Brad with an apologetic shrug.

Brad put his arm around her, then reached out and squeezed Irene's hand.

Irene smiled. "Do you think it's time?"

Brad nodded. Confused, LuAnn looked around to see Leo, Grant, Wendy, Saffron, Tess, and Janice also nodding.

Irene let go of Giana's hand and laced her bony fingers together in a prayer pose on her lap. "You all need to know that this was my idea. It never really mattered whether or not we found the deed, because we've known for some time what we were going to do with the house. Leo is heading off to Africa, and Thelma and I are moving on to a new adventure, but the house needs to stay in the family."

LuAnn looked at Grant and then Wendy and Saffron. Did Grant want the house? Or his girls? How perfect for his artsy daughters to have a place for their—

Brad stood, turned, and knelt in front of LuAnn. She shook her head. What was going on? He'd already proposed…

"LuAnn soon-to-be Grimes, would you do me the honor of becoming the mistress of the Bickerton mansion?" He held out a set of keys, opened her hand, and placed them on her palm. "We will have our entire honeymoon to talk about how we're going to fill all those rooms, but I heard someone say it would make a wonderful retreat center. And it just might be the perfect setting for some immersive theater productions."

"Shut your mouth, Lu," Tess whispered, and the room erupted in laughter as LuAnn wrapped her arms around her almost husband and began to sob happy tears.

When she'd finally composed herself and used half the wad of tissues Winnie stuck in her hand, LuAnn sat back, allowing Brad to get off his knees and sit next to her again. She wrapped both arms around his arm and was about to lay her head on his shoulder, when a thought registered. She pointed at the brass box and then to Giana. "Did you open it?"

Giana gave her a questioning look. "Yes. The pictures were in it."

"But did you use the code?"

"Code?"

Brad was pulling out his wallet. He handed LuAnn the code card. "You read, I'll twist and turn."

"Okay. Turn over, then twist right front right two turns."

"Twist the leg? It must be." He twisted one of the small brass buttons that served as a leg. Metal grated against metal in protest, but it turned.

"Turn over."

"Again?"

"There's probably a ball bearing rolling around when you turn it," Leo said. "I saw something like this on the History Channel."

"Now twist the right back to the left, turn on its right side, and tap it. While right side up, turn the left back leg left. The bottom should—"

They all jumped as the bottom of the box sprang loose, clanging on the table.

"It's a false bottom," Brad said, sliding his hand in to carefully remove several folded pieces of paper. He set them on the table, then opened the top paper and grinned. He turned it around.

Whereas, Howard Bickerton, of London, England, has deposited in the GENERAL LAND OFFICE of the UNITED STATES a certificate of the Register of the Land Office…

The paper was signed by President Franklin Pierce.

"There's something else." Brad pulled out a string of pearls and held them up. Ivory in color, each pearl a unique shape glowing softly in the lamplight. He handed them to LuAnn.

"Marta's pearls," Irene whispered. She reached out and took LuAnn's hand. "You should wear them tomorrow."

LuAnn nodded. "You can never have too many somethings borrowed, right?"

"Right."

Tess set a giant bowl of popcorn on the table in their fourth-floor gathering room. "Your last night here…and what a night it's been."

LuAnn, comfy in pajamas and slippers, tucked her feet beneath her. "I can't believe you two knew about the house the whole time I was choosing the paint colors and curtain fabrics."

There were those Cheshire cat smiles again. "We're very good at keeping secrets." Janice settled in a chair with a throw over her legs.

"Are you happy about it?" Tess asked.

"Happy doesn't even come close. I'm still in shock." She couldn't stop grinning, and her face was beginning to ache. "Every time Brad mentions retiring, I get this panicky feeling, scared we'll become those old people who sit in their matching recliners eating off of TV trays and watching *Wheel of Fortune* every night. But now… It's like a whole new world of possibilities has opened up. For all of us. I don't know what it's going to look like yet, but I know the Bickerton mansion and Wayfarers Inn are going to work hand-in-hand."

CHAPTER TWENTY-FOUR

On her last morning as a resident of Wayfarers Inn, LuAnn took a long bubble bath, spent a leisurely hour reading in her favorite chair—which would soon be relocated to the master bedroom at the Bickerton mansion. Her copy of Prudence's journal lay open on her footstool, open to the page about Asher and Salome's wedding. One line stood out to her as she glanced at it and reminded her of another passage she had read two years ago. Could the two be related? She turned back one page.

What joy! Only God could orchestrate this. A sheriff's deputy from Millwood arrived this morning with a package. They have captured the thief and confiscated Z's ransom. He has asked me to keep them for him, but only after insisting S borrow them. If Z's mother is looking down on him, she is beaming with pride at her boy with the generous heart.

Was "Z's ransom" the necklace Prudence mentioned in her account of Asher Bailey's wedding? She wouldn't have spoken of a necklace as "them" unless...they were pearls. Marta's pearls. LuAnn felt her eyes smart. She would not be the first, or the second, bride to wear them. Who would be next?

She took her time, finishing packing for her honeymoon before heading downstairs to breakfast.

Was it her crazy imagination, or did the din of conversations in the café lessen when she walked down the stairs? Several people stared at her with knowing smiles. Harry, Thorn and his wife, Beverly, Maybelline, Axel, and their granddaughters. Of course, even though they'd only invited close friends and family, the whole town knew about the wedding. Still, something about the looks seemed odd.

Giana and Erica—*Gwen*—motioned to her from a table near the window. They wore matching purple blouses.

"Go sit with them," Tess said, sneaking up behind her.

"Okay...." She took the chair Giana pushed out with her foot.

Gwen smiled sheepishly. "I wasn't sure you'd want me around, but I'd really love to finish your photos."

"If you wouldn't mind, we'd love to go with you to your hair appointment," Giana said. "It might help you be a little less nervous."

But she wasn't nervous. That had been the impetus for a simple wedding. No stress. No nerves. Still, this might be an opportunity to get to know Giana and the real person who'd posed as her photographer. They would, after all, be crossing paths at bridal showers and, very likely, another wedding in the near future. "That would be...fun." She'd almost tripped on the last word, but, as she said it, it actually rang true.

They ordered yogurt parfaits and eggs Benedict, and LuAnn mostly listened as the sisters told stories of their childhood. When they finished eating, LuAnn looked at her watch. "I'll meet you down here in five minutes, okay?"

Up in her room, she opened her closet to get a sweater. An empty space on the top shelf caught her eye. Her shoes were gone. Again.

When she got downstairs, she cornered Janice. "Do you know where my wedding shoes are?"

"Shoes?" Janice was a horrible liar.

LuAnn suddenly laughed. She'd seen this before, though it was usually a prank pulled on the groom. They'd write something like "Help!" on the bottom of her shoes. With a shake of her head, she walked over to the twins. "My car's in back. We can go through the kitch—"

"I'll drive!" Gwen held up her keys. "I'm right in front, and the bride should be chauffeured, right?"

Giana sat in the middle of the back seat. LuAnn checked the time on the dashboard. "We have a few extra minutes. I want to stop at the church and just make sure the unity candle arrived and check on the decorations." Tess had said the deaconesses had offered to put the bows on the ends of the pews.

"Are you sure we should?" Giana asked. "It sounded like Tess and Janice had everything under control. And you might end up talking to someone and be late for your appointment."

"I'll just be a minute." She gave Gwen directions to the church, telling her to park in front, and ran in.

The sanctuary was just as they'd left it last night. Not a bow or candle or deaconess in sight. Had the women forgotten? She ran to the office. The church secretary looked shocked to see her. When asked about the deaconesses, she sputtered something about someone being sick, and they would surely get it done this morning, and she'd call Paige right away.

As they entered Curl Up & Dye, LuAnn had the same feeling she'd had when she'd walked into the café. Knowing smiles, secretive glances. Did the women of Marietta have nothing more important to do than titter over a sixty-five-year-old bride?

Corrine, who'd been cutting her hair for two years, gave her a giant hug. "The glorious day has arrived," she effused. She draped a cape over LuAnn's shoulders and sent her to the shampoo sink while she set two folding chairs in her station.

Warm water and coconut-and-honey shampoo washed away all tension. By the time Corrine had dried her hair and swung her around to face Giana and Gwen, her thoughts were once again aright. Today she would become Mrs. Bradley Grimes. LuAnn Grimes. Today was going to go exactly as planned.

Gwen took pictures, and she and Giana kept up a steady flow of stories as Corrine tugged and curled and sprayed.

Why was she spraying? LuAnn had specifically told her she wanted her hair to be soft and natural. What was the woman doing? When she tried to crane her head around to see the mirror, Corrine blocked her view. "I want to look like me when you're done, you know."

"You look beautiful," Giana said. "It's perfect."

An hour later, Corrine stepped back. "There. All done." Corrine removed the cape and turned her around.

It took every ounce of self-control LuAnn could muster not to burst into tears. Corrine had created a ridiculously elaborate updo with a center part and coils around her ears. She looked like she belonged in one of the old oval sepia-toned photos that had graced the walls of the mansion library before she'd redecorated.

Giana, Gwen, and Corrine looked at her with such enraptured smiles, she didn't have the heart to say a word. She'd simply have to brush it out and redo it when she got back to the inn. Would a flat iron be able to bring her back to looking like LuAnn rather than something conjured by her time machine imagination? With trembling hands, she pulled out her wallet.

Corrine waved away her money. "It's all paid for. Go, get married. And bring me pictures!"

Great. Now she'd have to avoid Corrine for the rest of her life.

The nerves her lists were supposed to prevent began battling like caffeinated butterflies in her belly on the way back to the inn. Her appointment had taken longer than planned. Would she have time to get ready and get to the church and check on all the details? Though Giana and Gwen did their best to get her talking about her dress and the cake and flowers, it only made things worse. She'd never heard back from the bakery or the florist. What if they hadn't made her changes? What if Tess and Janice had dropped the ball...multiple balls?

What if they delivered the wrong cake and flowers and there were no decorations and no shoes and she couldn't tame the awful vintage hair?

When they parked at the inn, she forced herself to look out at the calm Ohio reflecting a cloudless sky. Today was her wedding day. Even if everything wasn't perfect, it would still be wonderful.

Giana motioned for her to lead the way into the building. She put her hand on the heavy iron door handle, remembering the first time she'd walked through these doors and into a world of secrets and magical potential and—

Tess stood just inside the door, wearing the long rust and sage-green plaid dress she'd worn for their Heritage Tour back in October. Her copper hair was pinned back, and a chignon of curls was fixed at the back of her head.

"What are you—"

"Welcome to your time machine wedding, Miss Sherrill."

"Please step through the portal, ma'am." Janice, in her long blue and green vintage dress, swept her hand around a wrought-iron arch entwined with flowers. Thorn stood just around the corner, drill in one hand and flowers in the other, grinning.

"What...?" Numbly, LuAnn took a step. "Where am I?"

The café tables were gone. The entire first floor was filled with folding chairs, all facing the fireplace, which was covered in dusty-rose flowers and sage-green branches. Antique candelabras—that had likely come in a huge box from Indianapolis—lined the walls. Tess and Janice led her to the stairs. "Time to get you dressed," Tess said.

Feeling like she was in a dream, LuAnn walked up to the fourth floor and into their apartment. "What's...going on?"

Janice stood back, letting LuAnn walk ahead of her into her bedroom. In the closet, where her simple dress had once hung, was the most gorgeous gown she had ever seen. Ivory silk, three tiers forming the skirt, an off-the-shoulder V neckline and pleated bodice, a deep V waistline, three-quarter sleeves, and a train that puddled on the floor next to... "My shoes!"

The same shoes but now accessorized with silk roses that matched the dress.

"We took them because we were going to have them dyed blue, but then we found these flowers," Tess said. "Sorry to make you think you were losing it."

LuAnn laughed. "I was losing it! And all I week I thought you two were..." She shook her head. It didn't matter now. "What did I ever do to deserve such wonderfully amazing, sneaky friends?"

"You were just you," Janice said, wiping the dampness from her bottom lashes.

"Okay, enough of that." Tess pulled a tissue from a hidden pocket in her full skirt. "We have work to do."

Eyes smarting, LuAnn did what they asked, slipping out of her clothes and raising her arms as her best friends of forty-plus years slid the rich confection of a dress over her head. She slipped on her shoes then put on the earrings her mother had worn at her own wedding. Tess fastened the diamond necklace and then Marta's pearls around her neck.

"Now comes the hard part," Janice said. "We have to do your makeup, and you absolutely cannot cry it off until after pictures."

That only made her eyes smart more, but she sat and let Janice do her face while Tess pinned a gauzy ivory veil to the hair that was perfect for the dress.

They walked out into the hallway, and Tess handed her a bouquet of dusty-pink and ivory roses interspersed with day lilies, black-eyed Susans, and Queen Anne's lace. "If you don't want the wildflowers, we can—"

"They're perfect. Absolutely perfect."

Janice tucked an antique handkerchief trimmed in blue tatting into the sleeve of LuAnn's dress.

"We're going to go down first," Janice said. "When the music changes, it's your turn."

LuAnn stood on the second-floor landing, gazing down at every person who had enriched her life in the past two years and some before that. Several former students and coworkers, Tippi Coddlesworth, Maybelline and her family, Elliott MacIntosh, Emma, Harry, Paige, Tess and Janice's children and grandchildren, Thorn and Beverly, Robin, Taylor…

While Asher and Salome had celebrated their wedding with "a lovely sponge," the smells drifting from the kitchen told her Winnie would once again delight guests with her butterscotch cake instead of the sheet cake she'd put on her list. LuAnn smiled. Absolutely nothing about this day had gone according to plan. And she couldn't be happier. She stepped down one step, and her eyes were drawn to the fireplace where

Pastor Ben stood, in total solemnity, wearing a double-breasted coat. The collar of his white pleated shirt stood up beneath a wide black cravat. And on his left...

Brad stood, hands behind his back, beyond striking in a navy-blue jacket with gold buttons and gold epaulets and two shining medals on his chest...dressed just the way Prudence described Lieutenant Asher Bailey on his wedding day.

Prudence's words came to mind: *"It is with hope, and because of love" that we set out...* With her heart full to overflowing, LuAnn walked down the aisle toward a future that promised to be anything but boring.

After all, who could resist a historical building with secrets and potential?

And those blue eyes...

Dear Reader,

Every time I write the last line of a book manuscript, I celebrate. It may only involve a cup of tea and a nap, or might be as wild as a spa pedicure, but I always do something to mark the occasion. This time feels a little different. I find myself echoing LuAnn's emotions as she realizes that "As with so many of life's adventures, she had to leave something behind in order to experience something new." In this case, I am leaving behind the beautiful, history-rich setting of Marietta, Ohio, and three characters who have come to feel like real friends.

I'm also very aware that this means you, dear reader, are also saying goodbye to LuAnn, Tess, Janice, Brad, Tom and Huck, Winnie, Thorn, Irene and Thelma, Prudence, Jason, Moses, Patience, and all of the Wayfarers Inn friends, guests, and suspects. I hope it's been a delightful journey filled with mystery, mirth, and muffins, and maybe a few faith steps and lessons learned right along with the Inn Crowd.

Let's celebrate this "leaving behind" together. First, let's put our feet up on the coffee table and savor a gigantic slice of Winnie's Old-Fashioned Butterscotch Cake. Then, let's put our hands together and join our voices in a pact.

Ready?

"We will never be boring or bored, and we will never act our age!"

Thanks for joining us in Marietta. May God bless you as you move on to something new.

Hugs,
Becky Melby

About the Author

Wisconsin author Becky Melby and her husband have four married sons and fifteen grandchildren. *Old, New, Borrowed, Blue* is her twentieth published title.

When not writing, reading, or spoiling grandkids, Becky may be found plotting and brainstorming on the back of their Honda Gold Wing motorcycle or traveling the country with their camper.

Connect with Becky at beckymelby.com, Becky Melby Author Page on Facebook, or Becky Melby Books on Instagram. She is also a regular contributor to Fill My Cup, Lord on Facebook and would love to have you join her and six other authors for daily online inspiration that feels like "coffee with girlfriends."

THE REVERSE UNDERGROUND RAILROAD

The deplorable practice of kidnapping free black Americans and fugitive slaves from free states and transporting them to slave states for sale as slaves was known as the "Reverse Underground Railroad."

Organized gangs of "man-stealers" used physical abduction and trickery to apprehend their targets. The Reverse Underground Railroad operated for eighty-five years, from 1780 to 1865. Much of their nefarious activity occurred in free states that bordered slave states.

In 1827, an article in *The African Observer* described how several Philadelphia children were lured on board a small sloop anchored in the Delaware River with the promise of peaches, oranges, and watermelons, then immediately put in chains in the hold of the ship. After a week-long journey on the sloop, they were marched through swamps and cornfields, again "kept in irons for a considerable amount of time," then eventually taken by ship to Maryland where they landed and were forced to walk for "many hundred miles" until they reached Mississippi.

The same article described a network of Reverse Underground Railroad posts "established from Pennsylvania to Louisiana."

In the West, kidnappers rode the waters of the Ohio River, stealing slaves in Kentucky and kidnapping free people in Southern Ohio, Indiana, and Illinois, who were then transported to the slave states.

Even before the Fugitive Slave Act of 1850, state and city governments had difficulty preventing kidnappings. The Pennsylvania Abolition Society compared records of apprehended blacks to try to free those who were wrongfully detained, kept a list of missing people who were potential abductees, and formed the Committee on Kidnapping. However, these efforts proved to be expensive and therefore unsustainable.

Citizens, particularly free black citizens, were active in lobbying local governments to adopt stronger measures against kidnapping. Due to the lack of cooperation from these institutions, free blacks were frequently forced to use their own methods to protect themselves and their families, including avoiding strangers and keeping their freedom papers with them at all times.

Constable Samuel Parker Garrigues of Philadelphia took several trips to southern states to rescue children and adults who had been kidnapped from the city's streets. One such case was Charles Bailey, kidnapped in 1825 at the age of fourteen, and finally rescued by Garrigues after a three-year search. Unfortunately, the beaten and emaciated youth died a few days after being brought back to Philadelphia.

When a kidnapping was recognized and taken to trial, the verification of the black's freedom was extremely hard to prove. Not all blacks carried freedom papers, and those who were kidnapped were often stripped of their papers. Since freedom papers could easily be forged, some judges would not allow them as evidence.

The forced resettlement of free Negro and fugitive slave African Americans into southern slavery ended with the Union victory at the end of the American Civil War and the passing of the Thirteenth Amendment abolishing slavery, and the Fourteenth Amendment to the United States Constitution giving African Americans full citizenship rights.

SOMETHING DELICIOUS FROM OUR WAYFARERS INN FRIENDS

Winnie's Old-Fashioned Butterscotch Cake

Ingredients

Cake:

2 large eggs

Nonstick baking spray

2½ cups sifted cake flour (sift before measuring)

2 teaspoons baking powder

¼ teaspoon salt

1½ cups light brown sugar

¼ cup granulated sugar

1½ cups half-and-half or whole milk, at room temperature

¾ cup safflower oil or canola oil

2 teaspoons pure vanilla extract

Frosting:

4 tablespoons, plus ½ cup water

2 teaspoons unflavored powdered gelatin

2 cups light brown sugar

½ cup half-n-half or whole milk

1¼ pounds unsalted butter (5 sticks), at room temperature

2 teaspoons pure vanilla extract

Butterscotch Sauce:

4 tablespoons unsalted butter

1 cup light brown sugar

1 teaspoon fresh lemon juice

¼ teaspoon salt

¾ cup heavy cream

2 teaspoons pure vanilla extract

Directions

For the cake:

1. Separate eggs. Place whites in medium bowl and yolks in small bowl. Let stand at room temperature, about 20 minutes.
2. Preheat oven to 350 degrees F and line the bottom of 3 (9-inch) round cake pans with parchment paper. Spray with nonstick baking spray. Set aside.
3. Sift together flour, baking powder, and 1/4 teaspoon salt in a large bowl. Add the brown sugar. If there are any large clumps of brown sugar, break them up with a spoon. Stir, then set aside.
4. Whip egg whites to soft peaks with an electric mixer. With mixer running, slowly add granulated sugar and continue to whip to stiff peaks. Add egg yolks, half-and-half, oil, and vanilla to the flour mixture. Mix until just combined.
5. Fold whipped egg whites into cake batter a third at a time. Divide batter among prepared cake pans and bake 18 to 20 minutes or until a toothpick inserted in center of cakes comes out clean. Let cool.

For the frosting:

1. Place 4 tablespoons water in a small bowl or ramekin. Sprinkle gelatin powder over water, making sure gelatin is moistened. Let stand 5 minutes to bloom.
2. Place brown sugar, half-n-half, and ½ cup water in medium saucepan. Stir. Cook over medium-low heat, stirring occasionally until sugar is dissolved, about 5 minutes. Turn heat to low and add bloomed gelatin. Stir. Cook 2 to 3 minutes,

until gelatin is dissolved. Remove from heat and cool to room temperature.

3. Whip butter in a standing mixer until fluffy. Add cooled gelatin mixture and begin whipping. This will look like a curdled hot mess but keep whipping, and in 10 to 15 minutes it will become a beautiful buttercream. Mix in vanilla.

For the butterscotch sauce:

1. Melt butter in a 2-quart saucepan over low to medium heat. Add brown sugar, lemon juice, and salt. Cook, stirring occasionally, until sugar is dissolved and mixture is bubbling, about 5 minutes.

2. Remove pan from heat and add heavy cream. The mixture will bubble. Whisk until cream is incorporated. Return pan to low heat and cook 10 minutes without stirring, until slightly thickened. Remove pan from heat and add vanilla. Stir. Let cool to room temperature. Sauce will thicken as it cools.

3. Fill and frost the cooled cakes, drizzling sauce between the cake layers and on top of the frosting, and also on top of the cake.

Invite some friends (or an author!), make a pot of coffee or tea, and enjoy!

Read on for a sneak peek of the first book in another exciting new mystery series from Guideposts Books—Savannah Secrets!

THE HIDDEN GATE
by Marlene Chase

D o you think Flannery O'Connor really taught a chicken to walk backward?"

Meredith Bellefontaine stopped in midbreath. Captivated as she had been with the fragrance of camellias drifting in through the open window of her car, Julia's question had the effect of a sudden blast of cold air. She gave her old friend a quick glance. "What?"

Julia Foley leaned forward and rolled her eyes at Meredith. A lock of silver hair fell over her forehead. "Well, do you think she did?"

"It's spring," Meredith said. "The camellias and dogwoods are blooming everywhere, and you're asking me about chickens!"

Julia sat back and folded her arms over her soft cotton blouse. She'd tossed her mauve Preston & York suit jacket into the back of Meredith's 2017 marine-blue Nissan. Meredith had picked her up this morning so she could leave her Hyundai at the shop for an oil change. "Well, we just drove past her childhood home and museum. Call me curious. What can I say?"

"Well, to answer your question, she did," Meredith said, feeling a bubble of laughter rise. "She wrote an essay about it back in 1961. She called it 'Living with a Peacock.'"

Any historian living in Savannah had to know about Flannery O'Connor, who wrote ironic, subtly allegorical fiction about deceptively backward Southern people who experience transformations of character. These transformations were often accomplished through pain, violence, and ludicrous behavior in the pursuit of the holy. Meredith had often told visitors to Savannah about O'Connor's nineteenth-century Greek revival townhouse that was even now undergoing major renovations. The living room on the parlor-level floor was open to the public. The walled garden in the backyard, where the five-year-old O'Connor was said to have taught a chicken to walk backward, was added in 1993.

"Well, I guess you would know," Julia said.

Meredith could tell Julia was digesting her brief historical sketch, eyebrows raised in her high forehead. Analyzing it, no doubt, as someone with the legal mind and experience of a retired court judge would. Meredith waited, glad for the company of her friend and now business partner.

They'd roomed together their senior year in college and later kept in touch, over the miles, with Christmas cards and occasional notes. After University of Virginia Law School, Julia had practiced in Atlanta. However, when she returned to Savannah fifteen years ago to become a presiding judge in Chatham County's Juvenile Court, they had quickly renewed their close friendship. They had become a foursome—Julia and Beau, Meredith and her husband, Ron, sharing life and supporting each other. But four had become three when Ron died in September almost two years ago.

Meredith had been content with her work as head of Savannah's Historical Society. Well, *content* was a relative term. Some things weren't easy to dismiss. Maybe a complete change was in order—especially after her own scary heart attack on the first anniversary of Ron's death had made her reexamine her priorities. Reopening her husband's detective agency and serving the community certainly qualified as a complete change. And Julia's critical thinking and experience made her the perfect choice for a partner.

"Still wearing your historian's hat," Julia said warmly, giving Meredith's arm an affectionate nudge. "Fits you well, but so does your new one. And I love being back in the day-to-day grind with you." She leaned forward again and said, "Let's take the long way. It's a drop-dead gorgeous day." She sighed. "No time to sit back and let life happen around us. Beau is happy as a clam with a nine-iron or a fishing pole in his hand. Goodness knows he's earned a rest after those years championing the new children's wing at the hospital. But retirement's not for me."

Beau, better known as Beauregard Eugene Foley, expressed no qualms about his wife joining Meredith to reopen the detective agency. But was her old college friend being set up to fail? Meredith felt a twinge of the old fear nudging at the back of her mind. She'd always been interested in what Ron was doing—she'd even gotten her PI license so she could assist him by gathering historical background for his cases, but what did she really know about the day-to-day ins and outs of the detective business?

"You sure about this, Mom?" her oldest son, Carter, had asked when she told him her plans. He'd run a hand through thick chestnut hair that was so like his father's and jingled the keys in the pocket of his pleated Chinos. A banker had to dress the part, and Carter's trim waist wore pleats well. He was skeptical about her decision, though he tried not to show it. But Meredith recognized the gesture—the jingling keys that always signaled some inner conflict. Ron had done the same.

Wise, compassionate Ron with his hardheaded determination and terrible sense of justice. He'd joined the police force right out of college, but he hadn't been satisfied with his vocation. He'd wanted something more, some way to bring hope to those lost in the struggle of living with no one to fight for them.

A wave of sadness washed over her with such force that for a moment she thought she might drown. The surprise of it left her winded. She had worked through all that—moved ahead with her life—hadn't she?

"You all right?" Julia asked softly.

Meredith drew in a breath, embarrassed by her own reflections. And chastened too. She'd gotten through those difficult first days, her faith holding her up like virtual wings. And she had been sure—well, most of the time—that she was attuned to God's leading in reopening the agency. Still, she couldn't tamp the doubts all the way down, even with the help of Julia, who was clearly a stabilizing force.

Julia had needed her too. She'd had a successful career, but she'd needed something on which to focus her still bright energies, a cause that would give her a sense of renewed purpose. Meredith believed that joining her in reopening Ron's detective agency had been good for Julia—good for them both.

Meredith glanced at her watch. "Maybe we should head to the office instead of meandering through country roads smelling the oleander." But she took a long, slow breath as the road narrowed, and centuries-old trees arched overhead like a leafy cathedral. "Suppose there are clients waiting?" She grinned wryly. *Sure. Like they're beating down our doors clamoring for us to solve their dilemmas!*

Julia snatched her new iPhone from her lap. When she wasn't clutching it like a physical appendage, it was close at hand. Julia liked the latest gadgets and used them with ease. She brought the phone to her ear, put it on speaker mode, and pressed the number that would undoubtedly summon Carmen Lopez.

They really couldn't afford a receptionist, but they had to at least *look* like they were successful. Meredith hadn't been left without means, but they'd sunk a lot of money into the agency. Julia was happily contributing to the renovation too. She had worked hard cleaning up the back garden where charred items had been thrown after a fire in Ron's office shortly after his death.

The fire had been attributed to faulty wiring and was quickly extinguished, but a credenza, a reading lamp, and several cardboard file boxes had been lost. Before it was all hauled away, they had painstakingly picked through everything.

While clearing away leaves and grass in the back garden, Julia had found a key—a small, outdated, unimpressive bit of metal, which despite numerous tries had fit nothing in the agency. Nor did it match the lock in the burned credenza. They had put the key away safely but not before making up mysterious stories, each one more outlandish than the last, over a pot of Earl Grey.

Inside renovations were still in progress. They had decided to update the reception area and two of the offices, leaving Ron's old office, which required extensive drywall work, for later.

"It's long past time that the place had a face-lift," Julia had said. "This floral wallpaper went out of style years ago. Besides, it's coming loose in places. I even saw some crumbling plaster on the rug last week."

Julia had also recommended the hiring of Carmen Lopez, citing her remarkable intuitive sense where people were concerned. Now Julia's voice rose over the phone she had placed on SPEAKER. "That you, Carmen?"

"Uh, just a minute. I'll check," came the mellow voice, tinged with her usual good-natured irony. Who else would be answering the phone?

Carmen, twenty-something and street smart, had come from Guatemala with her parents. But when they were killed in an automobile accident, and there were no siblings or relatives for her to go to, ten-year-old Carmen became a ward of the state and not with the best result. Tossed from one foster situation to another, she had pretty much raised herself.

Meredith pictured the attractive young woman with glossy black hair and dark eyes that revealed no secret. She was seldom at a loss for words, and tact had, so far, eluded her. She was most at home in jeans and a sweatshirt but showed a good sense of career-woman style.

"Cute," Julia said dryly into her phone. She rolled her gray eyes at Meredith as she continued her conversation with Carmen. "We'll be along pretty soon. Anything going on?"

"No, just the demolition derby giving me the *dolor de cabeza.*"

Carmen's English was more than acceptable, but she liked throwing in the occasional Spanish phrase. Meredith couldn't restrain a laugh picturing the wily receptionist with hand to brow feigning a headache.

Julia clicked off and dropped the phone in her lap. "She's a trip, but ya gotta love her, right? Actually, she's come a long way since showing up in my court a few years ago." Julia pursed her lips in thought. "Petty thefts, disorderly conduct—that sort of thing. It's a wonder she turned out so well considering the start she had in life."

That was vintage Julia. A heart attuned to others.

Julia's voice broke into Meredith's reverie. "Let's go by the old Besset plantation. Since the news about Geoffrey Besset, I haven't been able to get that place off my mind."

The wealthy plantation-owner-turned-lawyer had practiced in Charleston, South Carolina, but the *Savannah Tribune* had carried the obituary three days ago. At the age of 82, Geoffrey Philpott Besset was dead.

Under his great-grandfather's control, the plantation had been one of the richest in Savannah—a thriving concern with its cadre of slaves. Years later, Geoffrey's grandfather, and then father had overseen sharecroppers. The property was nothing now but overgrown trees, a crumbling antebellum mansion, and a terrible secret. Geoffrey's twelve-year-old sister, Harriet, had disappeared almost sixty-five years ago. She was presumed to have been killed, but her body was never found.

They parked on the street in front of the mansion, and Julia climbed out of the car, that can't-wait look turning her cheeks pink. Meredith knew something about the place through her work with the Historical Society. She had learned that Geoffrey Besset left the plantation shortly after his father's death, posting a prominent notice of non-admittance on the door of the mansion.

The city occasionally monitored the old place to be sure it didn't become the target of vandals or drug dealers. Beatrice Enterline, who replaced Meredith as head of the Historical Society, seemed bent on seeing the plantation restored. What a feather that would be in the Queen Bee's bonnet.

"Now that we're in the business of solving crimes, maybe we'll crack that old case," Julia said, grinning as they approached the pitted driveway. "Besides, I don't like to see the old place turned into a haunt for ghosts. All for the sake of commerce, of course. Nothing like a good ghost story to lure folks to the historic homes tour."

Meredith felt the heaviness of old sorrow. Old regret. Though Harriet's body had never been found, you couldn't stop people from speculating. Tales of cruelty and repression seemed to cloak the overgrown acres like a pall. But no one wanted to remember, much less talk about, that sad epoch of pre-war slavery and the continued denigration of an entire race fighting for equality.

Meredith sighed, wondering what cracking the six-and-a-half-decades-old case might mean. "Once we have some time on our hands, of course," she responded wryly, because they had nothing *but* time on their hands. "One thing is for sure. Geoffrey Besset won't be any help now."

They walked among arching cypress and live oak trees dripping with Spanish moss. Enormous swaths of it hung from twisting branches like old women's hair. The dangling moss was considered picturesque and charming in most settings. But here Meredith felt a chill, like being transported to an ancient cemetery with names no one knew anymore or wanted to know. She shivered.

In the distance loomed the remains of the mansion, forlorn in the May sunshine. It had once been magnificent with its huge pillars, a handsome balcony running along the outside edge of the house, large windows, and big center entrances at the front and rear. Grand gardens with geometrically cut hedges had likely complemented the symmetry at one time. Meredith paused, surveying the overgrown grounds. "Let's just walk a little and enjoy the beauty of this splendid day." She stepped into a narrow path, where a yellow pine warbler twittered on a tangle of low pine scrub.

Julia followed, pushing branches and weeds aside. "Good thing I wore my flats today," she said laughing. She seldom wore anything else. She was tall, slender, straight, and even more imposing in her judge's robe.

They walked in silence for a while before Julia spoke again. "Imagine, these were once thriving fields of cotton with hundreds of slave families working the land, even little children, their fingers so swollen by nightfall they cried themselves to sleep." She thrust back a branch, and it cracked with the force of a whip. "I read some people back then said their lives must not be so bad, because they could hear them singing in the fields."

Meredith paused. "They weren't just singing, they were praying," she said almost in a whisper. "And they were rising. 'Everything that rises must converge.'"

"Flannery O'Connor again," Julia said, dropping down to rest on a nearby boulder.

"She got the title from Pierre Teilhard de Chardin, the French philosopher and Jesuit priest. He wrote about moving upward toward greater consciousness and love." Meredith paused again, surprised at her own recall of a quote that had often inspired her. "'At the summit you will find yourselves united with all those who, from every direction, have made the same ascent. For everything that rises must converge.'"

"Our society has risen higher since those awful pre-Civil War days, that's for sure," Julia said after a few seconds in which she was once again processing the words. "Our beautiful Savannah has come a long way."

But not far enough. Meredith knew they were both thinking the same thing. She found it hard to believe there were people still left in this world who politely tucked their racism in their pockets every day, kept it handy when it suited their aspirations. She couldn't imagine robbing oneself of the richness to be found in relationships with those who might look or sound different. "Heavy thoughts on a brilliant morning," she said aloud as she got up from the boulder on which they were resting. "Just a bit farther, and then let's take our weary selves back to civilization."

"I'm with you, girlfriend. Guess we're not going to learn anything about that old mystery this way." She tucked her arm through Meredith's, and the twinkle was back in her eye. "So, what do you suppose it was like for folks who worked here back in the 1950s?"

"I was just a child then," Meredith said. "Maybe *you* can tell me."

Julia laughed. "Yes, you're a whole eight and half months younger than me." She sobered. "We know that things were far from restful. People fought against racial discrimination for centuries, but during the '50s, the struggle entered the mainstream of American life."

"Even for a child of privilege like Harriet Besset those years could have been tumultuous," Meredith added. "Girls were expected to identify as wives and mothers with no encouragement beyond domestic bliss. When I was a girl—"

"Ouch!" Julia, who had dropped Meredith's arm when the path grew narrower and was now in the rear, tripped, knocking Meredith to her knees into a bed of pine needles along the path.

There in front of her, just beyond a cluster of loblolly pines, Meredith saw the broken-down remains of a gate, some of its iron bars still welded into the stone gateposts. Most of the overhead arch had fallen in, but the posts rose in a tangled mass of woody vines and black gum branches. Just beyond the crumbling gate was a partial stone structure with a low wall.

"It looks like it could be what's left of an old summerhouse." She stood unsteadily, feeling her heart pound triple time. With a little gasp, she bent to creep under a rusted bar.

"I wonder why this wasn't demolished with the rest of the old shacks and outbuildings," Julia said in a whisper. "I can just imagine young Harriet stealing away from the heat and bustle of the house and coming here. Maybe meeting someone."

"Or maybe she just wanted the solitude of a place like this." Meredith sat down on the low wall, feeling a strange hush. "I remember a place like this at my grandmother's house. She had a gazebo painted white with wild roses twining through the slats. I'd take my Diet-Rite cola and curl up on the seat to read. I can still feel the prickles from the rosebushes that kept poking in. But *Heidi, Winnie the Pooh,* and *Anne of Green Gables* took me away."

"I used to love *Little Women,*" Julia breathed.

Meredith tented her fingers at her lips. Why were they whispering? The silence was deep, yet it seemed to echo so loudly around them. Was it just the crackling of small creatures stirring in the brush or the warble of a bird launching itself into the brittle air? Or was someone there, peering through taut branches ready to snap? "It feels like someone is watching," she whispered. "Watching or waiting for something—or someone."

Julia shifted uncomfortably on the low wall. "I think it's time to go." Glancing around, she clutched her arms as though chilled. "I feel it too. Maybe it's the eyes and voices of the past, the long march of history that won't stop, still rising to converge."

A NOTE FROM THE EDITORS

We hope you enjoy Secrets of Wayfarers Inn, created by the Books and Inspirational Media Division of Guideposts, a nonprofit organization that touches millions of lives every day through products and services that inspire, encourage, help you grow in your faith, and celebrate God's love in every aspect of your daily life.

Thank you for making a difference with your purchase of this book, which helps fund our many outreach programs to military personnel, prisons, hospitals, nursing homes, and educational institutions. To learn more, visit Guideposts Foundation.org.

We also maintain many useful and uplifting online resources. Visit Guideposts.org to read true stories of hope and inspiration, access OurPrayer network, sign up for free news-letters, download free e-books, join our Facebook community, and follow our stimulating blogs.

To learn about other Guideposts publications, including the best-selling devotional *Daily Guideposts*, go to ShopGuideposts .org, call (800) 932-2145, or write to Guideposts, PO Box 5815, Harlan, Iowa 51593.

Sign up for the
Guideposts Fiction Newsletter
and stay up to date on the books you love!

You'll get sneak peeks of new releases, recommendations from other Guideposts readers, and special offers just for you . . .
and it's FREE!

Just go to Guideposts.org/Newsletters today to sign up.

Guideposts®

Visit Guideposts.org/Shop or call (800) 932-2145

Find more inspiring fiction in these best-loved Guideposts series!

Tearoom Mysteries Series

Mix one stately Victorian home, a charming lakeside town in Maine, and two adventurous cousins with a passion for tea and hospitality. Add a large scoop of intriguing mystery and sprinkle generously with faith, family, and friends, and you have the recipe for *Tearoom Mysteries*.

Sugarcreek Amish Mysteries

Be intrigued by the suspense and joyful "aha" moments in these delightful stories. Each book in the series brings together two women of vastly different backgrounds and traditions, who realize there's much more to the "simple life" than meets the eye.

Mysteries of Martha's Vineyard

What does Priscilla Latham Grant, a Kansas farm girl know about hidden treasure and rising tides, maritime history and local isle lore? Not much—but to save her lighthouse and family reputation, she better learn quickly!

Mysteries of Silver Peak

Escape to the historic mining town of Silver Peak, Colorado, and discover how one woman's love of antiques helps her solve mysteries buried deep in the town's checkered past.

**To learn more about these books,
visit Guideposts.org/Shop**